Praise for
MAGGIE PRICE's
LINE OF DUTY miniseries

"A quick paced, action packed romance."
—*The Romance Reader's Connection* on *Sure Bet*

"Maggie Price's riveting, intense plot makes this
an exciting reading experience."
—*Romantic Times BOOKreviews* on *Hidden Agenda*

"Get ready for chills, thrills, and shivers of delight
as a super-stud cop and his sexy, stubborn,
soon-to-be-ex wife go after a murderous cop."
—*USA TODAY* bestselling author Merline Lovelace
on *Shattered Vows*

"The cleverly developed plot is filled with
unexpected twists and turns."
—*Romantic Times BOOKreviews* on
The Cradle Will Fall

"Combines romance, mystery and crime into one
page turning, exciting and sensuous story."
—*Reader 2 Reader* on *Trigger Effect*

"A taut, romantic drama."
—*The Romance Reader* on *Most Wanted Woman*

MAGGIE PRICE

A former police-crime analyst for the Oklahoma City Police Department, Maggie Price has never tried to distance herself from her dark "cop side" when writing the riveting romantic suspense that has become her trademark. If anything, that meshing of the cop side with the romance side is a natural blending...and her stories show us that sometimes, love can kill.

The authenticity of police work and sizzling passion she brings to her novels have earned Maggie numerous awards, including a National Readers' Choice Award, a Booksellers' Best Award and a coveted RITA® Award nomination. Other honors received include a *Romantic Times BOOKreviews* Career Achievement Award for series romantic suspense, and a Reviewer's Choice Award for Best Silhouette Intimate Moments.

Maggie invites readers to contact her at 416 N.W. 8th St., Oklahoma City, OK 73102-2604. Or reach her on the Web at www.MaggiePrice.com.

THE RANSOM

MAGGIE PRICE

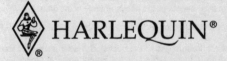

HARLEQUIN®

TORONTO • NEW YORK • LONDON
AMSTERDAM • PARIS • SYDNEY • HAMBURG
STOCKHOLM • ATHENS • TOKYO • MILAN • MADRID
PRAGUE • WARSAW • BUDAPEST • AUCKLAND

ISBN-13: 978-0-373-19890-0
ISBN-10:   0-373-19890-6

THE RANSOM

This edition published by arrangement with Harlequin Books S.A.

® and TM are trademarks of the publisher. Trademarks indicated with ® are registered in the United States Patent and Trademark Office, the Canadian Trade Marks Office and in other countries.

www.eHarlequin.com

Printed in U.S.A.

Dear Reader,

While a civilian crime analyst for the Oklahoma City Police Department, I snagged an assignment to a task force investigating the abduction of two preteen girls from the state fair. During that time, I was in contact with the distraught parents. Their despair and suffering touched my heart and gave me an insider's view of what it means to lose a child to an unknown evil.

That experience inspired me to tell the story of a divorcée whose small son is kidnapped for ransom. And the only person she dares turn to for help is the ex-cop who walked away a decade ago with a piece of her heart.

The Ransom is the story not only of the struggle to save a little boy's life, but of the rekindling of a love that refuses to die.

Warmest regards,

Maggie Price

To Pam Hopkins, my supersonic agent whom I've been blessed to have in my corner for over a decade.

PROLOGUE

Cross C Ranch
Layton, Texas

KATHRYN CONNER was coming home.

Kathryn Conner *Mason,* the man sitting on the ranch house's shady front porch amended. He had one hand clenched around a coffee mug and that morning's newspaper draped across his blue-jeaned thigh.

He could hear himself breathe.

Feel the sweat trickle from the pores of his underarms.

Taste his fear.

His spine stiff, he propped a shoulder against one of the porch's vintage white columns and stared out across the pristine lawn.

The July sun beat down without mercy, but the smothering heat couldn't touch the icy fear that crouched darkly inside him. He owed a Dallas gambling syndicate over a half million dollars and he had less than three weeks to come up with the money. *In full.*

He could no longer sleep. Had lost interest in food. Could barely breathe. For weeks he'd been popping pills that did little to ease the smothering sensation of being buried in a pit from which there was no way out.

And then he heard about Mrs. Devin Mason's imminent return to Layton, Texas. Kathryn was coming home.

And bringing her son.

Dropping his gaze to the newspaper, he focused on the picture that showed the smiling images of Kathryn, her pretty-boy actor husband and their son. *Ex-husband* now. The divorce had become final just weeks before Senator Sam Conner's death.

Kathryn hadn't even come home for her grandfather's funeral. Had never stepped foot on the Cross C after she went off to college ten years ago.

Why, he didn't know. Couldn't care less. All that mattered was she would arrive the following day.

And she was filthy, stinking rich.

Kathryn was his lifeline. She would save him.

And so would her son.

CHAPTER ONE

KATHRYN CONNER HAD vowed to never again set foot on the Cross C Ranch until her bastard of a grandfather was dead.

Now he was.

"You're home," Owen Daily remarked, braking his black Cadillac beneath the massive oak that shaded one end of the porch of the two-story ranch house.

Home. The word leaped into Kathryn's mind while she sat in heart-pounding silence beside the man she'd hired to handle her Texas legal affairs. Staring out the windshield, the knots in her stomach clenched tighter while she struggled to come to terms with her surroundings.

Bathed in afternoon sunlight, the house with its wraparound porch looked welcoming. For Kathryn, it had only felt that way when Sam was away in Austin dealing with senate business.

Always the wood had been painted white with butter-yellow trim. The wide porch had latticework at the eaves and long, sturdy columns. The swing—where she had sat so many evenings writing stories and spinning her private dreams that always took her far away—still hung from chains at the porch's far end.

Racked by emotion, she swept her gaze across the immaculate lawn toward the distant barn, the stables, the out-buildings, all surrounded by post-and-rail whitewashed fences. In her ten-year absence she had forgotten the Cross C's beauty—and only remembered her pain.

Her gaze returned to the house where yellow roses wound their way through the porch trellises. The bright blooms blurred in her vision while a nagging unease moved around the edges of her awareness, undefined, barely formed, a gray shadow.

She lifted a hand to her throat where a choking dread had settled.

"Something wrong?" Owen asked.

"I just…" Kathryn ran her other hand over the hip of her red linen slacks. "For a second it felt like someone stepped on my grave."

Owen gave the house a considering look. "You haven't said as much, but I have to figure your not coming home since that summer you left for college means not all your memories of the Cross C are good."

That summer. If only she had been wiser, more mature, she might have avoided making a fool of herself. Even now humiliation crawled through Kathryn, as hot as the hunger she'd felt for a man who'd been rumored to have an unlimited number of willing women on speed dial. But she had wanted Clay Turner since she'd been a starry-eyed schoolgirl who was stupid enough to think *she* would be the one who could change him. And by the time she turned eighteen that crush had transformed into love. So she'd made sure to ride over to the Double Starr the day Clay showed up to work on his uncle's neighboring ranch like he did every summer. She could still see him that day, leaning against the corral's top rail, all tough and rangy and fit in a white T-shirt and faded jeans. Still see his dark eyes, focused like a laser on her as she sat astride her mare. "Well, look who's all grown up," he drawled.

There'd been no love in his gaze. Not even affection. Just dark, dangerous lust that slammed her heart into her ribs and zinged its way right to her toes.

And even though he made it clear he wanted only good times and fast rides, she leaped off the cliff.

As if pulled by some unseen force, Kathryn's gaze shifted to the east. From talking to the Cross C's longtime housekeeper, she knew Clay had moved to Layton two years ago after his parents' tragic deaths at the hands of their kidnappers. He now managed the Double Starr, so it was inevitable they would cross paths.

Ten years had passed since she laid eyes on him. A decade, during which she had married another man, given birth to his son, agonized over Matthew's health, won an Emmy for screenwriting and had her crumbling marriage to Hollywood's "heartthrob" dissected by the tabloids. Yet the thought of seeing Clay again had a dark foreboding surfacing inside her with such corrosive force it seemed as if no time had passed to dull the pain.

"Well, there's someone who's anxious to see you," Owen said.

Kathryn looked back toward the house. All the pain of the past winked away as she watched Willa Mc-Kenzie—short, stocky and clad in the usual gray dress and white apron—bustle across the porch. Just the sight of the housekeeper who'd raised and loved her had Kathryn's heart swelling.

Willa was one of the good memories. And one of the people Sam had done a truly good, unselfish thing for.

Turning, Kathryn looked over her shoulder. Matthew hadn't stirred since he'd fallen asleep almost before they'd driven out of the airport. He was a sturdy five-year-old with thick blond hair and brown eyes that sparkled with mischief. Now, though, he looked almost cherubic, stretched on the back seat in his jeans and Western shirt, his miniature dachshund, Abby, curled against his stomach.

No one would suspect he'd been near death two years ago.

She gave him a gentle shake. "Wake up, Matty. We're here."

Thick blond lashes fluttered off his cheeks. Yawning, he pushed up off the seat, fists rubbing his eyes. The movement had Abby stirring. The dachshund levered up on her short legs and shook her head, the sunlight turning her reddish coat a deep mahogany.

Willa pulled the car's back door open and leaned in. "Is there anyone who can help me find a missing chocolate chip cookie?"

"Grandma Willa!" Grinning wildly, Matthew unhooked his seat belt then propelled himself into the housekeeper's arms. Abby rocketed after her master.

Kathryn climbed out, wincing as a gust of hot wind and dirt hit her in the face.

"Welcome to Texas," she murmured, shoving her sunglasses farther up the bridge of her nose.

"Bet I can find that cookie," Matthew insisted to Willa.

Willa's eyes sparkled. "Think so?" A wayward strand

of gray hair that had slipped from the bun at her neck waved like wheat in the breeze.

Standing on tiptoes, Matthew poked a hand into one apron pocket, then the other. "Right here!" he exclaimed, pulling out a cookie the size of a man's fist.

"How do you suppose it got there?" Willa slid a hand into a pocket on her dress and pulled out a rawhide chew bone. "Well, I'm carrying around all sorts of surprises today." Abby barked, her entire body waggling like a bass on a hook. "Guess you'll make good use of this," Willa said before tossing the bone a short distance away.

Owen grinned at Kathryn, his denim shirt and jeans making him look more ranch hand than attorney known for his scorched-earth tactics. "They've done this before, right?"

"A standing routine," she answered. "It started about the time I flew Willa out to California for Matthew's third birthday." Her heart brimming, Kathryn stepped into the housekeeper's welcoming embrace.

"Lord, child, it's good to have you home."

Kathryn shot a furtive glance at the house. In a flash of memory, she pictured herself the last time she crossed the threshold, bruised, bleeding and lying on a stretcher.

No, she told herself and ruthlessly forced away the harsh image. She couldn't allow herself to think about that. She'd returned to the Cross C because doing so was in Matthew's best interest. She could do this for her son.

Inching back, Willa cupped a palm against Kathryn's cheek. "Every time I see you, you look more and more like the pictures I've seen of your momma."

To Kathryn, the parents who had given her life and died when she was an infant had only ever been faded names in the Conner family bible. With her grandmother already deceased, it was Willa who had raised her when Sam took in his only grandchild.

After giving Willa another hug, Kathryn slipped an arm around her waist. "Matthew has chattered for weeks about living on a ranch with Grandma Willa." Kathryn glanced back toward the house. "Did our things get here?"

"I should say so. Pilar and I have spent days unpacking boxes." She ruffled the boy's blond hair while he munched on his cookie. "I expect you can wage a small war with all the tanks and toy soldiers."

"A *big* war." He glanced around in expectation. "Can I see the outlaw tunnel?"

"After supper," Kathryn answered. The tunnel, connected to the basement, had been dug by her great-great-great-grandfather Conner so his bandit son could sneak into the house for visits. Matthew took exceptional pride in the fact one of his ancestors had been a real life outlaw.

Willa gave Kathryn another squeeze. "The decorator finished up the remodeling you wanted done yesterday. You won't recognize your old bedroom."

That's the idea, Kathryn thought. She knew she would never walk into that room again without thinking about the final vicious fight she'd had with Sam. So she had instructed Willa to put her clothes and other belongings in one of the spacious bedrooms that the senator had reserved for guests.

Willa looked toward the porch. "Pilar, come get reacquainted with Kathryn."

Pilar Graciano came down the porch steps where she paused and gave a polite nod. "Señorita Conner, it is nice to see you after so long," she said in the hesitant, accented English Kathryn remembered.

"Thank you, Pilar." Kathryn smiled at the thin, small-boned woman with black hair plaited into a braid. The maid had always been as skittish and shy as a newborn colt. "How is Nilo?" Kathryn asked, referring to the swarthy ranchhand who'd won Pilar's heart.

"My husband is well."

Willa patted Matthew's shoulder. "This is Pilar. Do you remember me telling you she has a boy named Antonio?"

Matthew nodded. "You said he has a horse named Gringo."

Pilar quietly welcomed Matthew. That done, she slid her hands into the pockets of her dress and stood in silence as if awaiting orders.

A distant shout drew Kathryn's attention beyond the vast lawn to the stables. She recognized Johnny Sullivan's lean, craggy build. The Cross C's longtime foreman appeared to be involved in an intense discussion with a tall, blond man who looked distinctly out of place in a gray suit.

Kathryn turned to Willa. "Is that Brad Jordan with Johnny?"

"It is." Willa shrugged. "I expect the banker's fussing at Johnny for not getting permission before calling Doc Silver out to look at the horses you shipped here."

Kathryn's eyes narrowed. "Johnny doesn't need to check with Brad before calling the vet."

"Tell that to Brad." Willa blotted her damp brow with the back of her hand. "Everything changed once Sam's will was read and the bank got control over the Cross C."

The reminder of the last-minute codicil Sam added

to his will before cancer killed him had Kathryn setting her jaw. Because all Conner land and money was held in a series of age-old trusts, there was no way Sam could disinherit her or Matthew. So her grandfather had done all he could to hobble her when it came to running the ranch. It was Sam's way of reaching out from the grave and slapping her one last time, just to prove how totally he had loathed her every day of her life.

Even now, Kathryn had no idea why her grandfather had hated her like poison.

"The bank doesn't control Cross C business," she said, forcing back the anger she'd carried with her since she learned the contents of Sam's will. "It oversees expenditures, is all."

"Well, Brad's been doing a lot of overseeing," Willa commented. "I have to show him receipts for the groceries and everything else I buy. Waste of time when I've got a house to run. I expect he'll bring all that up at the meeting you said you've got scheduled with him in the morning."

"No doubt." Kathryn looked back toward the stables in time to see Brad slide behind the wheel of a blue Jaguar. A moment later, he steered the car toward the road.

"Well now," Willa said, cupping Matthew's chin. "How about we find some milk to wash down that cookie?"

A smear of chocolate on the boy's cheek lengthened when he grinned. "Okay."

Willa and Matthew walked hand in hand toward the house, Pilar and Abby following in their wake.

Kathryn waited until they were out of earshot to turn to Owen. "You're sure about the codicil? Positive the terms will stick?"

"They'll stick," her lawyer confirmed. "You know how Sam was—he didn't do anything without thinking it through. Same thing goes for the codicil. And don't forget the clause that states if you contest the will, a corporation made up of your grandfather's political friends has authority to take over the running of the Cross C."

"Meaning, everything stays in the Conner name, but there wouldn't be a Conner at the helm."

"Basically." Owen raised a brow. "Do you want me here in the morning when you meet with Brad?"

Kathryn pulled in a deep breath, drawing in the scents of mown grass, fresh hay and animal flesh. It was a shock to discover that the scents and the land itself still called to her.

That land—and all the responsibilities that went with it—were now hers. There were always cattle that needed to be rounded up, fences to mend, grain to be planted or harvested. No matter the barriers Sam had erected in his will, it was up to her to deal with every aspect of running the ranch. She understood full well that all of Layton would be watching to see if the Hollywood screenwriter had enough of her grandfather in her to operate the Conner empire.

Watch me. Standing there, she could almost feel the mantle of her new responsibilities drop onto her shoulders. Those responsibilities would be in addition to the writing career she'd worked so hard to establish and intended to continue.

Turning, she looked back at Owen. "Yes, since I'm not familiar yet with all the terms of the financial noose Sam put around my neck."

"That's what you pay me for." Owen checked his

watch. "You need me for anything else before I head back to Layton?"

"No. Thank you for picking us up at the airport. It was good to have a chance to discuss business face-to-face." Kathryn squeezed his arm. "I'm sorry, Owen, I got so caught up talking about Cross C matters that I haven't asked after your father."

A muscle ticked in his cheek. "The stroke left him weak, but his mind's as sharp as ever. I expect he'll be back in the office in a couple of weeks."

"I'm glad to hear it." She wondered, but didn't ask, if Owen partly blamed Sam for his father's stroke. How could he not, the way Sam had so suddenly and ruthlessly jerked all his legal dealings away from the man who'd not only been his attorney for decades, but a close friend since childhood?

While Owen's car headed down the driveway, Kathryn turned toward the house. It was hers now. Hers and Matthew's. She would make him a good home here, a *happy* home. And over time she would wipe away the darkness of the past.

A past that, right now, hung heavy around her as she scaled the steps. Her pulse beat dull and thick as she moved across the porch toward the massive front door. She knew there would be ghosts. But if she was going to make a good life here for Matthew, she was going to have to face them.

Better to get that over with she told herself, then eased the door open and stepped inside.

And was instantly flung back in time.

Her breath shallowed as she remained unmoving in the dim entryway. The same drop-leaf table still stood against the wall holding her late grandmother's crystal vase that was eternally filled with yellow roses. The familiar antique mirror in the gleaming brass frame hung over the table. The long rug still ran muted colors along the length of the wide hall that stretched from the front door to the back.

Gathering her courage, she shifted toward the staircase that swept up two stories. As always, the wooden railing and newel post gleamed with polish.

The ghosts of the house circled around Kathryn, whispering taunts, making her feel as if her nerves were crawling under her skin. An ache settled in her heart. Yet, she couldn't cry. The tears had frozen inside long ago.

Damn you, girl, you'll do as I say!

She pressed a hand to her stomach while the memory of that last awful fight snapped out at her like fangs.

Squeezing her eyes shut, she reeled against the onslaught of pain and remorse that pounded her with the force of a sledgehammer. Two of the most important men in her life had rejected her. Sam had taken her in after her parents died solely for the sake of appearances. Clay Turner had wanted her only for a good time, a pleasant diversion during a searing-hot summer. Then he headed back to Houston and his job as an agent in the U.S. State Department's diplomatic security service.

She had seen him only one time after that when she woke to find him sitting beside her hospital bed. He hadn't had to speak the words for her to know he regretted her fall, but nothing more. The child she had lost would have been a complication, one of those strings he'd told her up-front he didn't want.

But *she* had wanted. Oh God, she had wanted both Clay and their child.

She grimaced as she realized what she was thinking. *Everything* about that summer was a part of the past, she reminded herself. She had Matthew now and she'd come back to the Cross C for his sake. Not only because he deserved a life away from the fishbowl of his father's fame—she could have taken Matthew to live any number of places where he'd be sheltered from the unrelenting media attention that was a byproduct of Devin's stardom. No, she'd brought her son to Texas because *this* had been Conner land for nearly two hundred years. The Cross C was Matthew's heritage. His future. *His right*. She would make it their home and run the ranch to the best of her ability until Matthew was old enough to take over the reins.

For her son, she would deal with the memories that taunted her, the pain she'd buried deep and anything else that came along. Including the inevitable unavoidable encounters with Clay Turner.

Squaring her shoulders, Kathryn gripped the banister with a damp palm, then headed up the stairs.

CHAPTER TWO

"Pow! Pow! You aim the staple gun like this 'n pull the trigger. Pow!"

Matthew pointed a finger at an invisible target as he bounded down the staircase beside Kathryn. Abby followed in their wake, the dachshund's short legs taking her down each step in a seesaw swagger.

"Sounds like important work." Kathryn held back a smile at the sight of her son in his desert-camouflage shorts and a T-shirt. As fashion statements went, the cowboy boots he'd begged to wear didn't quite make the outfit.

She paused to slick back his blond hair, still wet from the shower she'd had to insist he take after his outing to help mend a fence. Above them, Kathryn caught sight of Pilar Graciano moving as silent as death along the hallway, a stack of linens in the maid's arms. It had been Pilar's husband, Nilo, who'd taken his own son and Matthew out that morning.

Kathryn felt immense relief that in the three days they'd been at the Cross C, Matthew was fast on his way to making a new friend in Antonio.

With the staircase behind them, she and Matthew walked hand in hand, he swinging her arm to-and-fro as they traversed the hallway's glossy wood floor. Abby trotted beside Matthew, her toenails tap-tapping lightly as she went. After turning a corner they came even with the door of Sam Conner's study. Although Kathryn felt her grandfather's heavy presence each time she walked into the room, she was determined to use it for her own office. After all, generations of Connors had ruled the Cross C from inside those dark-paneled walls. She had already set up her computer on the massive desk and was in the process of organizing files on the screenplay she was currently writing. In time, she would go through all of Sam's files and purge him, page by page.

Arms swinging, she and Matthew continued down the hallway. The kitchen was at the back of the house, a cheerful room eternally filled with the heady aroma of Willa's cooking. The room's ash walls were painted white, butcher blocks covered the countertops and work island. Chains hung from the high-vaulted ceiling, suspending racks heavy with brass and copper pots. The kitchen was as modern as Sam Conner's money could make it; the oversize refrigerators, dishwashers and ovens had been installed to ease Willa's supervision of the extra help brought in for the lavish parties hosted for constituents and anyone else deemed capable of furthering the senator's various agendas.

Still, Kathryn had to admit that not everything Sam did had some political motive behind it. When Willa's husband suffered a heart attack, Sam had kept the ranch hand on the Cross C's payroll until his death three years later. It was only his granddaughter whom Sam never opened his heart to.

"Lunch is almost ready." Willa sent a bright smile

across the center island while spreading peanut butter on bread.

Kathryn's gaze flicked to the oak table in the alcove where Brad Jordan sat, a half-eaten piece of apple pie on the table before him. Beside the banker was a stack of receipts. Kathryn supposed Willa was trying to use her take-you-to-heaven pie to ply some goodwill from the man who now had his hand on the Cross C's purse strings.

Not his fault, Kathryn reminded herself when heat rose under her skin. Brad wasn't to blame for what was in Sam's will.

Matthew lifted his chin and sniffed. "What smells so good?"

Brad pointed his fork at his plate. "Willa's apple pie."

Matthew's face brightened as he peered around the center island. "Hi, Mr. Jordan!" He tugged from Kathryn's hold and headed across the kitchen. "What are you doing here?"

Brad feigned a look of horror as Matthew climbed onto a chair. "You've got a serious case of the wet look, son."

While Abby settled beneath his chair, Matthew scratched his head. "Mommy made me take another shower."

"Two in one day?" Brad asked, meeting Kathryn's gaze.

"Couldn't be helped," she replied. "Matthew had a pound of prairie dirt on him."

Brad Jordan was tall and wiry with dark hair and intense eyes. The smile he now flashed at Kathryn was the same one that had once had handfuls of females at Layton High School melting. But the star quarterback had eyes only for head cheerleader Felicia Smith. Their wedding had been *the* social event of that long-ago summer.

It was Brad's father-in-law—a crony of Sam's—who owned Layton National Bank. And it was Garner Smith who insisted the codicil be enforced with microscopic exactness. Brad had assured Kathryn he would work with her to make their transactions painless. She knew that wouldn't be the case if she were forced to deal with Brad's dour-faced father-in-law.

She retrieved a carton of milk from the refrigerator. "Brad, did we have an appointment I forgot about?"

"No. I had to go by the Double Starr this morning to discuss business with Clay Turner."

Kathryn tightened her grip on the carton. Dammit, the part of her that had loved Clay was hollowed out. So why did just the mention of his name put a hitch under her ribs?

"Since I had to be out this way," Brad continued, "I decided to drop off the check that you'll present to the hospital board at the fund-raiser on Friday night." He winked at Willa. "I got lassoed into having pie."

"In a movie, my daddy tied up a bad man with rope," Matthew said. He smiled up at Willa when she served him. "Can I have some pie?"

"I think your momma is taking you for dessert after you meet Dr. Teasdale." She finger-combed his damp hair before moving back to the counter. "Kathryn, I almost forgot to tell you two things."

Kathryn rolled her shoulders, trying to ease the tension that the mention of Clay had settled there. "What things?"

"First, Johnny needs to update you on what Doc Silver found when he checked that mare with colic.

Second," Willa continued, pulling a piece of paper from her apron pocket, "Shannon Burton called again. The *Layton Times* is sending her to the fund-raiser, and she wants to interview you about the wing you're funding for the hospital."

"Thanks." Kathryn took the paper from Willa. "I'll talk to Johnny before Matthew and I drive into Layton." As for the reporter, Kathryn knew Burton had written articles in the *Times* that put a harsh light on her missing Sam's funeral. Marriage to the country's top box-office actor had taught Kathryn numerous ways to deal with that type of reporting.

Brad gave Matthew a considering look. "Are you going to see Dr. Teasdale because you don't feel good?"

"No." Matthew took a bite of sandwich. "This is a…Mommy, what kind of 'pointment is this?"

"An introductory appointment," Kathryn said while opening a carton of yogurt. Even after two years, she still found herself gripped by a terrible panic when she thought about how ill Matthew had been when his kidneys had failed. After months of hospital stays and dialysis, a transplanted kidney had saved his life.

Now, a daily dose of an antirejection med and an occasional checkup kept Matthew on a healthy, even keel.

Glancing Brad's way, Kathryn pulled a spoon out of a drawer. "Matthew and Dr. Teasdale are going to get acquainted today."

"I've got two girls of my own," Brad told Matthew around a bite of pie. "They both go to Dr. Teasdale."

"Is he nice?"

Brad nodded. "He's so nice, he has permission to deputize little boys. And give out special deputy badges."

Matthew swiveled in his chair. "Mommy, can I be a deputy? And get a badge? Then I can arrest the outlaws in our tunnel."

"We'll ask Dr. Teasdale." Kathryn slid into the chair beside her son, and pretended not to notice the bite of pie Brad snuck onto Matthew's plate. Yes, when it came to banking, she much preferred dealing with him than with his father-in-law.

CLAY TURNER strode out of Layton City Hall into the fiery heat of the late afternoon sun. He was tall, nearly six foot four with a rangy, disciplined build more accustomed in the last few years to a rancher's denim than the body armor and holstered weapons that were a part of his past. A well-worn Stetson shaded a tanned face that was lean and square-jawed. A scar slashed across his right cheek, disappearing into the dark hair at his temple. The scar was a reminder of a time he would never leave behind.

By the time he'd crossed the town's busy main street, Clay's white dress shirt was damp with sweat and he was sucking in air as dry as old bones.

He glanced at his watch, frustrated that so much of the day had gotten away from him. He'd spent the morning repairing fence near the road bordering the north side of Double Starr property. Fortunately he'd been able to continue working while talking financial business with Brad Jordan. Then he'd had to clean up and drive into town where he'd just wasted a couple of hours in a meeting of the Layton Municipal League, of which his uncle was chairman.

While an agent for the U.S. State Department's diplomatic security service, Clay had attended so many meetings he'd grown to hate just the thought of sitting through another one. But his uncle was out of town on ranch business and he'd asked Clay to attend in his place. Since Les Turner was also his employer, Clay couldn't very well say no. So he'd crammed the tail of his dress shirt into a clean pair of jeans, lashed on a damn tie and driven to town.

The tie was now loosened, his shirt's upper buttons undone and its sleeves rolled up on his arms. He glanced toward the end of the block where a digital display scrolled beneath the bank's sign. One hundred two degrees. Clay gritted his teeth. No man was supposed to live in these temperatures.

Lucky for him he'd been as good as dead nearly two years.

His eyes narrowed against a blast of hot wind and brutal memories. He feared he would hear his mother's screams, his father's shouts for the rest of his life.

His parents were dead. He was at fault. Blame weighted his shoulders, a heavy, unyielding albatross.

He dragged an unsteady hand across his jaw, swallowing the bile that rose like poison in his throat. The only thing that held back the guilt was work. Physical and mental labor, preferably to the point of exhaustion.

Clearly he hadn't done near enough work today.

With his uncle out of town and the cook off, Clay decided to pick up his supper before he left Layton. When he got back to the Double Starr he would eat while he inputted the banker's latest figures into the spreadsheets he maintained on the ranch's finances.

Since his pickup was parked in front of a new place

that featured sandwiches, ice cream and designer coffees, that's where he headed. Pulling open the door, he stepped into the brightly lit glass-and-tile-lined café. To his left was a glossy black counter and a display case full of pastries and cookies the size of hubcaps. The tables that dotted the floor were covered with butcher paper and in the center of each was a glass holding colored pencils. The place looked good. And the air conditioner was set on *arctic*.

Clay glanced toward the far corner. Six teenage girls, each licking on her own ice-cream cone, were clustered around one of the tables, giggling and sharing secrets. A man and woman whom Clay didn't recognize sat at one of the booths that lined the front window.

Easing back the brim of his Stetson, he scanned the menu board on the wall behind the counter.

"Afternoon, Clay. Glad you came in."

He nodded to the plain-faced middle-aged man behind the counter. Norman Adams and his wife were teachers at the high school. Clay recalled hearing talk that a bad investment in the stock market had tumbled the couple into debt, and they'd opened the café to supplement their incomes. "The place looks great, Norman."

"Thanks. So far, business has been good." He sent Clay a smile that was shaky around the edges. "What can I get for you?"

While he ordered, Clay heard the café's door open and close. He pulled money out of his billfold at the same time a child's voice said, "Mommy, look at the football player in the window."

"That poster he's on lists the high school football games. We'll have to go to some this fall."

Clay froze. *That voice.* For an instant, he thought it was just another from his past, come to haunt him.

Throat tight, he forced himself to turn toward the door. A hot ball of awareness settled in his gut as he took in the woman clad in slim white slacks and a sleeveless crimson blouse who was leaning down, one arm around a small boy's waist. She spoke to him softly while nodding toward the poster in the window.

He'd known she was coming back. With the newspaper running pictures and articles, and all of Layton buzzing about Kathryn Conner Mason's return, there was no way Clay couldn't have known.

What he hadn't known was that studying every picture of her he'd come across had been the easy part. Seeing her in the flesh was the equivalent of a fist smashing into his solar plexus.

The eighteen-year-old girl he'd walked away from was now a woman. The raven-black hair she had worn to her waist now barely skimmed her shoulders, framing a face that had become more fine-boned with maturity. The slender, angular body that he'd known every dip and hollow of had developed a woman's seductive curves. Studying her, Clay felt his heartbeat spike. His mouth went dry. And the floor beneath his boots shifted due to some age-old emotion, coupled with regret. Dragging regret over the choices made by a young man who had not fully understood repercussions, hadn't thought long-term. Hadn't wanted to.

A band tightened around his chest. On nights when his nightmares woke him he lay alone in a cold sweat, thinking about Kathryn Conner. Wondering which direction their lives would have taken if back then his mind hadn't automatically done a quick sidestep at the thought of a woman, *any woman*, tying him down.

If only he'd responded differently when Kathryn pressed for a commitment. If only he'd taken time to explore the emotions he'd been so quick to deny that had drawn him to the spirited dark-haired girl. Maybe then he would have taken her to Houston with him when his vacation ended. Doing so might have saved their child. If so, his parents would have moved back to the States like they'd always promised they would when he settled down and gave them a grandchild.

His gaze went to the boy. *Kathryn's son*. He was blond and brown-eyed, the image of his superstar father. *Matthew Mason, five years old*, Clay thought, his cop's mind pulling back the information he'd read in the newspaper.

And in the *People* magazine he'd secretly bought to sate his curiosity about the woman who'd brutally clung to his thoughts over the past two years.

Her laugh drifted on the cool air as she cupped her son's chin, gave him a kiss, then straightened and turned toward the counter.

With her gaze locked with Clay's, Kathryn went still while everything around her slipped out of focus. A shudder shot down her spine and onward to bury itself behind her knees.

If she took two short steps she could reach out and touch him. Touch the man whom she had once wanted more than she'd wanted even to breathe. The man she had made such a fool of herself over.

She fought back humiliation along with the urge to

grab Matthew into her arms and run as fast as she could away from Clay Turner, away from the past. The pain.

But all she could do was stare back at him while she struggled for words that wouldn't come. His face was thinner than she remembered, the hollows of his cheeks deeper. Lines were scored into the corners of his eyes and mouth. His body was trim, muscled and looked hard as granite. A white dress shirt, open at the neck, revealed curling black hair as rich in color as the hair that brushed the shirt's collar. Beneath the brim of his Stetson, his dark eyes looked as sharp as a sword.

Her gaze slid to his right cheek, now marred by a thin scar that slashed upward across his temple. A memory came: her own fingers stroking a similar scar on his back as they lay on rumpled sheets.

"Hello, Kat," he said quietly.

"Clay." Despite the blood pounding in her cheeks from his use of his private nickname for her, she kept her voice casual and controlled.

"Been a long time," he said.

Not long enough. "It has," she managed to say through stiff lips.

"Mommy, you're squeezing my hand too tight!"

Jolting, she loosened her grip. "Oh, Matty, I'm sorry."

"You going to introduce us?"

Her gaze whipped back to Clay. She needed to breathe, but she couldn't quite remember how. "This is my son, Matthew. Matthew, this is Mr. Turner."

Matthew tipped his head back so far in order to meet Clay's gaze that the boy rocked on the heels of his cowboy boots. Kathryn placed a steadying hand on his shoulder.

"Hi, Mr. Turner."

"Hello." Clay stepped closer and crouched, putting them eye to eye. He noted that Kathryn kept her son's hand firmly in her own.

"Nice to meet you, Matthew." Clay skimmed a fingertip across the plastic badge pinned in the center of the boy's T-shirt. "You the new law in these parts?"

He nodded, his brown eyes sparkling. "I got to spit into Dr. Teasdale's hand and that made me a deputy."

Clay raised a brow. "Sounds like the doc knows a good man when he sees one."

"Now, I can arrest the outlaws in mommy's tunnel. Have you seen the tunnel?"

The outlaw tunnel. Lifting his gaze to Kathryn's, Clay saw that her face had paled. Was she thinking about all the nights she'd used the tunnel to sneak out of her house? About how he'd ride over to the Cross C after dark and wait for her in the stand of scrub oaks that hid the tunnel's outer entrance so it couldn't been seen from the house? Did she remember the time when a rainstorm whipped in and they'd had hot, wild sex in the tunnel?

When she tore her gaze from his, Clay had his answer. *Yeah, Kat, you remember*. He struggled against the urge to tell her there was no way she could detest him more than he detested himself for the way he'd treated her.

Instead he looked back at Matthew. "I've seen the tunnel. It's a long stretch of land. Are you sure you can rustle up those outlaws all on your own?"

Matthew nodded. "Me 'n Abby can do it."

"Who's Abby?"

"My weenie dog."

"Clay, your order's ready," the café owner said.

"Thanks, Norman." As he spoke, Clay kept his gaze on Matthew's compelling face. "Time for me to go, Deputy. I'll be sure I stay on the right side of the law so you and Abby won't have to come arrest me."

"Okay."

"Matthew," Kathryn said while Clay rose, "you can look in the display case and choose one cookie."

"Okay, Mommy."

Realizing the café had gone quiet around them, Clay checked across his shoulder. The man and woman in the booth, and all the teenage girls were staring holes through Kathryn. Since she didn't seem to notice, he assumed her years of marriage to the heartthrob actor had made her immune to that kind of attention.

When he looked back, her expression was impenetrable, her eyes unreadable.

"I was sorry to hear about your grandfather," he said quietly.

"Thank you." She closed her eyes for an instant. "And I'm sorry about your parents. Losing them that way must have been devastating."

Clay felt the bright, swift pain twist inside him. There was no way she could know how closely linked she was in his mind to their deaths. He tightened his jaw.

"Guess we've both had our share of loss to deal with," he said. "You're doing a good thing by building the wing onto Layton's hospital in Sam's memory. He'd have been proud of you for continuing all he did for folks around here."

She smiled now, her lips as thin as a blade. "I'm sure," she said then looked toward the counter. "Hello, Mr. Adams, how are you?"

"Fine. I'm just fine, Kathryn. Seems like only yesterday you were sitting in my English class." A blush settled under his skin and a muscle ticked in his cheek. "It was real nice, you mentioning my name when you won your Emmy award."

"You taught me about writing. I owe a lot of my success to you." She looked back at Clay. "You mentioned you were leaving. Don't let us hold you up."

Clearly she wasn't interested in letting bygones be bygones. Couldn't say he blamed her.

He touched a finger to the brim of his Stetson. "See you, Kat. Bye, Matthew. Norman."

"Bye," the boy responded. Norman nodded. The fact that Kathryn said nothing sliced Clay into a thousand pieces.

With guilt and regret sitting in his stomach like jagged rocks, he snagged his sack off the counter.

He headed for the door, deliberately distancing himself from Kathryn Conner for the second time in his life. This time, though, he was the one who felt all the pain.

KATHRYN WOKE the following morning feeling as if a spider had woven a thick, sticky cobweb inside her brain.

The sun's rays slanted into her second-floor bedroom through the gauzy curtains, reflecting off the brass bed's ornate grillwork. The light felt like ice picks stabbing into her eyes. She shoved at her tangled hair, thinking surely she hadn't overslept. In the time she'd been back at the Cross C she had woken each day before dawn. As had Matthew.

She told herself to get up, *willed* herself to, but her eyelids felt heavy and refused to stay open. On top of her lethargy, faint waves of nausea lapped at her stomach. Sick, she thought hazily. She'd picked up a bug. Since Matthew hadn't been in to pounce on her bed like he did almost every morning it was possible he'd come down with it, too. The thought shot a sharp pang through her. Her concern wasn't just a mother's general worry that her child might be ill. Any sort of bug—even a cold—could have devastating effects on his transplanted kidney.

That knowledge had Kathryn swallowing the sick taste in her mouth and drawing on all her inner strength. She forced her eyes open, instantly squinting against the sun's glare. Her concern took on added weight when she focused on the clock on the nightstand. *Ten o'clock.* Good God, sick or well, she never slept this late!

Nor did Matthew.

She knew the distress she felt wouldn't be rocketing toward the ozone if Willa were home—she sometimes kept Matthew occupied before breakfast in the kitchen. But just as she had done every Wednesday since Kathryn could remember, Willa had driven to Dallas yesterday evening to spend the night with her daughter. Today was her day off. And Pilar wasn't coming this morning to clean because she had to take Antonio to the dentist. It was just Kathryn and Matthew in the house.

Matthew, she thought as she clamped her teeth on her bottom lip.

She pushed herself up against the bank of pillows lining the headboard, which intensified the nausea. A headache worked its way up from the base of her skull. Swallowing convulsively, she put her head back and waited for the sick feeling to pass.

Several long, slow breaths later she shoved back the sheet and antique wedding-ring quilt. Not trusting her legs to hold her, she flattened one palm against the nightstand and pushed herself up. Beside the clock sat the empty wineglass she'd sipped from the night before. She wished the glass was full of water so she could ease the dryness in her mouth. Thoughts of stopping in her bathroom to get a drink dissipated when her bedroom whirled once, then righted itself. She'd be doing good just to get down the hallway to Matthew's room without adding a side-trip. Working hard to even her breathing, she forced her unsteady legs to take tentative steps, feeling like a drunk staggering against a current.

Although her head still felt like it was packed with gauze, her stomach seemed to be settling now that she was on her feet.

Good. This is good.

Dressed in a yellow cotton camisole and sleep shorts, she left her robe on the bed's footboard and made her way across the bedroom, the wood floor cool beneath her bare feet. Her hand shook when she reached for the doorknob. She stepped into the hallway; except for the low hum of the central air-conditioning the house was ominously silent.

"Matthew?" Her shout seemed to hang in the air around her.

From down the hallway came Abby's muffled bark. The dachshund's toenails scraped against the closed bedroom door.

Since Abby stuck loyally to Matthew, Kathryn reasoned both dog and boy were still in his bedroom.

Her movements felt hazy, almost dreamlike as she

made her way along the hallway. Although the distance between the bedrooms was short, she had to stop several times when the trembling in her legs worsened.

The closer she got to Matthew's room, the more urgent Abby's barks. The instant she swung open the door the dachshund leaped out, weaving frantic circles around her mistress's bare feet.

"Matthew?" Kathryn stumbled over the dog into the large, airy room with windows that looked out over the front driveway.

Her gaze swept the bed. The jungle-theme sheets and spread were rumpled, as if her son had just climbed out. His robe lay on the end of the mattress. Kathryn swiveled toward the waist-high bookcases built into the far wall. Toy tanks, airplanes and platoons of soldiers crowded the shelves. Several Jeeps and Humvees lay in a jumbled pileup on the braided rug.

"Matty, where are you?"

Pain pulsing behind her eyes, Kathryn walked toward the adjacent bathroom, Abby on her heels. Glancing down, Kathryn frowned. There was something odd about the way the dog moved, as though she had a slight catch in one hip.

"Matthew?" The silence that pressed like fingers against Kathryn's eardrums told her before she got to the bathroom that she'd find it empty.

It was.

Her concern growing, she shoved at her hair. Considering it was past ten, she wasn't surprised Matthew was out of bed. What bothered her was Abby. Matthew never went anywhere without the dachshund in tow. Unless, Kathryn reasoned, he hadn't gone far.

"Are we playing hide-and-seek?" she asked, stepping to the closet.

When she slid the door open, Abby darted inside, snuffling into each shadowy corner. A whine rose up her throat when she failed to locate her master. Kathryn lifted her gaze to the closet's shelves, but she saw nothing out of place.

When two short beeps sounded, she stepped to the bookcases. Her heart tattooed in her ears while she waited for the beeps to sound again as she scanned the shelves, trying to figure out what toy had emitted the un-familiar electronic signals.

When the beeps sounded again, she whipped around toward the bed. Her gaze settled on the nightstand and her eyes widened. A cell phone lay beside the miniature airplane that doubled as a lamp. Matthew didn't have a cell phone. And even if he'd found one that had been laid aside, she knew for sure the phone hadn't been there last night when she'd tucked him into bed and dropped a kiss on his rumpled blond hair.

She crossed the room in two strides, grabbed the phone and flipped up its cover. The screen displayed the text message icon.

Kathryn's fingers made trembling, fumbling stabs at a series of buttons. When the message displayed, its first line sent fear pressing against her heart so she could hear the panicked beat of it roaring in her ears.

WE HAVE YOUR SON.

CHAPTER THREE

"MATTHEW..." Terror crimped Kathryn's voice. A growing pressure around her heart made it beat in hitchy strikes. Her entire body shaking, she forced herself to read the entire text message.

We have your son.
We will kill him if you contact the police. We are watching you. Get one million dollars in various denominations. Keep the money and this cell phone with you. Don't change your routine. We will call and tell you what to do. Screw up, the kid dies.

The words blurred while heat traveled in a wave up Kathryn's spine.

"No, no. Matthew..." Panic clawed at her throat; for a moment, the shapes and colors in the room seemed to shift. She felt herself sway.

With a flurry of barks, Abby raced to the bedroom's door, her right hind leg lifting out of sync with the others. Turning, the dog rocketed back, tramping across Kathryn's bare feet. The contact snapped her back. She forced herself to breathe. Struggled to think.

Think. Whipping around, she dashed into the bathroom, moving so fast she plowed one hip into the sink. The pain didn't even register as she wrenched open the door on the medicine cabinet.

A ball of ice dropped into her belly as she stared at the large amber bottle containing the antirejection pills Matthew took daily. *Had to take daily*. Missing even one dose could jumpstart his system into an attempt to reject his transplanted kidney.

"Oh, God." The terror burning in her had her stomach heaving. She leaned over the sink and gagged. Nothing came up but a stream of saliva.

Rinsing her mouth, she heard Abby dashing in and out of the bathroom, felt her nipping at her ankles. The doxie's frenzied barking had Kathryn's brain clicking to the possibility that whoever had taken her son might still be in the house.

Did she still have time to save Matthew?

Fueled by that hope, she jammed the cell phone into the pocket of her shorts and darted out of the bathroom. As if connected to the dachshund by an invisible leash, Kathryn sprinted after Abby.

Her incessant barks now deep, throaty rumbles, the dog shot down the hallway, a discernible limp in her gait as her long, thin nose skimmed the wooden floor, then lifted as if scenting the air for her master.

Kathryn ran, shouting her son's name while her chest tightened and the breath sobbed out of her lungs.

Her heartbeat battered her ribs, her temples in a savage, pulsing rhythm. She couldn't face the possibility of losing her child. Refused to think it. She would find Matthew. Save him before some faceless monster carried him away.

Abby bounded off the staircase, her paws skittering

across the waxed floor. She turned a corner, scurried along the hallway toward the rear of the house, her snout sweeping to and fro.

"Matthew!" Kathryn ducked into the living room, Sam's study, then the dining room, searching for some sign of her child.

Abby slowed, turned and began retracing her zigzagging steps along the hallway. At the bottom of the staircase, she looked up at Kathryn and whined.

She'd lost Matthew's scent. Breath sobbed out of Kathryn's lungs. "We can't give up looking." Turning, she dashed toward the kitchen, her shouts for Matthew echoing through the empty house.

AFTER SEARCHING the kitchen and Willa's rooms, Kathryn hammered down the basement stairs, grabbed a flashlight and checked the outlaw tunnel, desperately hoping that she'd wake up from this nightmare and find Matthew playing there.

He wasn't.

With the tunnel's dank, musty air still in her lungs, she sprinted back upstairs, yelling his name while she checked each room, closet, looking beneath every bed. She found no sign of her child.

As she raced back down the staircase, the fear that had been pounding at her now screamed into her mind, bursting through her body like a storm of ice.

Matthew was gone. Taken by some faceless someone. *We have your son.*

The pain inside her was so huge it reached to the bone.

Intent on searching the stables, she bolted off the bottom step and plowed into a solid, unyielding frame.

"Sweet Jesus!" Reece Silver's voice was as hard as the hands he clamped onto her shoulders.

"Where is he?" Half-crazed, Kathryn shoved at the veterinarian who'd tended the Cross C's animals since she was a teen. "What have you done with him?"

"Who?" Reece loomed over her, controlling her with hands well-used to keeping strong horses in line. His face was slender, almost gaunt, and the brown eyes staring down at her were filled with confusion. "Johnny? He and I came up here to talk to you. About the mare that came down with colic yesterday? He went down the hall to the kitchen to see if you were there."

"Not Johnny," Kathryn gasped. "*Matthew!* He's gone." The hallway with its dark wood walls and floor seemed to be closing in on her. In desperation she fought against Reece's hold. "Let go!"

"Not while your eyes are glassy and your face is as pale as a boiled egg." While he spoke, the vet half-nudged, half-dragged her into the living room. "You need to sit, catch your breath." His face was grim as he prodded her into one of the wing chairs that ringed the fireplace.

"Can't…" She tried to pull in air. "Breathe."

"Lean over." Crouching beside her, Reece placed a palm against the back of her head and shoved it between her knees. The movement forced the air out of her lungs. Staring at the colorful braided rug, Kathryn pulled in a deep breath, then another.

"More," Reece said. "In and out."

She gave a vague nod. There were steel wires around her chest, around her head. Tightening, tightening.

The echo of boot heels coming down the hallway had Kathryn jerking her head up. When the Cross C's foreman stepped into the room, she nearly sobbed. Johnny Sullivan had put her up on her first horse, he'd taught her to ride, how to use a rifle, to rope a steer. He, along with Willa, had taught her how to love.

Dressed in worn jeans, a plaid shirt and scuffed boots, Johnny gripped his sweat-stained straw hat in one arthritic fist. When he spotted Kathryn, the clear blue eyes in his leathery tan face narrowed. "God Almighty, girl, you look sick as a dog."

"I'm not sick." She straightened in the chair. "It's Matthew. He's gone. Johnny, they took my baby."

"Who?" He moved to her, exchanging an uncertain look with Reece when the vet rose to his feet. "Who took our boy?"

Reece scrubbed his palms down his jeaned thighs. "I think she thought I did."

"I thought they might still be in the house," Kathryn said, her breath coming in pants. "When I ran into you…" She shook her head. "They left a cell phone in Matthew's room with a message. They want money. They'll kill him if…" Kathryn's entire body trembled. "His medicine. He *has* to take it every day. He could die if he doesn't."

"We're not gonna let that happen." Tossing his hat onto the nearby coffee table, the foreman settled a hand on her shoulder, squeezed. "I'd best get Sheriff Boudry over here."

"No!" Kathryn grabbed his hand, felt the familiar rougher-than-sandpaper calluses. "They'll kill Matthew if I go to the police." She dug the cell phone out of the pocket of her sleep shorts, and gripped it tight, the sole lifeline she had to her child. "I have to do what they say, or they'll kill him." She paused, her mind reeling in a hundred directions. "Devin. I have to call Devin and tell him. Call the bank."

Reece's concerned gaze skimmed over her face. "My advice is bring in a security expert before you do anything." He stepped around the leather couch and headed to the wet bar. There, he opened the small refrigerator, pulled out a bottle of water and twisted off the cap.

"A security expert," Kathryn repeated. Watching Reece walk back toward her, she struggled to control her thoughts. "Devin uses a security company in L.A., but I don't know the name. I'll find out." She squeezed her eyes shut. "Devin's in Tibet, making a movie."

"You don't want rent-a-cops or bodyguards." Reece set the bottle on the table next to Kathryn, then settled on the chair beside her. "You need someone who knows how to deal with kidnappers. A negotiator."

"He's right," Johnny said and gave a curt nod. "I can call over to the Double Starr and talk to Clay Turner."

"Clay?" For a crazed moment, Kathryn stared up at the foreman, wondering if he'd somehow found out about what happened between her and Clay during that long-ago summer. "No, Matthew isn't… I lost…" She clenched her jaw. *Matthew*.

Reece leaned in. "Did you hear about Clay's parents getting kidnapped in Colombia a couple of years ago?"

Kathryn nodded. Right now, she could remember only one detail. "They died. His parents died. Horribly."

"T'wern't that negotiator's fault." The foreman's hand tightened around hers. "A lot of things went wrong then. This is now. Clay was on duty in Colombia when his parents got taken and he got shot. The state department sent in some fella who knew how to deal with kidnappers to work with Clay. He can tell you how to reach that man. Say the word, I'll get Clay on the phone."

Kathryn picked up the bottle, took a long, slow drink of the cold water. She wasn't going to fall apart, wouldn't *let* herself. Doing so could cost Matthew his life. She would do whatever she had to do. Deal with whomever she had to in order to get her child back. *Just get him back.*

Setting the bottle aside, she met Johnny's gaze. "Find out where Clay is," she said levelly. "I'll go talk to him myself."

"TRACTOR THREW A ROD," Eddie Woodson informed Clay. "Second time this year." His straw hat shading his eyes from the straight-up-noon sun, the young, muscled ranch hand with corn-colored hair lapping across a sunburned neck used a rag to scrub smears of grease off his stubby fingers.

Clay sent the tractor a disgusted look. "Ever wonder why equipment always breaks down when it's in the middle of a field instead of near the work shed?"

Eddie shot Clay one of his good-natured grins. "My ma says stuff like that happens to people who have black clouds hanging over their heads."

Thinking about his past, Clay couldn't disagree.

Glancing down, he tested the soil with the toe of one boot. Too dry, he thought and made a note to turn on the system that irrigated this section of pasture earlier than programmed. Also on his mental to-do list was assigning a couple of the hands to start rotating cattle from pasture to pasture.

The designation of chores, the buying and selling of

cattle and horses had been his province for the past two years as his uncle gradually turned over the day-to-day operation of the Double Starr to Clay. Ironic, he thought, that the work he'd had no real heart for during his youth was now his whole life.

"Guess we can also blame those black clouds on how things break down when we don't have parts on hand to fix stuff." Eddie jammed the rag into the back pocket of his worn jeans. "You want me to drive into Layton now and pick up what we need?"

"Yeah." Clay adjusted the brim of his Stetson lower to shade his eyes. "I want to check Cimarron, so you can drop me at the barn," he said, referring to a mare near her time who always had difficulty foaling.

"Doc Silver's planning on being here for the birth, right?"

"Right." Studying Eddie, Clay slid the fingers of one hand into the back pocket of his jeans. Because he knew all too well how a young man with a circus going on in his pants operated, he inclined his head in the kid's direction. "I want this tractor running again today. Which means you can drop by the drugstore to rub up against that cute blond checker. What you can't do is spend a couple of hours there."

Eddie's sunburned face turned even redder. "I enjoy talkin' to Andrea, is all."

"Nothing wrong with *talking* when you don't have a tractor sitting idle."

The sudden thunder of hooves had both men looking across their shoulder. Clay narrowed his eyes. He didn't recognize the chestnut galloping flat-out over the rise, but he had no trouble identifying its rider.

He would know her if he'd spotted her five miles away. Kat had always looked more natural on horseback than she did on her own two feet. Still did.

As the chestnut thundered closer Clay noted Kathryn was hatless, her dark hair flying behind her as her boots pumped against the horse's sides. Its hurtling hooves puffed clouds of dust into the still air.

Since she'd made her feelings for him clear during yesterday's impromptu encounter, he couldn't even guess at what had brought her riding his way, hell bent for leather.

"That looks like…" Eddie squinted, then looked at Clay. "Is that Kathryn Conner?"

"Mason. It is." Clay noted that the kid was ogling Kathryn the same way the customers had in the café.

"Ma's gonna drop into a dead faint when she hears I met Devin Mason's ex."

"Put a lid on it," Clay ground out. Frowning, he watched Kathryn jerk the reins back so sharply the chestnut nearly skidded into the side of his pickup. Before the horse came to a full halt she slid out of the saddle, a movement as graceful as ballet. Still holding the reins, she turned his way.

And Clay's gut tightened. Her face was pale. Tense. Lines of stress fanned from the corners of her mouth. Shadowy smudges clung beneath her eyes.

Something was wrong. Bad wrong.

"Ma'am." Oblivious, Eddie dragged off his straw hat and stared with undisguised curiosity at the woman who'd been the talk of Layton for the past weeks. "Welcome to the Double Starr, Mrs. Mason."

Giving Eddie a vague nod, Kathryn released her

grip on the reins. While the chestnut trotted a few feet away, she kept her gaze locked with Clay's while she clenched one hand on the cell phone clipped to the waistband of her jeans.

"I need to talk to you." Her voice shook. "Alone."

Clay shifted his gaze. "Eddie, go on now and run that errand."

"Sure." Cramming his hat back on his head, the young ranch hand walked to the pickup, swung open the door, then paused. "How you gonna get back to the barn, Clay?"

"I've got my cell. I'll call one of the other hands."

"Okay." Eddie shot Kathryn another look of interest. "Ma'am."

Clay sliced a hand toward the kid. "Take off."

Eddie slid behind the wheel and turned the key; the powerful engine rumbled. Clay noted the way Eddie lifted his chin in order to keep Kathryn framed in the rearview mirror as his drove off.

"I need your help," Kathryn blurted, at the same instant Clay stepped toward her.

"What—"

"They took Matthew. My baby. He's gone."

Clay furrowed his brow. His first thought was that she and Mason had some sort of custody dispute going over their son. "Who took him?"

"I don't know." She jerked the phone off her jeans, flipped open its cover and jabbed buttons. Her hand trembled so badly the phone shook when she handed it to him. "Johnny and Reece Silver said you could help. You have to help." Her voice shuddered as badly as her hands and her words tumbled over each other. "Matthew needs his medicine. They left it. He could reject his kidney. They said you can help me. They left the phone."

Struggling to makes sense of her jumbled words, Clay looked down at the phone's display. His lungs stopped working the instant he began to read. His gaze whipped up to meet hers. "When did you get this?"

"Two hours ago." She wrapped her arms around her waist. "I overslept. Woke up sick. I could barely make it to Matthew's room. He was gone. Abby tracked them downstairs, but lost his scent. He's gone. They took Matthew."

Dread clamped a vise on Clay's chest as he pictured the compelling little boy with sparkling brown eyes and a plastic deputy's badge pinned to his T-shirt. He knew all too well what could go wrong during a kidnapping. Which was the last thing Kathryn needed to hear.

"How far did Abby track Matthew's scent?"

"Just to the bottom of the staircase. They shut her in Matthew's room when they took him. She's limping. I think they kicked her."

Clay rescanned the text of the ransom message, hoping to find something that might dull his initial fear for the boy's well-being.

He didn't.

"They'll call soon, won't they?" Kathryn asked, her voice reedy with terror. "Tell me how to get Matthew back. He needs his medicine. I'll do whatever they say. Give them anything they want. *I have to get him back.*"

"They'll call, but I'm not sure when," Clay said while his thoughts veered to his parents. His father had been the number two man at the U.S. Embassy in Bogota, his mother the ambassador's executive assistant. The rebels who'd snatched them had believed the U.S. would put pressure on the Colombian government to release jailed compatriots. A patient group, the rebels had waited two weeks to make initial contact. The hostage negotiator brought in by the State Department had told Clay that kidnappers knew every minute they delayed contact made those left behind more desperate. More afraid. More willing to pay.

And so Clay had waited for the call, then after that for his parents' safe release while his mind replayed the instant the rebels ambushed his parents' car while he was at the wheel. To Clay, it didn't matter that he'd taken a bullet during the attack—he'd been a cop, he should have sensed the danger closing in, should have protected his family. *Should have done something.* He knew he would never be rid of the guilt nor the mistrust of his own instincts that prompted him to turn in his badge. And there was no way in hell he'd risk Matthew's life by letting Kathryn rely on those faulty instincts.

"I can help you only so far." Closing the phone's cover, he offered it to her. "You need someone who knows how to deal with kidnappers. That isn't me."

From under the brim of his hat he watched her face, saw fury flare in her eyes so white-hot it could have sparked a pasture fire.

"Damn you, Clay Turner, I know I meant nothing to you." She tore the phone out of his hand with the intensity of an erupting volcano. "But if you think I'll let you turn your back on me a second time when my son's life is a stake, think again."

He said nothing for a moment. How could he when her words sliced to his core?

"I'm not turning my back," he countered levelly. "While I worked for the State Department, I had some training on what to do right after a kidnapping occurs. Which is how to keep things calm until someone who knows what they're doing arrives on the scene. The best way I can help you is to put you in touch with a hostage negotiator I know. A man who does this for a living. His name is Forbes. Quentin Forbes. He's the best there is. He knows kidnappers in and out. Knows how to negotiate—"

"I don't want to negotiate," Kathryn hissed. "I want to pay the million dollars. I'll pay whatever they want as long as I get Matthew back."

The desperation in her voice tightened the knots in Clay's gut. Another lesson Forbes had hammered into his head was that to pay too much too soon was to make kidnappers think they could squeeze more money out of the family. That doing so sometimes resulted in the extortion of a second ransom for the same victim. And prolonged the heart-wrenching wait. Not to mention they had no proof of life, which would be the first thing Forbes would demand.

Clay scrubbed a hand over his jaw, his callused fingertips scraping across the scar on his right cheek. The scar was visual proof of how cold-blooded a kidnapper's determination could be. Better to let Forbes deal with Kathryn on the issue of negotiating the ransom, Clay decided. With everything. Considering his own track record, the farther he stayed from this, the better chance Matthew had of getting out alive.

"Whether or not to negotiate the ransom amount is something you can talk over with Forbes. He'll also advise you on what to say and what not to say when the kidnappers call."

The wind picked up, slapping strands of her dark hair against her cheeks. It seemed to Clay that she swayed beneath its force. Her face was white as death now, the gleam of shock in her eyes subsiding as realization set in.

Knowing the fire that had pushed her this far was fading fast, he gave thought to taking hold of her arms and shoring her up in case her legs gave out. Suspecting she would prefer a rattlesnake bite to his touch, he opted to tug his cell phone out of his shirt pocket.

"Forbes can help get Matthew back safe," he repeated. "You can trust me on this." And she could. After all, he had always been honest with her. Brutally so.

"It'd probably be best if you talk to Matthew's father first," Clay added. "Better if you both decide what to do about Forbes." And if the unthinkable happened, *she* wouldn't have to live with the hellish guilt that the sole responsibility for her child's death lay with her.

She shook her head. "I tried to call Devin. He's in Tibet, shooting a movie. I couldn't get a good connection. It might take hours to get through to him." She pressed her fingertips to her eyes. "I can't just wait and do nothing. If the man you know, this…"

"Forbes. Quentin Forbes."

"Forbes." Dropping her hand, she looked up at Clay, her eyes dark pools of anguish. "I feel like I'm going crazy. I can't concentrate. All I can think about is Matthew. Clay, they might kill my baby."

"No." Because he could no longer stop himself, he reached out, played a hand down her arm. It had to be ninety degrees, yet her flesh was ice-cold. "They don't want to hurt him. They only want you to believe they will. The kidnappers want money," he continued. "Keeping Matthew unharmed is their only guarantee of getting it. Hang on to that, Kat."

Nodding, she looked away. Clay watched as she raked her fingers through her hair, leaving it a dark, rumpled frame around her ashen face. He remembered, perfectly remembered, the silky softness of that hair against his hands.

Again, he felt the hard knot of regret for how callously he had treated her. For all that he'd given up. Thrown away. Lost.

When Kathryn remet his gaze her eyes were expressionless, her face as calm as carved stone. "Call him, Clay. Call your Mr. Forbes."

"All right." Clay's chest tightened. He would do everything he could to save Kat's son. Just as he'd done all he could to try to save his parents.

Beneath his hand, he felt Kathryn shudder. Until Forbes arrived, Clay knew he was the only man who could help her.

And the last man who should.

CHAPTER FOUR

AFTER LEAVING a message for the negotiator, Clay swung up into the saddle on Kathryn's mare, then held out a hand to her. When he saw her hesitate, he felt a quick, nasty slice to his heart that he struggled to ignore.

Hard to do when on its heels came a flash of memory: Kat at eighteen, slim and leggy, with black hair to her waist, a young woman not entirely aware of her effect on him. Granted, her schoolgirl crush had her chasing after him for years, but one look at her that summer and he'd let himself be caught…not captured. Still sowing his wild oats, he'd refused to admit there was more to the relationship than the lustful, sweaty need of a man for a woman. Yet, when he reported back to work in Houston, Kat had stayed on his mind. And still he denied his feelings, telling himself he had time to get a handle on things.

Time ran out when she phoned and told him she was pregnant. He'd headed for Layton, his emotions warring. Age-old emotions of the rounder he'd been with those of the man whose heart was trying to lead him for the first time.

But when he arrived in Layton, Kathryn had miscarried. And the pale young woman lying in the hospital bed no longer gazed at him with love shining in her eyes, but with hurt and indifference.

So he kept his uncertain feelings to himself, took her to the friend's house where she wanted to stay, then left when she told him to go.

And tried to put her out of his mind. Which was something he'd done pretty well, until his parents died and all the guilt and regret flooded over him.

Clay's thoughts jerked from the past when Kathryn slid her hand into his.

With ease that came from a lifetime of climbing onto a horse, she fit her left foot into the stirrup and settled in front of him in one smooth move. The scent of her hair filled his head. When her backside nestled into his thighs, he felt his insides jolt, like a boulder teetering off a cliff.

Ah, hell. The last thing he needed was a reminder of the heat that had always arrowed straight to his loins whenever they touched.

Thinking of Matthew in a kidnapper's clutches, Clay set his jaw, reined the mare around and moved off.

After reaching Cross C property, they left the mare to graze and approached the house from the rear where a flagstone terrace spilled out of tall French doors. Yellow mums sat amid the wrought-iron furniture; the clear water in the swimming pool glittered like diamonds beneath the bright sun.

"Did you notice if any doors were unlocked this morning?" Clay asked while studying the house. "Any windows open?"

"I didn't check the doors." Kathryn dragged her fingers across her damp forehead. "If a window had been open, I probably would have noticed, but I'm not sure."

"What about Willa? Did she hear anything last night or early this morning?"

"She's not home. Willa spends every Wednesday night at her daughter's house in Dallas."

"Every Wednesday?"

"Yes. She's done that for as long as I can remember."

"Is there any other live-in help?"

"No. Pilar Graciano comes in daily and helps Willa." Kathryn met his gaze. "You might remember her or her husband, Nilo. Matthew went with Nilo and his son, Antonio, to string fence." She pressed her fingertips to her lips. "Yesterday. It was just yesterday morning."

When her world was still on an even keel, Clay thought. "Did Pilar come to work this morning?"

"No. She had to take Antonio to the dentist."

Interesting, Clay thought, that the kidnapper struck the one night of the week Willa was gone. He wondered if the kidnapper knew the maid wouldn't show this morning. Forbes would want to give everyone privy to that kind of info a hard look.

Thinking of the negotiator reminded Clay how out of his league he was. But until Forbes returned his call, he could at least look around and at the same time keep Kathryn busy. Giving her as little time as possible to think about the uncertain fate of her child was the best thing he could do for her.

"Kat, I need you to walk me through everything you did this morning, starting from when you woke up. Retrace your steps."

"I looked for Matthew everywhere. Even the outlaw tunnel." She closed her eyes. "I didn't find *anything*."

Clay gripped her elbow, turned her to face him. She

looked afraid. Vulnerable. "You were searching for Matthew. We need to see if we can find a trace of himself the kidnapper might have left. Something that may lead us to him. To Matthew."

"All right." Her lips trembled. "He needs his medicine. We have to find him, Clay. We have to."

"We will," he said. And hoped to hell that when they did, Matthew was still alive.

BY THE TIME Kathryn finished walking Clay through the house, it was late afternoon. Now, she stood in Matthew's bedroom, her arms wrapped around her waist while she stared out the window at the distant stables and barn. Beyond them sat two houses. Nilo and Pilar Graciano and their son resided in the larger of the two. Johnny Sullivan lived next door to them.

Behind the houses land stretched toward the horizon. Matthew was out there. Somewhere. Scared. Wanting her. Needing her. Crying for her.

She closed her eyes. The helplessness—the awful knowing she could do nothing to lessen her child's terror—wrapped around her like a suffocating straitjacket. She felt ill from the fear burning inside her. A horrible, all-consuming fear that she was destined to stand at this window for the rest of her life, wondering what had happened to her child.

"So, after you talked to Reece Silver and Johnny, you changed clothes," Clay said. "Then rode over to find me."

"Yes." Kathryn turned. Clay stood across the room, studying the cork board on the wall above Matthew's desk. Pinned to the board were drawings of odd-shaped horses sketched in a rainbow of crayons. A snapshot of Matthew, grinning ear to ear while propped in the crook of Devin's arm, was pinned in the board's center.

She studied Clay, his profile tough, contained, grim. Being with him, having him here when he'd been gone from her life for so long made everything seem even more surreal. Yet she knew his presence was the only thing keeping her sane.

"Do you think Mr. Forbes will call soon?" she asked.

"If he doesn't, I'll try him again." Clay moved to the braided rug beside the bed, crouched and rubbed Abby's head. The dachshund's tail worked like a metronome set on high.

"Kat, when did Willa leave for Dallas?"

"Before supper. Matthew and I made pizza…." Her voice caught as she pictured her son's mischievous grin while he formed pepperoni slices into a happy face. She couldn't bear the thought that she might never see him grin again. Laugh again.

"After that?" Clay prodded.

She clamped down on emotion. "We watched TV. Later I put Matthew to bed."

"Then what?"

"I checked the doors." She paused, thinking. "Poured my glass of wine, then went to bed and read. I couldn't keep my eyes open so I turned off the light after about ten minutes."

Clay cocked his head. "You said, 'I poured *my* glass of wine.' Do you always have wine before you go to bed?"

"Yes." She'd needed something to help her relax when she learned Devin was having an affair with his then leading lady.

"Who knows you always have a glass of wine before bed?"

"I guess Willa. Before we arrived, I asked her to add a couple of bottles of Merlot to her shopping list. She said it was too bad Sam got sick before he had time to stock the wine cellar he'd had built in the basement."

"Where's the bottle you filled your glass with last night?"

"The living room. In the cooler behind the bar."

"Was last night the first time you'd drank from that bottle?"

"No, I opened it the first night I was here."

"Since you've been back, have you woken up sick any other morning?"

"No. Clay, why do you want to know about the wine?"

"Because you said you felt sick this morning and overslept." He gave Abby a final rub of her ears, then rose. "I don't think you picked up a bug. More like someone laced your wine."

Kathryn's mouth went dry. "That would mean whoever took Matthew knows my habits."

"And a lot more. If I'm right, the kidnapper knew Willa would be gone. With you drugged, the threat of exposure was minimal. Then there's Abby."

Kathryn looked down at the doxie. "What about her?"

"You said she was limping, like she'd been kicked."

"Yes. You don't think she was?"

"No. One reason is how she greeted me when I got here. She'd never seen me before, but she trotted over and licked my hand. It's logical to think she acted the same way when the kidnapper showed up. If Abby knew him, she would have been more welcoming. And if they wanted to keep her quiet, why *kick* her?"

Kathryn shoved a hand through her hair. "Doing that wouldn't make sense."

"You told me Abby would have had a barking fit over being left behind when they took Matthew. The kidnappers couldn't be sure you'd pour yourself a glass of wine last night or how much you'd drink if you did. So they wouldn't want any noise that might wake you. The sole threat Abby posed was barking when they left with Matthew. The best way to deal with that would be to give her a shot of a fast-acting sedative. It'd keep her quiet for hours, and cause the limp you saw."

Guilt descended over Kathryn like clammy heat. "Matthew was virtually unprotected. It would have been nothing for me to have an alarm installed before we arrived here. I could have hired a security company to patrol the ranch—"

"It's not your fault, Kat."

"He depended on me to keep him safe. He's gone because—"

"Some greedy bastard came in here and took him," Clay said as he gripped her shoulders. "Another thing I learned from Forbes is how committed kidnappers can be. That whomever they plan to take, they take. If you'd had this place secured like Fort Knox, they would have gotten Matthew some other way."

"Devin has bodyguards," she tossed back. "I should have hired someone to watch Matthew."

Clay gave her a firm shake. "Your blaming yourself won't help your son."

She gripped his wrists. "I don't know how to help him."

"You stay calm, is how." Clay felt the knots in his gut jerk tighter. Dammit, every hour that went by put Matthew into greater peril. Why hadn't Forbes called?

Beneath his palms, he felt Kathryn tremble. Her face was chalk-white, her eyes gleamed with a mix of fear and absolute helplessness.

Easing out a breath, he thought about the conclusions he'd come to. If he was right about the wine and the dog, whoever took Matthew had done a lot of research. "Kidnappers," Forbes had once told Clay, "plan to the last inch." The articles Clay had read in the *Layton Times* and *People* magazine about Devin Mason had mentioned his son's kidney transplant.

"What type of medicine does Matthew take?"

"An immunosuppressive drug. Transplant patients take them to prevent rejection of their transplanted organ."

"So, with research, the kidnapper would know that," Clay reasoned. "This guy came prepared. Maybe he left that way, too." He looked toward the bathroom. "You said you saw the prescription bottle with Matthew's medicine. Can you find out if extra pills are missing?"

"I had the prescription refilled two days ago. There should be only two pills gone from the bottle."

"Count the pills, Kat."

"You think the kidnapper took some? To give to Matthew?"

"I think we'd be smart to check." When she started to turn, he held her in place. "Even if all the pills that should be in the bottle are there, it doesn't mean Matthew won't get his meds. Not when it's easy to buy drugs over the Internet."

"Okay." Kathryn closed her eyes. "If I could just be sure Matthew's taking his medicine."

"It's my bet he is." At least Clay hoped so.

His phone rang just as Kathryn stepped into the bathroom. Relief rolled through Clay when he saw Forbes's name displayed.

That relief lasted only until Forbes advised he was in England, negotiating the release of an earl's kidnapped wife.

With tension coiling through him, Clay briefed him on Matthew's abduction. And the conclusions he'd come to.

"I think you're right about Mrs. Mason and the dog being drugged," Forbes said in his perpetually calm voice. "And that a check needs to be run on everyone with access to the Cross C." Clay pictured the gray-haired, scrawny-necked man who never showed emotion, even in the face of impending disaster. Forbes's air of quiet confidence went a long way to soothing and calming.

For three months, the man had kept Clay sane.

"What about the cell phone the kidnapper left?" Forbes asked. "Can it be traced?"

"No, it's a brand I've never heard of, so I went online and checked it out. The phone's a disposable one, sold by a company that doesn't require a purchaser to sign a contract or have a credit card. All someone has to do is walk into any convenience store, lay down cash and they've got a phone with a preset amount of calling minutes on it."

"With no audit trail assigned to the phone there's no way to trace who bought it. So, that's a dead end."

"Right," Clay agreed.

"The ransom amount puzzles me," Forbes continued. "Devin Mason is wealthy. Why ask only one million dollars for his son's safe return?"

"Good question." Clay tightened his grip on the phone. "Look, I understand why you can't come to Texas, but I need to get another negotiator fast. Who do you recommend?"

"You."

Old memories, like the ghost of past sins, knotted Clay's gut. "No way in hell." For two years he'd lived with guilt over his parents' death that gave him night sweats and a dull, skittering sense of panic. The last thing he wanted was to take on the responsibility of Matthew Mason's life.

"You know the normal goings-on in the community," Forbes persisted. "Since the kidnapper insists Mrs. Mason maintain her regular schedule, we can assume he's in a position to watch her. You're a friend, a neighbor, you can place yourself near her without alarming the person holding Matthew. And perhaps spot someone who seems overcurious about her."

Clay set his jaw. From the instant Kathryn handed him the phone with the ransom message he'd had the sensation of having stepped in quicksand. Now, he felt himself getting sucked farther into a black hole. How could he help her when he couldn't trust himself to make the right moves?

"Kathryn is a celebrity," he said. "Everyone is curious about her, so you'd have Layton's entire popu-lation on your suspect list. The best way I can help her is from a distance."

"I disagree. Mrs. Mason needs someone she can trust

staying close to her to assess the people she interacts with. Someone who will know if a person's normal body language has changed, if they're showing signs of nervousness and stress. You're a former police officer, you're trained to do that."

"Are you forgetting my instincts are so screwed I didn't sense the danger closing in on my parents?"

"What happened in Bogota was not your fault. And even if I were able to come there," Forbes continued, "I would be dependent on you to advise me on the people, their backgrounds. You already know who, if anyone, on the local police force can be trusted to be approached. I can consult for Mrs. Mason by phone if you'll agree to work with her there."

"Dammit." Clay lowered his voice to a whisper. "I don't want to be responsible for another person dying."

"You have never been responsible for that."

Just then, Clay saw Kathryn step from the bathroom, the pill bottle gripped in one hand. He explained to Forbes about Matthew's medicine, then held the phone so that the negotiator could hear Kathryn.

"Ten of the pills are gone."

"You're sure?" Clay asked.

"I counted them three times."

"Okay. Is there any chance Matthew could have gotten that bottle out of the cabinet? Taken the missing pills, thinking they were candy? Or maybe to hide them?"

"No. He's spent weeks in the hospital, years going to various doctors. He understands why he has to take medicine."

Clay put the phone back to his ear. "You hear that?"

"Yes, ten pills," Forbes said. "I wonder if that's the

kidnapper's timetable? Ten days from the snatch to delivery of the ransom. Or do they plan to demand the ransom be paid sooner? They possibly took more pills as a cushion in case something unforeseen requires they hold the boy longer than planned. If that's the case, why not just take the bottle?"

"Would have made more sense," Clay said.

"You said Matthew's father is in Tibet?"

"Yes. He insisted on coming here to deal with the kidnappers. I talked him into staying put, at least for now."

"And you claim you can't handle things?" Without waiting for a response, Forbes added, "Let me speak to Mrs. Mason."

Clay handed Kathryn the phone. "He wants to talk to you."

"He's coming, right?" she asked. "Mr. Forbes is coming?"

He met her desperate gaze. "No, Kat, he can't come."

AFTER TALKING to Forbes, Kathryn handed the phone back to Clay, then clenched her hands to keep from burying her face in them and weeping. Because her legs had turned to water, she lowered herself onto the edge of her son's bed.

"We can bring in another negotiator," Clay said.

"How long will that take? Another day? Two? Three?"

"There's no way to know until I make a few calls."

Kathryn pleated the rumpled sheet. The bed was in the same condition as when she stumbled into the room that morning. She thought of the stories she'd read about parents who left the bedrooms of their missing children unchanged. Her heart had ached for those people. Now, she was one of them.

She looked at the phone she'd placed on the nightstand. "Why don't they call? God, why don't they *just call*?"

"They will," Clay said. "When they do, remember what we went over."

"No matter what they…threaten, stand firm," she said, her voice raspy. "Insist they get the ransom only after I have proof Matthew is alive."

"Staying calm while they swear they'll kill your child will be the hardest thing you'll ever do."

She met Clay's grim gaze. "You know that, because of when your parents were taken, right? You had to stay calm while talking to the people who…" *Killed them.*

Kathryn's throat tightened when she saw the pain in Clay's eyes a second before his expression hardened. Now that the stunning shock that had held her in its grip was subsiding, she realized how difficult her situation must be for him.

"When Reece and Johnny said you could help me, I didn't think twice. I just found you. It didn't occur to me how dredging all this up would be for you. I don't guess I cared. But it has to hurt, remembering what happened to your family."

Clay stared down at her. There was no way for her to know that his pain was twofold, that his parents might never have been kidnapped if only he'd made a different choice where she was concerned. So many regrets, he thought. So much pain.

Pain that he was going to have to shove back into the dark pit inside him since the weight of responsibility for Matthew's life had dropped like lead onto his shoulders. Though he'd wanted to avoid that, Clay knew this wasn't about what had happened to his parents, or himself. This was about a five-year-old boy whose life was at stake.

And the ashen-faced woman staring up at him.

He crouched beside the bed, bringing his face level with hers. "Matthew's situation is different," he said evenly. "My parents were grabbed by rebels who wanted to force the Colombian government to release their imprisoned pals. A Colombian general lost patience and ordered an attack on the rebel camp. My parents got caught in the crossfire."

Reaching out, Clay tucked a wisp of dark hair behind Kathryn's ear. When heat arrowed straight to his gut, he nearly jerked his hand away. He knew the only way Matthew would stay alive was for everyone involved to keep emotion out of the mix. For him, that wasn't going to be easy.

"Matthew doesn't have opposing groups warring over him," he continued. "His kidnappers want money. You're willing to pay. We'll get him back safe if we're careful."

Kathryn pulled her bottom lip between her teeth. The man crouched before her bore only a vague resemblance to her lover from a decade ago. Then, there'd been no furrows creasing his forehead. No crinkles at the corners of those dark brown eyes. No lines fanning from the mouth that had so often curved into a cocky grin that had added to the instant, sexual punch. No scar slashing a diagonal line across his right cheek and temple.

She had given him her heart and he'd shattered it. Her own fault, she conceded, since Clay had never pretended his feelings mirrored hers. Nor had he lied about his intentions, or anything else. Knowing that, she now pulled his words to her heart, clinging to them like a safety line to her child.

"Was Mr. Forbes with you in Colombia? Advising you what to do?"

"Yes. It would have been a lot worse if he hadn't been there."

She looked toward the window. Already late afternoon shadows had set in. Evening would creep up, then darkness. She couldn't bear to think about Matthew alone in the dark.

"My appointment with Brad Jordan is in the morning. When I called to tell him Devin was wiring a million dollars to my account and I needed it in cash, I could tell Brad was holding himself back from asking me why. The hospital benefit is tomorrow night. Shannon Burton will be there. She keeps calling, wanting to interview me about Sam. She'll ask about Devin. About Matthew."

Kathryn shook her head, overwhelmed by the prospect of making a misstep that might alert someone about her child's plight. "The ransom message said not to change my schedule. I can't cancel anything while we wait to get another negotiator's advice." She shuddered. "How am I supposed to act normal when I have no idea where my son is? No idea what he's going through?"

"You'll do it for Matthew's sake," Clay said quietly. "I've got an idea how you can deal with Jordan so getting that much cash doesn't pique his interest. We'll talk about the best way to handle Burton. My uncle is on the hospital's board of directors, so we'll take you to the benefit, give you support there."

Kathryn stood and wandered to the far side of the

room. She paused before the wall of built-in shelves crowded with tanks, Humvees and soldiers. To her right, her laptop computer sat on Matthew's small desk. Yesterday she had sat there with him on her lap while they wrote an e-mail to his father.

Her gaze went to the picture on the cork board; tears burned her eyes, blurring her son's face. She took a choked breath. She hadn't let herself cry. Couldn't. With fear imbedded deep inside her she was afraid if she started sobbing she would never stop. And no amount of tears would get her son back.

She turned to face Clay. "Mr. Forbes said I can put full confidence in what you tell me. That you know the right things to do."

She saw a flicker in Clay's eyes. "I'll do what I can to help. But you need someone here to give you expert advice."

"You're the reason I've gotten this far without falling apart, Clay." She wrapped her arms around her waist. "Mr. Forbes agrees with you that Devin should stay in Tibet."

"It's the best thing for Matthew."

"Which is what you've kept in mind this whole time." She rubbed her fingers across her throat. "If you hadn't told me to count his pills, I wouldn't know the kidnappers took any of them. I wouldn't have the hope they intend to keep Matthew healthy."

"It was a guess on my part."

"A good one. Everything Forbes told me, I had already heard from you. He's an expert and you know how he thinks." At that instant she realized what it had been that reached so deeply inside her when Clay spoke to her earlier with soothing softness. Forbes's voice had sounded much the same. Calm. Comforting. A voice that had taken an edge off her fear by instilling hope.

Her gaze returned to Clay. Seeing him yesterday had been a stark reminder of the vow she had made after her marriage crumbled to never again place her hopes, her needs, her wants in the hands of another man. But it wasn't her heart at stake now, it was her son's life. Forbes had told her she could put her faith in Clay. That, coupled with a deep, intuitive certainty told her that depending on him was the right thing to do.

Her mind made up, Kathryn retraced her steps across the room. "You're the best person to fill Forbes's shoes."

Clay shook his head. He hadn't been the best man for anything since he wound up in a pool of his own blood while his parents got dragged away. "You can't depend on my guesswork."

"Whatever you tell me won't be guesswork," she countered quietly, watching a muscle work in his jaw. "Because you learned from an expert."

"I wasn't sitting in a damn classroom." Clay scrubbed a hand across the back of his neck. "Forbes and I moved from one roach-infested hut to another while we followed rumored sightings of the rebels holding my parents. Inside, I felt as unsteady as you do right now. I picked up things from Forbes, but I can't guarantee I know what he would do."

"You know how he thinks, Clay," she countered. "And if you're not sure, you can call him. You know Mr. Forbes, you *trust* him. I don't want someone who neither of us knows guessing what I need to do to keep my son alive."

She moved forward until only inches separated them.

The familiar salty clean scent of his skin slid into her lungs. She remembered the swirling fire that scent had once ignited inside her. Remembered, too, the passion that had fueled the man when he'd gone after something he wanted, whether it be the job at the state department, the breaking of a wild bronc—even her for a short time. That same passion would drive him to do everything in his power to help her bring Matthew home alive.

"You know what it's like to be the one left behind." She placed her hand on Clay's forearm. Beneath her fingers, she felt taut muscle and shimmering tension. "The one waiting for the phone to ring. You know how terribly things can go wrong. Because of that, you'll be extra careful nothing does."

Clay's gaze lowered to the hand curled against his bare arm. In the next instant Kathryn felt it, a kind of quiet internal click. A reconnection, as if ten years had not passed. Emotion unexpected. And unwelcome.

She pulled her hand back, flexed her fingers and thought of her son. "You're who Matthew and I need. I trust you, Clay."

He stared at her a long moment, wishing to hell he trusted himself. "Think about this overnight. About how it will only take a few calls to get a pro here. Maybe by morning you'll see the sense in that."

She glanced across her shoulder at the grinning snapshot of Matthew, his brown eyes so brightly alive. Just the thought of him any other way shredded her insides. So she wouldn't let herself think the unthinkable. She would concentrate on bringing Matthew home alive. Listen to her instincts that told her the man who was a part of her past was her son's best hope for the future.

Looking back, she met Clay's waiting gaze. "I won't change my mind."

He saw the trust, the sureness in her eyes and it scared the hell out of him.

"All right, Kat, let's start now." He'd planned to wait until morning to bring up the subject on the off chance she could find a measure of peace overnight and get some sleep. Now, the point he needed to drive home was too important to put off.

"I want you to approve my going to Sheriff Boudry," he said bluntly. "To tell him Matthew's been kidnapped."

Clay set his jaw while he watched her eyes go wide.

"The…ransom message said no police." The only color left in her face was the arctic blue of her eyes. "They'll kill Matthew if we call the police."

"You need to sit down." Clay gripped her arm, nudged her toward the bed, then settled beside her. "Boudry moved here after you went off to college so you don't know him. I do. He's smart, knows how to keep his mouth shut."

"But he'll write a report. Someone might see it."

"I'm not talking about dialing 911 and making this official. I do that, Boudry is required by law to call the FBI. You've told me that's the last thing you want to do."

"The very last thing. How will your going to the sheriff be any different?"

Clay rested his elbows on his thighs. "Only Boudry will know Matthew's been kidnapped. He can have his deputies use their eyes and ears for our benefit without them knowing it."

"How?"

"The sheriff can work it so his troops watch for

activity that's out of the norm, for strangers in town." Clay pursed his mouth. "If there's only a single kidnapper, he can't watch you if he's got Matthew stashed too far away. Word would spread like a prairie fire if I went to a real estate office and asked for a list of every house in the county that's been rented lately. Boudry can get that information without causing a ripple."

"What if you're wrong about him?" Kathryn asked. "What if Boudry finds out where Matthew is? Suppose he orders his deputies to surround the place?" She shook her head. "The kidnapper might kill Matthew."

"Yes." Clay sat up slowly, locked his gaze with hers. "There's a chance I'm wrong about Boudry. I won't approach him unless you give me the go-ahead. This won't be the only decision like this you'll have to make. There will be more. That's why you should bring in an expert."

She reached for the rumpled sheet, began pleating it between her fingers. "If I bring in someone else to advise me, he won't know anything about the sheriff, who he is, what he might do." She lifted her gaze to Clay's. "I meant what I said. I trust your judgment. Go see Sheriff Boudry."

Despite the sick dread in his stomach, Clay nodded. "I'll talk to him in the morning. Right now, we need to try to figure out how the kidnapper got in and out." Clay gave Abby's ears a scratch, then stood. "You remember locking the doors before you went to bed. I've checked them all, and all the windows, and haven't found any sign of forced entry."

"So, you think the kidnapper has a key?"

"Or knows how to pick a lock." Clay shoved a hand through his hair. "Even with a key, he wouldn't risk using the front door. Not when he couldn't be certain one of the hands might have had a sleepless night and be standing outside, smoking."

"So, one of the back doors would have posed less risk."

Clay nodded. "If it were me, I'd use the outlaw tunnel."

"But the only lock on the outer door is on the *inside*. There's no way to get the door open from the outside."

"Not if it's locked," Clay pointed out. "But if whoever took Matthew *did* drug your wine, he or she was inside the house at some point before last night. The person could be familiar enough with how this place works to know where spare keys are kept. It would only take a couple of minutes to grab the key to the tunnel, slip downstairs and unlock both doors. The tunnel's outer entrance is far enough away it can't been seen from the house. Making it the perfect way for a kidnapper to get in and out of the house undetected."

"But we went to the tunnel when I walked you through what I did this morning. You didn't find anything."

"I only went about three-quarters of the way to the end because the light was too dim to do a thorough check, and I didn't want to mess up any evidence. We need to go back there and take our time looking around."

Kathryn rose. Instead of moving toward the door, she paused at the window. Memories, she thought, were hidden bombs, lying everywhere. "For years, I didn't think about the outlaw tunnel. Didn't want to because it reminded me…" Pain twisted in her heart. "I didn't tell Matthew about it until right before we got here. The tunnel was all he talked about. When he mentioned it to you at the café, I saw in your eyes that you remembered."

"I remember everything, Kat."

The thick rug muffled Clay's footsteps as he moved to stand behind her. Unwilling to face him while the past pressed in on her, Kathryn kept her gaze focused out the window.

"I regret the way I treated you back then," Clay said quietly. "I'll always regret that."

"You were honest," she said. "But I had so many stars in my eyes I chose to ignore what you said about not wanting strings. Commitment. I was sure I could change your mind."

"But there was a string," Clay said, keeping his eyes locked on her profile. "You were pregnant. If I'd been here when you found out, I wouldn't have walked away—"

"That wouldn't have changed how you felt about me." She pressed a trembling hand to her throat. "Wouldn't have stopped him... Stopped me from falling." She forced back the memory of the part her grandfather played in her miscarriage. She had another child to think about now. "None of what happened in the past matters now. What matters is getting Matthew back."

"You're right." Clay's throat ached with the words while regret filled the air around him like invisible smoke. "Nothing else should matter."

But it did.

She mattered, and he'd kept his true feelings for her locked away for years. The passage of time had only made him more certain that Kathryn Conner was the best thing that had ever happened to him.

And that he had no hope of getting back what he had tossed away.

CHAPTER FIVE

HE HAD THE KID.

Finally.

Crouching over the cellar's wooden door, the man used the heel of his palm to shoot home the shackle of the shiny new padlock. He tugged the lock, making sure it was secure on the hasp he'd bolted to the door. That done, he stood and turned his back on the boarded-up farmhouse hidden in the thick copse of trees. The late afternoon air was heavy with so much humidity that it felt like a wet towel against his skin.

After the gripping fear he'd been living with, the heat was a minor annoyance. What mattered was that in the wee hours of the morning everything had gone according to plan. He'd snatched the kid out from under Kathryn Conner Mason's rich nose.

Miss Hollywood had to be feeling powerless. Terrified. Frantic while waiting for the phone to ring.

His feeling of triumph abruptly fizzled. Despite knowing he had his ticket out of the mess he was in locked away, the man's insides still felt like a coiled rattler. No way could he let himself relax until he had the money. He had researched every document and case study he could find on the Internet about kidnapping, with an eye to finding out how others had screwed up.

He'd learned most mistakes happened at the point when the ransom was handed over. Which included ransoms "handed over" electronically.

He'd first planned on demanding the million be wired to an offshore account. But research confirmed that for every electronic transfer made, there was some computer whiz who could follow the electronic trail, no matter how complex or faint.

So, he'd opt for Plan B. And when it came time to collect the dough, he would have his associate show up at the drop site.

And *he* would watch from a safe distance. If the cops closed in, they'd have no reason to suspect him. He would fade into the shadows. Then show mommy dearest he meant business by sending her one of the kid's fingers with the demand for a second ransom.

Which was something he didn't want to have to do because he needed the damn money *soon*.

Once he had it, he could get his life back on track.

The man shoved on his sunglasses and strode to the gray sedan parked behind the house, his boot heels crunching through overgrown grass and weeds. He had good reason for not demanding a king's ransom, just one that Miss Hollywood and her superstar ex could put together at the speed of light. Money that would get him out of trouble. Save his neck.

Just thinking about the visit he'd had from the enforcer sent fear wafting up his spine. His hands began to tremble. He nearly fumbled the pill bottle he dug out of his shirt pocket.

He palmed two tablets into his mouth, dry-swallowed them.

He took a careful breath. It wouldn't be much longer, he told himself. A couple more days, then he'd be home free.

Safe.

He pictured the small boy he'd left lying drugged in the cellar. At last he held all the cards. *He* was in control.

As long as everything went according to plan, the kid didn't have to die.

WITH ABBY at her heels and Clay following behind, Kathryn descended the wooden steps to the basement, the air going from cool to refrigerator cold. The windows had been nailed shut and painted years ago, so the only light came from the overhead fixtures suspended from the joists.

A sparkling washer and dryer sat against one wall, vivid contrasts to the nearby ancient soapstone sink. A laundry line stretched overhead. Tucked into a nook were the water heater and furnace, its silver ducting extending in several directions.

Abby trotted to the opposite wall to sniff at the stacks of empty boxes and trunks that had held the items Kathryn shipped from California.

Despair pressed in on her at the thought of repacking those boxes with Matthew's belongings because he was no longer alive to use them. She curled her fingers into her palms while cautioning herself not to think that way. She couldn't give up hope—they would get him back, safe and sound. *They had to get him back*.

Legs unsteady, she moved to a metal storage cabinet

and swung open its doors. "Sam kept tons of flashlights in here," she told Clay, forcing her voice to remain emotionless. "For as long as I can remember, Johnny has come down every month or so to check them and change batteries when necessary."

Clay flicked a look at the cabinet's contents. "Meaning, the Cross C's foreman has unlimited access to the house. And the outlaw tunnel."

She met Clay's gaze. It wasn't a giant mental step to follow his thoughts. "Johnny Sullivan has worked here since before I was born. He helped Willa raise me. He wouldn't have kidnapped Matthew. He *couldn't* have."

"I'm not saying he did, Kat. But whoever took Matthew has a connection to the Cross C and needs a lot of money fast. That's why I've already got a private investigator running financial and background checks on all employees. We'll expand that to anyone with even the slightest connection to the ranch once we have that list of names. We also need to look at Sam's political associates and constituents."

"Sam?" Kathryn shook her head. "You think it's possible someone with a grudge against my grandfather took Matthew?"

"We can't discount anything. The kidnapper could just be someone who'd benefit financially from a ransom. Someone Sam invited to the lavish dinner parties he was famous for hosting."

Clay swept a hand in the direction of the intricately carved door to the wine cellar, which had been completed just before Sam learned his days were numbered. "My uncle Les is chairman of the Layton Municipal League. Sam invited the league's board of directors to dinner. Afterward, they came down here so the senator could show off the wine cellar he planned to stock with wine made from Texas vineyards. Uncle Les said the senator also showed off the outlaw tunnel while relating how his great-great-great-something-grandfather Conner built it so his bandit son could sneak in and out to visit his family."

Kathryn looked around. Had the monster who'd taken Matthew learned the layout of the house while a guest of Sam's?

"Let's say you find out that someone Sam entertained here has financial trouble," she said. "What then?"

"Look at any connection he or she has to someone who works here." Clay paused, his gaze steady on hers. "It's possible whoever snatched Matthew might have had help from someone close to you. Someone you've known most of your life. And trust."

Kathryn thought about the kidnapper striking on the night of the week that Willa habitually spent with her daughter in Dallas. Then there was the drugged wine. And the possibility the kidnapper knew Pilar wouldn't be in the house that morning.

Kathryn could find no argument with Clay's logic. "I know you're right." She didn't realize her hands were trembling until she reached inside the cabinet for a flashlight. Her shoulders were board-stiff and her pulse had kicked up a notch. With her emotions in turmoil, she realized she couldn't bear to step foot into the outlaw tunnel again that day.

Maybe it was because in her heart she knew it was how the kidnapper gained access into the house. And the route by which he'd taken Matthew away. If he had struggled, he could have been injured. She didn't trust herself to stay in control if Clay's intense examination of the tunnel unearthed drops of blood.

Add to that her reluctance to again venture with Clay into the dark confines of a place where they had once spent the good part of a rainy night making love.

At least for her, it had been making love. She was sure he'd considered that time just another hot, fast ride.

Standing before the open cabinet, she was suddenly aware he was near enough that she could feel the warmth from his body in the basement's cool air. His worn jeans and denim work shirt emphasized his strength and fitness. She longed to step into his arms, rest her head against his shoulder and find some comfort against her desperate fear. Instead she handed him the flashlight and moved away.

"If you don't need me, I'll go start work on the list of names."

"I can check the tunnel on my own." He turned, walked toward the rear of the basement, his boot steps leaving an empty echo against the concrete floor.

Kathryn watched him unlock the heavy wooden door, pull it open, then disappear inside. Abby raced in after him.

She remained where she was, the entrance to the outlaw tunnel staring back at her like a single black eye. The dank, heavy scent of earth drifted from the tunnel's open door. Everything she'd said to Clay earlier about trusting him with Matthew's life was true. Yet she found herself wondering again if she'd been right to agree to his going to Sheriff Boudry.

We have your son.

We will kill him if you contact the police.

A weight pressed against her heart so she could hear its panicked beat in her ears. What if letting Clay contact the sheriff got Matthew killed? She could still change her mind, she told herself. Tell Clay not to go to Boudry.

She scrubbed her hands over her face, wishing Devin was there to help her make decisions. But with the paparazzi watching his every move, there was no way he could get to the Cross C undetected. If Devin was here, the media would camp at the ranch's entrance. Clay and Mr. Forbes agreed that could turn a kidnapper lethal.

"Yoo-hoo? Kathryn, are you and Matthew playing down there?"

Kathryn whipped around at the sound of Willa's cheery voice coming from the top of the stairs. Oh, Lord, she hadn't given a thought to how to break the news of the kidnapping to Willa.

"I'm coming up." Squaring her shoulders, Kathryn headed for the stairs.

TWENTY MINUTES LATER, Kathryn sat at the table in the kitchen's windowed alcove, gripping Willa's hands. The housekeeper's eyes brimmed with tears and her skin looked almost as gray as the hair scraped back into its usual bun.

"Our poor baby." Willa's breath shuddered through her lips. "Matthew must be so scared."

"Yes." Kathryn blinked back her own tears. Dammit, she wasn't going to let herself cry. Crying wouldn't help Matthew.

"You're positive they took the medicine?"

"Yes."

Willa looked at the phone Kathryn had laid on the

table. "Why don't they call to tell you how to get our little boy back?"

"Clay said kidnappers know delaying contact makes those left behind more desperate. More willing to pay." Kathryn swallowed around the tightness in her throat. "He's right."

"Clay Turner." Willa shook her head. "Kathryn, after what happened between the two of you, how can you think you can depend on that man to save Matthew?"

Kathryn cast her gaze out the window where the swimming pool looked like a peaceful oasis in the pale pink evening light. During that long-ago summer she'd been a headstrong eighteen-year-old girl sleeping with a man five years her senior. If Willa had known, she'd have skinned her alive. So Kathryn kept her relationship with Clay hidden from everyone. Which had upped the thrill of having a secret love affair.

But after her accident, there'd been no keeping her short pregnancy—and the name of the baby's father—from Willa. Still, Kathryn's humiliation had left her unable to talk about what had happened between her and Clay. And after she recovered, she had gone off to college in California, intent on forgetting the man who'd broken her heart. Since then, neither she nor Willa had brought up that part of the past.

"I wish I had talked to you back then about what happened between Clay and me," Kathryn began. "But I was too embarrassed to tell you the truth, so it was just easier to let you believe the worst about him."

"What truth?"

"I'd had a crush on him for years, but he never gave me a second look. Certainly no encouragement. The summer I turned eighteen, I was convinced I was all grown up. I made up my mind to go after Clay and hook him. He told me up-front he didn't want any strings. No commitment. I was young and naive and convinced I could change his mind."

Willa's mouth thinned. "You were carrying his child. The man should have done right by you."

"Clay didn't know about the baby before he left here. When I called to tell him I was pregnant, he jumped in his car and headed this way. By the time he got here, I'd miscarried."

Kathryn squeezed Willa's hands. "What matters now is getting Matthew back. You know what happened to Clay's parents. He learned about how kidnappers operate. He knows what to do. If I hadn't had his help today, I would have gone insane."

"Lord, child, I wish I'd been here for you. To help you."

"You can help now."

"How?"

"Whoever took Matthew knows our schedules, routines. Clay needs lists of the people Sam entertained. And the waitstaff hired to help during the parties. Also the name of every person who has access to this house. That includes anyone who's made deliveries, or done repair work. I need your help to come up with those names."

"I've kept files on all the entertaining Sam did. The menu, the theme. Guest lists. Most of the maintenance and repairs are done by Johnny and his hands, but once in a while we have to call in someone from the outside."

"Do you have a record of what companies you use?"

"Yes. Everything's in a cabinet in my sitting room."

Kathryn eased out a breath. Compiling the lists would make her feel like she was doing something to help Matthew. "If you could bring everything in here, we can work at this table."

Instead of rising, Willa cupped an ice-cold palm against Kathryn's cheek. "Do you honestly believe Clay Turner can get Matthew back safe?"

Kathryn felt terror bubble up anew. So much could go wrong. Too much. She placed her hand over Willa's. "He's the only person who can help us."

Clay stood at the top of the basement stairs, listening. *He's the only person who can help us.*

He swallowed hard against swamping emotion. His parents were dead because his instincts had failed him. All it would take was one misstep on his part and Matthew would be dead, too.

His right hand clenched, sweaty and unsteady, around the item he'd found in the tunnel.

Just then, Abby scampered over his boots and headed for the alcove where Kathryn sat with Willa.

Swiveling in her chair, Kathryn met his gaze. "Did you find anything in the tunnel?"

"Yes, but I don't know if it has anything to do with the kidnapping." He noted that Willa McKenzie's face might be as pale as a sheet, but the housekeeper's eyes held the same distrust for him that he'd heard in her voice.

Over the past few years, he'd run into Willa several times in Layton. She had always given him a curt nod and a wide berth. He understood where the older woman was coming from: Kathryn was her chick and he'd been the big bad wolf.

He stepped to the table, gave the housekeeper a

nod. "Mrs. McKenzie, I wish I was here under better circumstances."

Willa's mouth thinned. "Kathryn said you were searching the outlaw tunnel?"

"Yes, ma'am." He opened his palm. "I found this toy soldier at the tunnel's far end. Would Matthew have had it with him last night?"

"Maybe." Kathryn stared at the small figure, but didn't reach for it. "Matthew has hundreds of those. He had some with him the day before yesterday when we went to play in the tunnel."

"So, he could have left this one then?"

"Yes. But he always has one or two stuffed into the pockets of his pajamas. So he could have had some with him last night." She raised her gaze from his palm. "Is…that all you found?"

Nodding, Clay settled onto the chair across from her. "Even though we have no proof, I'm almost certain the tunnel is how the kidnapper got in and out." He looked at Willa. "Has Kathryn told you about the list of names we need?"

"I've got a lot of the information in my room. I'll get it now so we can start working."

"There's something more important I'd like you to do first, if you would." Clay shifted his gaze to Kathryn. Under the kitchen's bright lights, her skin looked ashen, her blue eyes clouded. She was hanging on by a thread.

"I haven't been able to get Kathryn to eat today," he said, looking back at Willa. "Maybe you'll have better luck?"

"Child, you have to eat."

"I'm not hungry."

"You'll eat anyway. Otherwise, you'll make yourself sick." Willa rose, slid a palm down Kathryn's dark hair. "I'll grab a fresh apron out of the pantry, then get supper started."

Clay watched the housekeeper bustle away, then looked back at Kathryn. Her gaze was locked on him, her eyes fathomless.

"You did that for Willa," she said. "You know nothing's going to stop her from worrying, but keeping busy taking care of me will help her get through this."

"Something like that. And she's right, you need to eat." As he spoke, Clay slid the soldier into his shirt pocket. He hoped he was destined to return it to a living, breathing boy.

In what Clay knew was Willa's way of forcing a change of scenery on Kathryn, dinner was served on the flagstone patio.

"With the ceiling fans on, it's cool out here," Willa said, making room on the table for the platter of ham Clay carried.

"You could feed all the Cross C's ranch hands," he observed, taking in the bowls of potato salad and steaming baked beans.

"I had this fixed before I left for Dallas," Willa said, tucking a napkin beside each plate. "Figured that would give me time to make ice cream for dessert. That's Matthew's favorite." Willa looked away. "I can't believe he's gone."

"It takes time for something like that to sink in." Clay looked out across the back lawn toward a fenced pasture. There, a horse with a white blaze running down its nose grazed in peace, its black coat gleaming in the last rays of sun.

It would be dark soon, and still they'd had no contact from the kidnapper. One of the most dangerous times for the victim was between the snatch and the first contact with the family. The sooner contact was made, the better for the successful outcome of negotiations.

"Can someone get the door?"

Clay strode across the patio and pulled open the screen door. "I'll take that," he said, relieving Kathryn of a tray of chunky tumblers of lemonade.

The breeze from the fans tossed wisps of dark hair against her pallid cheek as she stepped onto the porch, Abby sniffing the floor behind her. The dark circles under her eyes had, with the advancing day, grown even darker. What she needed was a good meal and uninterrupted sleep, but Clay knew from his own experience that those were the last things on a person's mind when their loved one was in the hands of a potential killer.

"Clay, put that tray here," Willa said, shoving aside a pot of geraniums. She served the lemonade then waved them to chairs, hovering as Kathryn spooned potato salad onto her plate.

"While I was heating the food, I got to wondering about something," Willa said, handing Clay a bowl piled with buttermilk biscuits. "Kathryn said we all have to continue our usual routines because the kidnapper might be watching. And that we're not supposed to talk about what's happened with anyone else."

"Right," Clay said.

"Johnny and Dr. Silver were in the house, so they know Matthew's gone. What about other people? Brad

Jordan drops in to go over receipts for the bank. Yesterday Owen Daily dropped by legal papers for Kathryn. Pilar will be here in the morning to clean. What do we tell people who ask where Matthew is?"

"I hadn't thought of that." Kathryn looked up from the slice of ham Willa had forked onto her plate. "It hadn't occurred to me what to tell people."

"I've got an idea how to deal with that," Clay told her, keeping his voice level and calm. "Most people around here will believe it. I'm just not sure if the press will buy it."

"What?"

"Is it believable to say Matthew's in Tibet, staying with his father on the movie set?"

"It's not something Matthew's done before without me being there." Using her fork, Kathryn pushed a piece of potato around her plate. "But this is the first movie Devin's made since our divorce, so that's reason enough for me not to be there." She narrowed her eyes in concentration. "Devin has a private plane, so Matthew could have flown over with a nanny. And Devin's contracts require the studio keep the media out of sight of where he's filming. So there'd be no way for any reporter to disprove Matthew isn't on the set in Devin's private trailer."

"All right, we say Matthew's with his father," Clay said.

At length, Kathryn replaced her fork beside her still-full plate, and sat in silence. Despair—Clay could feel her despair as deep and black as the night that had quickly engulfed them. He'd felt the same way when he learned the rebels who'd shot him had dragged his parents away and disappeared into the jungle.

He'd been alone, bereft and scared as hell.

"Child, you've got to eat," Willa said in a firm voice, fully ignoring that she herself had taken only a few bites.

"I can't." Kathryn placed her hand on the older woman's arm. "I know you went to a lot of trouble to make this meal. But I look at the food and wonder if Matthew has anything to eat." Eyes full of torment, she shoved her chair back, its legs scraping against the flagstones.

Clay tracked her to the wrought-iron railing that rimmed the patio where she came to a standstill, head bent forward, shoulders slumped. Her posture said everything about her spirit.

He met Willa's concerned gaze. "Doesn't look like any of us have much of an appetite." As if on cue, Abby appeared from under the table and looked up at him, her tail fanning the air. He leaned, scooped the dachshund into his lap and ruffled her ears. "Except for this girl."

"I fed that little dickens before we came out here." Willa started stacking plates on a tray. "Kathryn, it just now hit me that Abby's the first dog we've had on the Cross C in twenty years."

Clay watched Kathryn turn. "Not since T-Bone," she said quietly.

"T-Bone?" Clay stood, holding Abby nestled in the crook of one arm while he rubbed her belly.

"He was a stray," Willa answered when Kathryn remained silent. "Looked like part bird dog and part mutt. He showed up one night while Sam and Kathryn were out here eating dinner. I'd cooked T-bone steaks, so that's the name Kathryn christened him. She and that dog fell in love the minute they saw each other. He used to walk her to the school bus in the morning, stay on the same spot on the side of the road until the bus dropped her off again. And protective…" Willa shook her head. "Sam used to say that dog was the best bodyguard Kathryn could have. Said he didn't worry about her as long as T-Bone was around."

Clay listened to Willa while watching Kathryn. Her eyes had gone cold. Hard. He lowered Abby to the floor. "What happened to T-Bone?"

"He got run over," she said, then turned and stared into the darkness.

From her reaction, Clay suspected there was more to the dog's death, but he let it go. He glanced at Willa. "Let me carry that tray in for you."

"No, you stay with Kathryn. I'll let you know when I get the kitchen cleaned up so we can start on those lists of names."

Clay moved to the railing to stand at Kathryn's side. Crickets chirped. Somewhere out on the prairie a cow bawled.

"They're feeding him, Kat," he said. "They wouldn't have taken the medicine if they didn't plan to keep him healthy."

"Why couldn't they have taken me?" she asked in a thick whisper. "If they want money, why couldn't they have taken me and left Matthew alone?"

Clay pulled details he'd learned from Forbes from his memory. "I know it doesn't feel like it, but you and your ex are the main target of this kidnapping."

"Devin and me?" She shook her head. "No—"

"But it would have been difficult for the kidnapper to attempt to physically take you or Mason. In a kidnapper's eyes, a child is a much more sought-after target. Children are small, they can be carried with little effort.

Hidden almost anywhere and kept under control with ease. It sometimes takes only a gruff voice to frighten a child into submission."

She lifted a hand to her throat. "It all seems so clinical. So matter-of-fact."

"To the kidnapper, it's all business. You control the Conner fortune and your ex-husband is the hottest ticket in Hollywood. So, the kidnapper takes your son, leaving you and Mason, who will move heaven and earth to get him back, to push the right buttons at the bank."

"Which is where I'll be first thing in the morning."

"Exactly." Clay glanced at his watch. "I need to take care of something. Why don't you work with Willa on the lists?"

Kathryn jerked her head toward him. "You're leaving?"

"I'm just going as far as the driveway to talk to Reece Silver. He's been at the Double Starr for a couple of hours dealing with a mare in labor. I want to talk to Reece in person about Matthew's abduction, so I called and asked him to drop by on his way home. He should be here anytime."

"You talked to Reece on the phone this morning and he agreed not to tell anyone about the kidnapping. Why do you need to see him in person?"

"To make sure he understands it's crucial he keeps what he knows to himself." And, Clay silently added, he wanted to read the body language of the vet who had free access to the Cross C and its employees. Not to mention drugs that could have been used on Kathryn and the dog.

Kathryn wrapped her arms around her waist. "I've heard you talking to your uncle several times today. I know he depends on you to help run the Double Starr. You can't be here every minute, I understand that. You have your work to see to. Your own life to live."

Not much of one, he thought. "Uncle Les will deal with Double Starr business for the time being." Clay paused. He knew she was worried if he left, that might be the time the kidnapper chose to call. An unsettling thought, even though she was the only one who could take that call. But he suspected the sudden panic he saw in her eyes wasn't due to her simply needing him to back her up. No, it went deeper.

Ten years deeper.

He cupped his palm around her elbow, her skin warm against his as he turned her to face him. "I've walked away from you before."

And by doing so, he'd cast a pebble in a pond that had sent ripples running long and wide. If only he'd known then how that one action would shift so many manner of balances.

But he knew now. Knew how it felt to be pinched and prodded by restless ghosts. To be jerked awake by nightmares that were cold, hard proof of how he'd failed on so many levels.

No one had to tell him if he continued his losing streak, Matthew Mason might die.

He slid his hand down Kathryn's arm, her wrist, his fingers brushing the slope of her palm before linking with hers. In the next heartbeat, electricity coursed from her fingers straight to his gut. Her hand twitched, as if she felt it, too, but she didn't pull away.

She just stared up at him while he watched her face pale, and her eyes go expressionless.

"Maybe you're thinking I'll take a another hike," he said. "Leave you alone to deal with all this." He tightened his fingers around hers. "I'm here, Kat. I'll be beside you all the way, until Matthew comes home. You have my word."

"Thank you." The words passed her lips in a trembling whisper. "I'm asking a lot. But I don't think I could stand this if you weren't helping me."

She pulled from his touch, her fingers sliding from his. Then she curled them into her palm and pressed her fist against her thigh. "I'll go in now. Help Willa."

He watched her turn. Watched her walk away in snug jeans that fit her like a second skin. He remembered every curve, every dip of her flesh. Remembered just where to touch to have her moaning and trembling beneath him.

His blood heated as he tracked her across the patio to the back door. Then she was gone.

He eased out a breath. He was beginning to think that even when this was all over, the last thing he would be able to do was walk away.

CHAPTER SIX

CLAY HAD JUST ENDED a phone call with his uncle when he heard the powerful thrum of Reece Silver's truck. Seconds later, its headlights licked across the front of the house.

When Silver braked the truck in the outspill of light from the porch's carriage lamps, Clay headed down the steps. Although Silver had made house calls to the Double Starr numerous times, Clay took a moment to give the idling pickup a closer look.

It was a Lincoln, big, black and sleek. The cargo area was protected by an automatic tonneau cover, which slid back to reveal the specially equipped drawers and compartments where Silver stored the equipment, supplies and drugs used in his veterinary practice. Clay estimated the vehicle's worth and cost of upkeep.

Big bucks, he decided.

Then there was the state-of-the-art clinic on the outskirts of Layton where Silver performed surgery. Outwardly it appeared the vet's practice had no cash flow problems that would give him reason to need a quick million. And even if he got behind in the rent, he had the Silver family fortune to fall back on, amassed from some sort of telecommunications business.

Clay pulled open the passenger door and slid in. The cool air smelled of new leather and hot sweat. Beside him, Silver wore a shirt that hung open and tattered jeans with dark splotches that Clay guessed were blood. His brown hair looked damp and was slicked straight back, making his face seem almost gaunt in the shadowy glow from the dashboard's lights.

According to Clay's uncle, Silver had spent a couple of hours in the foaling box at the Double Starr, which this time of year made the humidity in a greenhouse seem like a cool Spring breeze.

"Thanks for coming by," Clay said. "I figure you'd have rather just headed home after leaving the Double Starr."

"Not a problem." Silver shook his head. "I told your uncle how bad I feel about Cimarron's colt being breech and stillborn. I did all I could, but that doesn't make the loss any easier."

"Not your fault." Clay felt a twinge of guilt. Any other day it would fall to him to oversee disposal of the colt's remains, instead of leaving that chore for his uncle. But today had been far from routine.

"Doc, I need to talk to you about what happened here this morning."

Silver raked a hand through his hair, then reached for the open water bottle snugged into a holder in front of the leather-covered console. "Christ, dealing with Cimarron shoved Matthew's kidnapping out of my mind. How's Kathryn doing?"

"Holding on."

Clay no longer thought of himself as a cop, yet sitting there, he felt himself starting to tighten up. Felt the adrenaline, the hunting hormone, flow into his bloodstream. He'd always liked the feel of it, the stress of slipping into his cop's skin. And with his sixth sense now stirring, he couldn't help but wonder if it was meaningful Silver hadn't asked if they'd had word on Matthew. Was it because he knew they hadn't, or was it just the lawman in Clay being overly suspicious?

"Kathryn asked me to thank you for suggesting she get a negotiator. She wouldn't have thought of that if not for you."

"Johnny and I both recommended she do that."

"I got the impression it was your idea."

Flicking him a sidelong look, Silver replaced the bottle. "I guess it was. At first, Johnny wanted to call Sheriff Boudry. Kathryn nixed that."

"How'd you come up with the idea of calling in a professional negotiator? Most people wouldn't think of that."

But any kidnapper with half a brain would. A negotiator's main concern was the safe return of the victim, not the apprehension of the abductor. And the return of a living victim was almost always dependent on the ransom money being delivered without blips or bumps.

Silver's face tightened. "What's going on, Clay? Are we having this chat because you're suspicious about my suggesting Kathryn bring in an expert?"

"Call it curious," Clay said, staring out the windshield. In the distance, bright pools from security lights illuminated the stables and barn. He could see nothing beyond but relentless darkness that melted into a pitch-black sky.

"There's a scared little boy out there somewhere who has to take meds so his body won't reject his transplanted kidney. I want to get him home to his mother.

I'm not concerned whose toes I step on in the process. So I'd appreciate an answer."

"Yeah. Okay." Silver scrubbed a hand over his jaw. "I used to moonlight as a part-time vet at Red River Downs," he began, referring to the tony racetrack north of Layton. "A woman who owned a colt that looked like it might go all the way to the Derby got kidnapped out of her private box. The track stewards got nervous—it's bad for business to have the owner of a moneymaking horse snatched from under their noses."

"That it is," Clay agreed.

"The Downs hired a security firm to conduct a seminar for all employees so we'd know what precautions to take that might prevent a future kidnapping. We were also in-structed on what to do if an abduction did occur. One of the first things was to call in an expert negotiator to deal with the kidnapper." Silver regarded Clay for a long moment. "I'd forgotten you used to be a cop. Guess I'm getting a taste of your interrogation technique."

"This is more along the lines of an interview." Shifting in his seat, Clay glanced out the truck's rear window. "You carry a lot of drugs with you, right?"

"I have to. I can't anticipate what I'm going to need, especially if I have to deal with an emergency."

"Have you had any drugs come up missing? Some-thing that could be used to knock out a human?"

Silver nodded slowly. "A couple of weeks ago I did the usual inventory of my supplies at the end of the day. I was short one vial of Ketapromazine."

"Which is?"

"A fast-acting anesthetic. It can be used on both animals and humans. You may know it by its street name, KP."

"Yeah." Clay searched his memory for facts on the drug. "It can be both injected and swallowed. There's no taste to it, so it's perfect for those wanting to slip someone a mickey."

"Right. An injected dose acts almost instantly. Swallowed, it could take ten, maybe up to twenty minutes to take effect."

Clay nodded. Kathryn had said she'd read for only a short time after drinking her wine last night. "What are the symptoms in humans?"

"Unconsciousness, of course. Some people become nauseous after taking it." Silver flicked a look toward the house. "Are you asking because you think it's tied to Matthew's kidnapping?"

"It's possible," Clay answered. He wouldn't know for sure until the private lab analyzed the contents of the wine bottle he'd shipped off that afternoon. "Did you report the theft of the KP?"

"Sure. A deputy came by that same night and took a report."

Glancing again out the truck's rear window, Clay swept his gaze over the tonneau cover that sealed the cargo area. "How easy would it have been for someone to steal the drug?"

"If it was taken during my last stop that day, it wouldn't have been difficult. I was at the Newton Ranch doing a follow-up check on a mare I'd performed surgery on. The Newtons were hosting a birthday party for their twin granddaughters. There were carnival rides set up on the lawn and a swarm of parents and kids. Right at dusk they set off fireworks. The noise and lights spooked a stallion and he got himself tangled in a barbed wire fence. He was thrashing around, tearing up his front legs. I had to get him calmed down fast, so I grabbed a syringe and the drug I needed and raced off. I told the deputy sheriff I couldn't swear I remembered to lock the drug drawer."

"If that's the case, it could have been one of the Newtons' employees who stole the KP. Or a guest at the birthday party."

"Had to be." Silver rubbed his fingers over his jeaned thigh. His hand was wide and thick and looked like it belonged to a man who did hard labor. "I didn't say anything about this to Kathryn, but I first wondered if Devin Mason was behind Matthew's disappearance. Wouldn't be the first time a kid got snatched by one parent from another. But if the KP stolen off my truck was used, it sounds like someone local is involved."

Clay eyed Silver, trying to measure, to determine what, if any, his level of involvement was in the kidnapping, but saw nothing revealed.

"Thanks for coming by, Doc. Like I said on the phone this morning, it's important you keep everything you know about Matthew's disappearance under wraps."

"I haven't mentioned it to anyone. I won't." Silver's brow furrowed. "The other day I was in the stables here, checking on a gelding when Kathryn brought Matthew in. He must have asked me twenty questions about what I was doing. Cute kid. I don't want to think about what might happen to him."

Dread tightened Clay's chest. He had a tape-looping in his head of Matthew grinning up at him, a plastic deputy's badge pinned to his T-shirt. Clay couldn't shake the sensation that the window of time he had to save the boy was ticking away, and much more rapidly than any clock would indicate.

He'd felt that same sick dread while the rebels held his parents.

"Tell Kathryn if I can help with anything to give me a call," Silver said.

Clay nodded and shouldered open the door. "Will do."

THE FOLLOWING MORNING, Kathryn stood in Brad Jordan's office, a cup of coffee clenched in one hand as she stared out the floor-to-ceiling window. Her third-story perspective provided a prime view of Layton's busy town square on which the sun shown down with blazing intensity. Although she'd been gone for a decade, she recognized the majority of the people who went about their business, seemingly without a care in the world.

She'd been one of those people two days ago when she and Matthew crossed the square. They'd been on their way to the café that Norman Adams and his wife owned. Kathryn's main thought had been to introduce her son to the high school English teacher who'd helped her hone her writing skills. Then she and Matthew stepped into the café and she came face-to-face with Clay Turner. Another man who'd played a huge role in her life.

She'd had no idea that only hours later she would put all her hopes for Matthew's survival into Clay's hands. Or that, because Mr. and Mrs. Adams often moonlighted as serving personnel at Sam's lavish parties, their names would be on a list of possible suspects in her child's kidnapping.

Drawing in a slow breath, Kathryn turned from the window and placed her coffee cup beside a framed photo on the corner of Brad's desk. She noted that the fine tremor so conspicuous in her hands yesterday was now gone. Despite the sleepless night she'd spent, she felt steady. Beyond tears. A classic defense mechanism, she assumed. She had to push forward. Had to present a calm, unemotional face to the world while doing everything she could to save Matthew.

Which was why she would walk out of Brad's office with a million dollars in cash. And why Clay was at this moment across town, meeting on the sly with Sheriff Boudry.

Unwilling to again question her decision to go against the kidnappers' orders, Kathryn nudged the picture frame around and studied the studio portrait of Brad, his wife Felicia and their two young daughters. Wearing all black, they posed against a white backdrop, their smiles gleaming beneath the photographer's bright lights. Kathryn had been a sophomore when Brad and Felicia were seniors. They'd been the school's golden couple: he the star quarterback, she head cheerleader.

Kathryn flicked her gaze to the credenza where a trophy with a football player poised in action on top was displayed. Brad apparently was still basking in the glory of his sports days.

"Sorry to keep you waiting," he said as he hustled into the office. He shut the door while adding, "Garner pontificated longer than usual during this morning's staff meeting."

Kathryn raised a brow at Brad's reference to his father-in-law. Garner Smith had made no secret he thought his daughter used poor judgment when she set her sights on a man whose sole claim to fame was the ability to throw a football. Kathryn remembered Sam saying that making his new son-in-law vice president of the bank had been a huge burr under Garner's butt.

"I haven't been waiting long," she said, then tapped a fingertip on the frame. "You have a lovely family, Brad. Felicia is as gorgeous as ever and your daughters are beautiful."

"Apples of my eye, all three of them."

Smiling, Brad motioned Kathryn into one of the visitor chairs while he settled into the leather one behind his desk. "You can catch up with Felicia tonight at the fund-raiser."

"I look forward to it." In truth, she dreaded having to make small talk with Layton's elite while wondering if one of them had taken Matthew.

Despair cut through her, and she stiffened her spine against it. If cracks appeared in the wall she'd erected around her senses, it was essential she patch them before they became full-fledge fissures. Putting her emotions in cold storage was the only way she knew to keep the abject, debilitating fear for Matthew's welfare at bay.

She watched Brad position several file folders in the center of the desk blotter. With his dark hair cut short and clad in a pin-striped charcoal suit, white tab shirt and red and ivory tie he had the look of a consummate executive. Because his duties of overseeing the Cross C's expenditures for the bank made him a frequent visitor to the ranch, Brad's name had gone on the list of possible kidnappers.

When she felt her suspicion grow like a shadow at dusk, she dragged her gaze away. She had no reason to think he'd taken Matthew. Just as tonight at the fund-raiser she would have no firm reason to cast the same net of suspicion over everyone there. Even so, she knew she wouldn't be able to stop herself.

Kathryn closed her eyes. Somehow, someway she had to control the paranoia gnawing at the edges of her rational mind. Otherwise, she'd drive herself mad. She gave herself a moment to center herself before looking back at Brad.

"Do you have my withdrawal ready?"

"Almost." He flipped open a folder. "It wasn't long after you called yesterday that Devin Mason wired the funds. A bank our size doesn't have a million dollars cash on hand so I ordered it from a bank in Dallas. The armored car arrived with it half an hour ago. We're still processing the money, so it'll be a little longer."

Kathryn retrieved her coffee cup off the desk. "Fine."

Leaning back in his chair, Brad regarded her with curiosity. "A cash withdrawal that large isn't a request we get every day."

"I'd be surprised if it were." Knowing the transaction would raise suspicion from Brad on down to the lowliest teller, Kathryn had dressed in a royal-blue Prada suit. She knew it was important she convey the image of a woman transacting business instead of a mother desperate to save her child.

She sipped her coffee before replacing the cup on Brad's desk. "Since the funds were wired from Devin Mason and in no way tied to my inheritance from Sam, the bank doesn't oversee expenditure of the money. Meaning, you're not at liberty to ask why I want the million in cash." She sent Brad a cool smile. "Even so, you're dying to know."

"I'd be lying if I said I wasn't curious, but you're

right, it's none of my business." His brows drew together. "That doesn't mean I'm not concerned. And I don't like the idea of you driving around with all that cash. How about I follow you home?"

"I appreciate your concern, Brad. So much so that I'm going to let you in on a little secret. Several days ago, I got a call from a man whose land Sam intended to buy. I had already found a file in Sam's study with his notes, so I resumed the negotiations where they ended when my grandfather got sick."

"Land? What land?"

She angled her chin. "Not that I think you'd try to steal it out from under me for a better price, but I prefer to keep that information to myself until the deal is finalized. Just know I'm getting a sweet deal from the seller for paying cash."

A smile tugged at the corners of Brad's mouth. "I bet."

"When I told Devin about the offer, he suggested I put the land in Matthew's name and insisted on wiring me the money."

Kathryn paused. From the look on Brad's face, it was clear he believed her story. She sent silent thanks to Clay for inventing it. "And," she continued, "you don't need to worry about me driving around with all that cash. Clay Turner stopped by the Cross C this morning to discuss some business. He mentioned he was driving into town, so I asked if I could ride with him."

"It's handy to have a neighbor who's an ex-cop."

"It is," she agreed. In the presence of Clay's logical advice and cool confidence, she felt as though the mountain that had avalanched down on her had only partially buried her.

As if a door suddenly sprung open in her mind, her thoughts rolled like mist over the memories of the distant nights she'd spent in Clay's arms. She took a deep breath, then another. She couldn't let the gratitude she felt now be mistaken for anything more. Her love for Clay belonged to the past, an emotional dead end she had no wish to explore.

After checking her watch, she remet Brad's gaze. "Clay had a couple of errands to run, but he should be back soon to pick me up. Any idea how much longer until my withdrawal's ready?"

"Let me get your signature on a couple of forms, then I'll check. Light some fires under a few rear ends if I need to."

"I appreciate it," Kathryn said, and jerked her head toward her purse when a sound ripped her attention away.

A loud chirp from the cell phone the kidnapper had left behind on Matthew's nightstand.

CHAPTER SEVEN

KATHRYN'S HEART SLAMMED against her ribs as she jerked the kidnappers' phone from her purse.

She looked across the span of desk at Brad. His head was bowed while he shuffled the bank forms she'd have to sign before collecting the million dollars in cash.

"This… Brad, I need to take this call."

He glanced up. "Sure, go ahead."

She dragged in a breath. Clay had made her rehearse what to say when the kidnapper called. He had emphasized she had to stay calm. *Stay calm for Matthew*. Dear God, she desperately needed Clay with her. Needed his strength. His control.

"The call's personal. Could you give me some privacy?"

"Oh, sorry." Grinning, Brad rolled back his chair and rose. "I'll go check on the cash."

Kathryn stabbed the answer button before Brad shut the door.

"Hello?"

When no response came, she pressed the phone harder to her ear. Sweat pooled in the small of her back. "Hello?"

Nothing.

With her free hand, she gripped the chair's padded

arm. "Please talk to me," she said in a thick whisper. "Let me talk to my son."

The hollow hum of the connection skittered over her skin like the tiny feet of a dozen spiders. "I have the cash. All of it. Let me talk to Matthew. After that, I'll bring the money anywhere you say."

Closing her eyes, she sat unmoving through uncountable intensifying silent seconds.

Stay calm.

"Matthew needs…his medicine," she continued. "He'll get…sick without it." Her words came in faltering pauses. "You want money. I have it. It's yours, no questions asked. Just tell me where to bring it. Please, tell me."

There was only silence, and she realized the call had been disconnected.

"Matthew." With fear for her child clawing at her, Kathryn buried her face in her hands.

"POOR LITTLE KID," Sheriff Jim Guy Boudry said after Clay briefed him on Matthew's kidnapping. "Now I understand why when you called my office you asked me to meet you here on the sly."

Clay glanced around the dimly lit workshop located in a stand-alone building behind Boudry's house. "I figured your dropping by home wouldn't put you on anyone's radar screen," Clay stated. "Which made this the best place for us to talk."

"Agreed." Boudry's sandpaper voice sounded like the irreversible result of the three packs a day he'd smoked during his years as a state trooper.

The sheriff of Layton County was a good old boy, Texas style—a big, broad-shouldered man with gray hair, a weather-worn face and shrewd eyes. Clay had never seen Boudry in uniform; today he wore a dark green shirt and jeans, his gold star clipped to his belt. He wasn't carrying a gun, unless it was concealed in one of his scuffed boots. At present, he stood with one hip propped against a workbench strewn with tools, sawdust and wood shavings. A rack of dusty Ball jars hooked to one wall held an assortment of nails, nuts and screws.

"I didn't see your pickup when I pulled up," Boudry said. "Where'd you park?"

"The grocery store three blocks over. I cut through the wooded lots to get here. It's handy you live on the back edge of the neighborhood."

"Yeah." Boudry paused for a moment, staring gravely back at Clay. "How sure are you that Doc Silver and Johnny Sullivan will keep quiet about the Mason boy being kidnapped?"

"As sure as I can be. It's been twenty-four hours, so if either man had leaked the news we'd have heard about it by now."

"Can't argue that. My wife's at Inez Woodson's beauty shop this morning. Since Inez's boy, Eddie, works for you, I expect you're aware she's Layton's gossip queen. If information about the kidnapping had leaked, Inez would be doling it out, along with shampoos and perms. And my wife would've already called to ask why I hadn't told her about the son of that actor she swoons over getting snatched."

"Eddie was with me yesterday morning when Kathryn rode over to tell me about Matthew," Clay said, stroking the scar on his right cheek. "I sent Eddie off to pick up some parts for a tractor, but he was damn curious about her and why she was there. I'm sure by now all the Double Starr hands are wondering where I've gotten off to and why."

Boudry barked a laugh as rough as pine bark. "Hell, Clay, you think Eddie didn't mention to his momma about Mrs. Mason paying you a visit? And half of Layton is probably already talking about you dropping her off at the bank this morning. Word's gonna be there's a romance going on between you two."

Clay scrubbed at the headache brewing dead in the center of his forehead. While spending a sleepless night at the Cross C listening to Kat pace in the bedroom next to his, he'd thought about how their actions would be interpreted. Having the town's citizens gossiping about a supposed relationship between himself and Kathryn was the best way to create a smokescreen to hide the real reason he was now spending all his time with her.

Problem was, each minute in her presence brought back memories of the girl who had drawn him so intensely that long-ago summer. And even as he told himself it would be useless to search for a way back, that the fire was out, he felt the desire to have the woman she'd become burning inside him.

"It's gonna be a miracle if you can keep all this under wraps," Boudry said as he scanned the list of names Clay had given him. "There's a lot of folks been to the Cross C over the past year. I know most of 'em. Hard to believe any of Sam Conner's cronies would resort to kidnapping his great-grandson, but I agree it sounds like someone on the inside had a hand in it."

"Has to be. Too bad I have no idea who."

Boudry crossed his arms over his broad chest. "So far,

all you've asked me to do is have my deputies on patrol keep their eyes open for activity out of the ordinary. And to check at the real estate office to see what places in and around Layton have been rented lately."

"That's all I need from you right now, Sheriff."

"You're going to want background and financial checks run on everybody on this list."

"I'm having a retired cop pal who owns his own P.I. firm do that."

Boudry nodded the merest fraction. "Just keep in mind if you need me to do more, all you have to do is call. I'll meet you here anytime."

"I appreciate that." Clay glanced at his watch. "I need to get back to the bank so I can pick up Kathryn."

Clay squinted as he stepped out into the bright sun. Turning, he watched Boudry close the workshop's door, then use the heel of his palm to shoot home the shackle of a padlock through the hasp bolted to the frame.

Boudry slid on a pair of mirrored sunglasses. "Guess I won't offer you a ride to your pickup since it wouldn't be smart for us to be seen together until the boy's found."

Clay tugged the rim of his Stetson down lower to block the rays of the sun. "It's the thought that counts."

Boudry walked to his silver cruiser that displayed the Layton city seal on the driver's door. He paused, giving Clay a long look across the top of the vehicle. "Taking your background into account, it was a smart move on Mrs. Mason's part to go to you for help. But I sure don't envy the responsibility you're carrying around for that little boy's life."

Before Clay could respond, Boudry's cell phone

sounded. The sheriff held up an index finger, signaling Clay to wait.

Boudry answered, his eyes narrowing after a moment. "Lang again," he barked. "What the hell has my hot-shot deputy done now?"

While Boudry listened to his caller, Clay shifted his gaze to the sheriff's tree-shaded house that sat on the far side of the trim back lawn. Several lounge chairs with bright covers were positioned on the patio. Terra cotta pots and window boxes overflowed with fiery-red blooms.

He narrowed his eyes, remembering. The Cross C. Ten years ago. Sam Conner was away in Austin and Willa had gone to a church function, so he and Kat decided to go for an early evening swim. The edges of the fieldstone patio had been awash in red flowers. The same shimmering red as the excuse for a bikini she wore. He pictured her, slim and tan, a puddle of dripping water forming at her bare feet as she leaned over the padded lounge chair where he sat and pressed her mouth to his. "I love you, Clay," she murmured.

He'd felt something inside him shift, and on the heels of that an unfamiliar kind of panic. That a woman affected him both emotionally and physically was something new for him.

Something he hadn't been happy about. Something the squad room stud hadn't wanted to acknowledge.

So he'd simply tugged her down on top of him, then settled his mouth and his hands on her.

Two weeks later, he said goodbye and went back to Houston. Told himself what he felt for her was simply lust. Hot, sweaty lust.

He knew better now. Knew, too, he'd hurt her far too

much to ever hope he would have a chance to cure the mistakes of the past. But he hoped like hell he could make things up to Kathryn by doing something about her future.

And that was to get Matthew back. Alive. If he could manage that, Kathryn wouldn't have bad memories to keep her awake on dark nights for the rest of her life. Like he did.

WHILE CLAY MADE HIS WAY back to the grocery store where he'd parked his pickup, Deputy Vernon Lang was twenty-five miles away, bringing a smile to his married lover's face.

"Vernon, sugar, you've got a great mouth."

"Same goes for you, darlin'."

With Felicia Smith Jordan lying beneath him, Vernon had a prime view of the ripe lips that on numerous occasions had brought him to mind-blinding, shattering climax. He fisted his hands in waves of blond hair that splayed against the crimson pillowcase while he took in her cool green eyes, the curve of her throat, her nipples—still contracted into tiny bits of hard pink stone. He knew without looking that the long legs wrapped around him were the best he'd ever seen.

She was the best he'd ever seen. For months he'd tried to talk Felicia into leaving her loser husband, Brad. So far, Vernon had struck out. Content to flit in and out of his life, she saw him only during their meetings at her rich daddy's three-story lake house.

The more content she seemed to stay with Brad, the more obsessed Vernon became with putting his own permanent brand on her.

To do that, Felicia needed to view him as a man with the drive to make something of himself. Granted, he hadn't led the high school football team to the state championships like her husband. But that had been nearly fifteen years ago and Brad hadn't done shit since, except work at his father-in-law's bank.

"And it's not just your mouth I think's perfect." Dipping his head, he pulled her diamond-studded earlobe between his teeth. Feeling her shudder, he gave her a slow grin. "Every inch of you is."

Since Felicia couldn't remember the last time her husband had given her a compliment, she reveled in Vernon's words. And knowing they came from a lover ten years her junior made her downright giddy.

"Well, Deputy Lang, let me show you how perfect I think *you* are," she said, wriggling her bottom. Since he was still inside her, she had the pleasure of watching his eyes darken.

The newest addition to the Layton County Sheriff's Office was six feet of solid muscle with awesome shoulders, and a face softened by melted chocolate eyes. She'd first spotted Vernon looking all tough and sinewy in his uniform as he placed a parking ticket under the wiper of her lipstick-red Jaguar. She'd wanted to eat him alive. While Vernon watched, she'd folded the ticket and slid it into her cleavage. In less than a week, the deputy slid into her bed.

"Glad to know you think I'm perfect," he drawled.

Gazing down at her, Vernon felt his determination to have her intensify. Unlike her husband, *his* future lay ahead of him. He figured he had a good shot at being named to fill the vacant assistant sheriff's slot. And after biding his time, he planned to get elected to the job held by Jim Guy Boudry, who was getting a little long in the tooth to work in law enforcement. The politician in Vernon gave thought to the house around them with its soaring ceilings, balconies cantilevered over the living room area and massive stone fireplaces. Winning an election in Layton County would be a shoo-in with rich-as-God Garner Smith's daughter by his side.

But in order for that to happen, she had to dump Brad.

Feeling himself hardening inside her, Vernon sent Felicia a scalpel-sharp look. "If I didn't know better, I'd think you were using me for sex."

"Why, that's just not true." She raked her manicured nails across those magnificent shoulders and nearly purred. "You know I'm fond of you."

"Fond's something you feel for a pet dog." He set his teeth against the lust razoring into him. "I want more from you, Felicia. A lot more."

Sighing, she felt her impatience stir. If Vernon insisted on talking *again* about her leaving Brad, she might scream. She had finally found a handsome-as-sin man who was a rocket in bed. Why the hell did he have to mess up things by wanting her even when she had her clothes on?

Her tone went husky as she tightened her legs, pulling him deeper inside her. "How about we do something other than talk since I've got to leave soon to get my hair done for tonight?"

"What's tonight?" he murmured, nipping the soft spot behind her right ear.

"A fund-raiser for Layton Hospital." Her voice lowered, thickened against the heat surging in her blood.

"Kathryn Mason's donating a million bucks to help build a new wing on the hospital in her late grand-daddy's memory. Kind of strange for her to do that since she didn't set foot back home one time over the past ten years. Didn't even bother to show up for Sam's funeral."

Vernon trailed a line of kisses along Felicia's jaw. "Small world, darlin'. I'll be at the fund-raiser, too, working off-duty security. I have to keep an eye on the funds brought in on the silent auction items."

Beneath him, he felt her go as still as stone. "Really?"

"Really."

Her hands cupped his face, tugging his head up. Her green eyes had sobered. "Promise you'll act like you don't know me."

He arched a brow. "That'd be hard," he said, emphasizing the last word with a firm thrust. "Since I know you intimately."

"I'm serious, Vernon. You have to promise me that what's between us stays our little secret. Otherwise, we won't be seeing each other anymore."

Vernon set his jaw against a mix of anger and the need to take her that burned through him like a brush fire. Dammit, he had to work out a way to get her to see his worth. To make her understand they belonged together. And he would. It was a matter of time.

"All right, Felicia darlin', I promise." He kissed her brooding mouth. "But I'm going to make sure you won't be able to think of any other man tonight but me."

She sent him a sassy, under-the-lashes look. "Just how are you going to manage that?"

"Here's how." In one smooth move he pulled out of her, clamped his hands on her ankles and yanked her legs high. Using his mouth on her, he had the satisfaction of hearing his name rip up her throat on a moan.

"I MUST HAVE SAID something wrong." Kathryn sat in the passenger seat of Clay's pickup truck, clutching the cell phone, willing it to ring again.

"We've gone over everything you said," Clay commented as he steered away from Layton. "Nothing sounds wrong to me."

"Then why didn't the kidnapper say anything? Why didn't he let me talk to Matthew?"

"My best guess is he wanted to let you know who's in control."

"I know who's in control," she hissed, then gritted her teeth. Her heart was beating so fast her chest hurt.

With fence-line and endless pasture streaming past, Kathryn stared down at the phone. Her horror over the kidnapper hanging up on her had been so great it had pushed her beyond paralysis to a strange state of focus. She'd stayed in control while she signed Brad Jordan's endless forms. Walked coolly out of the bank with Clay carrying the million dollars in cash packed in the two briefcases she'd brought to the bank.

But when she slid into the pickup and told Clay about the phone call, she'd started to crumble slowly from the inside out.

"I told them I had the cash," she repeated, looking at Clay. With his gaze focused out the windshield, his profile was tough, contained. Grim. His jaw was darkened by stubble, his lips compressed. "All the cash," she continued. "That all they had to do was let me talk to Matthew and the money was theirs." Tremors settled into her hands and her breath started coming in short gasps. "They didn't…let me talk to him…because he can't talk, right? They killed him. They killed Matthew…."

"Don't, Kat." Clay swerved off the road onto the shoulder, crammed the pickup's gear into Park. Watching, hearing her suffer, made him want to slam his fist into something. Instead he took a deep breath and shifted in the seat to face her. "That's exactly what the kidnapper wants you to think, because it makes you more desperate."

She focused on the endless horizon. "It's working."

He was close enough to smell her lemony scent. Close enough to touch her, but he kept his hands to himself. The sun beaming in through the windows made her dark hair gleam. Her eyelashes were night-black and long enough to cast shadows against her pale skin. He wanted to kiss away those shadows. *Kiss her.*

"Remember what I told you yesterday about their plan?"

"They don't want to hurt Matthew. They only want me to believe they will."

"Right. Look in the back seat." When she didn't respond, he cupped a palm to her cheek and tugged her head around. "Look," he said, inclining his head. "The only way they get what's in those briefcases is to keep Matthew alive. They know that."

Clay was surprised when, instead of pulling away from his touch, she raised a hand and wrapped her fingers around his wrist. "When the phone rang, all I could think was I wanted you with me. That if you were there I wouldn't say the wrong thing."

"You didn't need me, Kat. You did fine on your own."

"Only because you'd spent hours drilling into my head what to say when the kidnappers called."

"Just doing my job." His thumb caressed her cheek while he wished like hell he still had the right to caress every square inch of her. "When we get back to the Cross C, there's some things I need to do with the ransom."

"What things?"

"Make a list of the serial numbers."

"I can help with that."

"All right." He glanced at the clock in the dash. "Hopefully the package I'm expecting from my P.I. pal will have arrived by now. If so, I'll plant a GPS chip in one of the bundles of money."

"What if the kidnapper finds the chip and refuses to release Matthew? Or worse?"

"The chip will be hidden. The majority of kidnappers collect the ransom then release the victim without taking time to count every bill. The GPS chip is added insurance in case something out of the norm happens."

Kathryn stared up into the smoky-brown eyes and firm mouth that she knew could light fires inside her. The stubble on his jaw was a blatant invitation for a woman's appreciative palm.

Abruptly she pulled away, forcing him to drop his hand. She needed Clay, she conceded. His strength. His knowledge. His logic.

What she didn't need was to feel his touch that made her want to lean into him and hold on until there was nothing left in her mind but the taste and scent of him.

She shifted closer to the passenger door. Doing so was safer than to risk reaching for him and have him walk away from her twice in one lifetime.

"We'd better get back to the Cross C," she said quietly.

CHAPTER EIGHT

THAT EVENING, Kathryn paused to check her reflection in her bedroom's full-length mirror. She'd drawn her hair back into a loose chignon; the flawless simplicity of her sleeveless black cocktail dress accentuated her slim build. The diamond choker—a wedding gift from her father to her mother—glittered at her throat.

The makeup she had applied painstakingly hid the shadows under her eyes. She looked calm and serene.

No one looking at her would guess she'd spent a few hours that afternoon recording serial numbers and stuffing banded packs of currency into a large duffel bag.

While she'd transferred the money, she'd watched Clay take one of the packs and slip the bills out, careful not to break the paper band around them. Then he cut the crisp bills like they were a stack of playing cards. Using a razor, he dug out a shallow circle about the perimeter of a dime. The small tracking device the P.I. had overnighted fit perfectly into the cutout hole.

With the device hidden in the middle of the stack of bills, Clay slipped the paper band back on. That bundle was now with the others in the fireproof closet in Sam's study.

With the ransom ready, all they could do was wait.

Moving to the bed, Kathryn slid the cell phone into

her black beaded bag. The phone hadn't rung since that morning at the bank. "Ring," she whispered, her voice a bare thread of sound. "Please ring."

When it didn't, she squared her shoulders, pulled open the bedroom door and stepped into the hallway. Earlier, she'd spoken to the chairman of Layton Memorial Hospital's board of directors who advised he expected a large turnout for tonight's fund-raiser. Her muscles as stiff as cardboard, Kathryn wondered again how she was going to manage to smile and chat with people, knowing it was possible one of them had Matthew.

You'll just do it, she told herself as she walked along the hallway wainscoted in dark, glossy wood.

Reaching the staircase, she paused to loop her purse's silver chain over one shoulder. When she glanced down into the cavernous entry hall, everything inside her went still.

Clay stood at the bottom of the stairs, his gaze focused away from her while he talked on his phone. He'd gone home for a short time to pack some clothes and change; now he wore black slacks, a starched white shirt and crimson tie. His black suit jacket was draped over the banister. With his chisel-cut features and his thick, black hair sleeked back, he radiated an aura of masculine power and control that made Kathryn intensely conscious of her own femininity.

She tightened her hand on the banister.

Ten years ago, she would have given anything to have him arrive at the front door and wait for her in the entry hall like the high school boys she'd dated. But Clay had been five years older, a man experienced in the ways of the world and in relationships with women. *For-*

bidden fruit. So from the very start of their affair she'd insisted on using the outlaw tunnel to sneak in and out of the house to meet him.

Even now, her cheeks burned at the thought of how eagerly she had sought him out. Of how crazy in love she'd been with a man who no doubt considered her little more than a convenience. What a fool she'd been, spinning fairy tales of love, marriage and babies to justify what had turned out to be nothing more than a walk on the wild side for a naive young girl. All those fairy tales had shattered the day she wound up bruised and bleeding in the very spot where Clay now stood.

Although she'd made no sound, he must have sensed her presence because he turned abruptly. With the phone still pressed against one ear, he lifted his dark gaze and focused on her. Slowly his eyes traveled down, all the way to her black, strappy high-heeled sandals, then back up again.

His intense examination settled heat at the base of her spine. Her eyes pricked so fiercely she had to look away. She didn't want this tightness in her chest, didn't want to be haunted by old, impossible longings. Apparently what she wanted didn't matter. The need refused to be shoved aside.

Struggling to get a grip on her composure, she descended the stairs while her unsteady fingers adjusted the purse's chain.

Just as she reached the bottom step she heard Abby barking wildly, and a boy's high-pitched laughter accompanied by the pounding of running feet. *Familiar sounds*. Ones she'd heard often since she and Matthew moved to the Cross C.

"Matthew!" Kathryn whipped around so fast she cracked her elbow against the newel post.

The desperate hope her son had somehow miraculously returned died like a flamed-out match when a thin boy with dark hair and an olive complexion darted into sight at the far end of the hallway, Abby scampering at his heels.

"Antonio." The seven-year-old's name came out perilously close to a sob. Kathryn knew that Pilar sometimes brought her son with her while she tended to her duties around the house. But it was early evening—much later than the maid usually worked, and Kathryn hadn't expected to see Antonio.

Oh God, why couldn't it be Matthew dashing down the hallway toward her?

"You okay?" Clay's voice was low, coming from just beside her.

Kathryn met his gaze. The concern crimping his eyes told her he knew she'd mistaken the boy's laughter for Matthew's.

"Fine." She looked back at Antonio at the same instant he spotted her and Clay. The boy came to a skidding halt, tennis shoes screeching against the waxed wooden floor. His shamefaced look was no doubt due to having been caught running indoors, something Kathryn had heard Pilar scolding him for.

"Hi, Antonio," Kathryn said while Abby whipped herself into happy circles around his feet.

"Mrs. Mason." Head ducked, he glanced at Clay. "Sir."

"Hello, son. Looks like you and Abby are having fun."

"Yeah." As if checking to see if the coast was clear, Antonio did a fast peek across his shoulder toward the rear of the house. "Mrs. Willa called to see if my daddy could come fix the leak in her kitchen sink. I came and helped Daddy."

Clay nodded gravely. "Did you get the leak fixed?"

"Almost. But Abby wanted to play really bad." He looked up at Kathryn. "Mommy said Matthew flew in a plane across the ocean to visit his daddy. I think Abby misses him."

"I think so, too." With a fist squeezing her heart, Kathryn stepped forward and used a palm to smooth the boy's thick, dark hair. "Next time I talk to Matthew, I'll tell him you're helping Abby not miss him so much."

"Okay. Maybe when he gets back we can go mend fences with my daddy again?"

"Matthew will like that."

"Antonio!" Nilo Graciano's voice boomed from the end of the hallway.

Kathryn watched the dark, swarthy man dressed in dusty jeans and a wrinkled shirt hustle their way. The longtime ranch hand was medium height and built as solid as a brick wall. The tool belt circling his thick waist flapped against his thighs.

"Antonio, what did I tell you about staying with me in the kitchen?"

"But, Daddy, Abby wanted to play."

Shaking his head, Nilo nodded to Clay, then met Kathryn's gaze. "I am sorry, Mrs. Mason," he said in his thickly laced accent. "My son knows better than to run through the house."

"I think we can overlook it this time. Especially since Antonio is helping you fix Willa's sink. That's very important work." She gave Antonio a somber look before returning her gaze to his father. "And I know Abby misses Matthew, so I appreciate Antonio taking the time to play with her."

"*Sí.*" Nilo settled a thick hand with stubby fingers on one of his fidgeting son's scrawny shoulders. "Playtime is over. I need my helper so we can finish the very important job."

"Okay, Daddy," Antonio said, before beaming a mouthful of teeth at Kathryn. "You look really pretty in that dress, Mrs. Mason."

"Thank you, Antonio." Kathryn watched father and son walk hand in hand along the hallway toward the kitchen. Abby trotted behind them.

"That was rough on you," Clay said, turning to face her.

"I thought… When I heard Antonio laugh, I thought…"

"Yeah." He angled his chin. "Things won't be any easier tonight with all the people who will ask about Matthew. Like does he enjoy living on a ranch compared to a Hollywood mansion?"

"I'll deal with the questions." Kathryn wrapped her arms around her waist. "What's going to be hard is knowing that some of them could come from the person who has my son."

"If things get to be too much and you need a break, give me a sign. I'll get you out of there for a while."

Kathryn nodded. She might not like knowing the only time she felt halfway steady was in Clay's presence, but it was a fact. Right now, the man she had planned to avoid at all costs when she moved back to Texas was her rock.

He shrugged on his suit coat, his eyes never leaving her face. There was such watchful carefulness, such rigid control in his gaze that an alarm shrilled in Kathryn's head.

"Something's wrong, isn't it?"

"No, Kat, nothing's wrong." He hesitated. "Nothing new, anyway."

She took a step closer while fear bubbled up inside her. "I saw you on the phone when I came downstairs. You found out something about Matthew, didn't you? It's bad and you don't want to tell me—"

"I don't have any news about Matthew. If I did, I'd tell you." His voice was soft, controlled. Soothing.

"I'm sorry." She closed her eyes for an instant. "I'm being paranoid. I know that, but I can't seem to control it."

"It's impossible to control," he said as he gathered the tips of her fingers onto his own. His hands were steady, his skin warm and callused. "If I have news, I'll tell you. I won't make you wait. You have my word."

She nodded. One thing she knew from experience was that Clay Turner could be counted on to keep his word.

When she started to turn toward the front door, he held her in place. "But there is something I want to say to you before we leave for the fund-raiser."

His warm, steady touch was tightening the knots already in her belly. "What?"

"I agree with Antonio. You look really pretty in that dress, Mrs. Mason."

THE HOME OF ARTHUR KERR, meat-packing tycoon and chairman of Layton Memorial Hospital's board of directors, was a breathtaking estate. Nestled within acres of lush green grasses, the stately house sat like a mammoth on top of a knoll.

"This is the first time I've been here," Clay said as he steered up the tree-lined macadam driveway that wound nearly a half-mile away from the main road. "How about you?"

"It's more like my twentieth visit," Kathryn answered.

Clay slid her a look. Up until this point, she'd remained silent during their half-hour drive. He suspected she'd needed the time to put a carefree outer demeanor in place while inside she was looking at a future too frightful for a mother to contemplate. He could at least try to take her mind off that for the few minutes left of their drive.

"So, why all your visits to the Kerrs?"

"Arthur and Odele have five sons who were total jocks and played about every sport Layton High School offered. Arthur was the driving force behind the inception of the parents' booster club. He used to bus students and teachers up here for pep rallies out on the front lawn. He even had a pit dug for bonfires. I was on the cheerleading squad, so I was always front and center at the rallies."

"A cheerleader," Clay said, infusing his voice with lazy interest. "I have this mental picture of you in a tight sweater and miniskirt while you frantically wave pompons. Am I close?"

"Right on target." Kathryn turned her head, her mouth settling into the smug curve he remembered from years ago. "I could do a mean double-backflip without dropping those pompons."

"Now, *there's* an image." He could smell the faint lemony scent of her perfume on the vehicle's cool air. Her black sleeveless dress emphasized her delicate build and showed off the lean muscles of her arms, the firm curve of her breasts. Her thick, dark hair was pulled loosely back, making her blue eyes seem huge.

There, in the outrageously beautiful woman, was the shadow of the girl he'd left behind.

He pulled to a stop under the house's portico while fresh regret washed over him. He wanted to tell her he would give anything if they could go back in time. That he'd been a damn idiot to walk away that long-ago summer.

Before he could say anything, a white-shirted valet swung Kathryn's door open.

She felt the light press of Clay's hand on her elbow as he escorted her across cobblestones that expelled the heat of the day. By the time they reached the front porch, the sun had dipped to just above the horizon, turning the summer sky into streaks of fiery-orange.

Clay's fingers tightened on her elbow, tugging her to a stop.

"One thing," he began. "I don't plan to stay with you the majority of the time tonight. It'll be easier for me to study the people who interact with you—and the ones who don't—if I stay in the background."

Kathryn looked past his shoulder at two elegantly clad couples making their way toward the house. Both of the women in the group smiled and waved. Forcing a smile, she returned the greeting. She had no doubt the next few hours would be torture, and she was tempted to insist Clay stay by her side. But pride held her back—she didn't want him to know he had become her personal mooring. And her clinging to him wouldn't help her get her child back.

"I hope to God you see something. Pick up a clue that leads us to who has Matthew." Her lips trembled, then firmed. "The waiting is awful. The not knowing." Conscious of the scar that slashed across his right cheek, she softened her voice. "You'd know that better than anyone."

"Yeah, I know," he said while bracing her shoulders with his hands. "Remember, if this gets to be too much, tell me. If necessary, I'll make our excuses and take you home."

"The ransom note told me not to change my schedule. So, I have to stay here. For Matthew."

Clay squeezed her shoulders. "You ready?"

"As I'll ever be."

Inside the mansion's cavernous marble foyer they received a hearty greeting from their host.

"You've taken me back thirty years," Arthur Kerr said while pumping Kathryn's hand. In his sixties, he was one of the richest men in Texas, and he looked it— large and imposing with sharp, defined features and thick silver hair. Kathryn recognized the cut of his dark gray suit as coming from a designer that Devin sometimes used.

Salt-and-pepper-eyebrows raised, Arthur continued to examine her. "If I didn't know it was you, I'd think your momma had just walked through my front door. And let me tell you, Lauren was a knockout." Arthur offered his hand to Clay. "You've got good taste in women, son."

"So do you," Clay said when Arthur's wife eased in beside him. Clay dropped a kiss on the cheek of the sharp-eyed, petite woman adorned in white silk.

"I just love having handsome men dote over me," Odele Kerr said, plucking flutes of champagne off the tray held by a hovering waiter. When they were all served, she raised her glass. "Kathryn, before you start mingling with the guests, I want to toast your generosity. The hospital board has talked for years about building a wing. Your donation is a godsend. And your stipulation that the wing be named after Sam makes us all proud. The senator was a wonderful man, bigger than life. I'm sure the Cross C just isn't the same with him gone."

"It won't ever be the same again," Kathryn agreed. Otherwise, she'd have never brought Matthew there.

Matthew. The ache in her heart for her child was burning, and she struggled to keep her anguish hidden. "I hope everyone who knew my grandfather will honor him tonight by bidding in the silent auction. Or giving a donation. It would be wonderful to have construction of the wing fully funded."

Arthur tapped his glass against hers so that the crystal sang. "I'll drink to that." After taking a sip, he turned to Clay. "There's a ton of folks here eager to talk to Kathryn about the hospital wing. And Shannon Burton's milling around somewhere. She's writing an article about the hospital and I told her I'd make sure she has a chance to interview Kathryn tonight. I hope you won't hold it against me if I keep your date busy for a while."

"Not at all." Clay dipped his head toward Kathryn. They'd known Burton would be here, that there was no way to avoid her. Kathryn had spent time on the phone that afternoon with Quentin Forbes while the negotiator coached her on what to say when the reporter asked about Matthew. "Kat, I'll catch up with you later."

"All right." Sending Arthur a smile, she slipped her hand into the crook of his arm.

Edging around knots of guests, Clay wound his way through the great room where stark-white walls provided a vivid backdrop for a magnificent art collection. Several groupings of plushly cushioned couches and antique tables were scattered among a profusion of potted plants.

He paused to exchange greetings with several ranch owners discussing the going price for grain. Yet, foremost in his mind was the exchange he'd just witnessed between Kathryn and Odele Kerr. On the surface, it had been a testament to Sam Conner. But Kat hadn't come home to see her grandfather for a decade.

For the first time, Clay wondered if the senator had visited her in California, or had they for some reason been totally estranged? Probably the latter, he decided, since she hadn't shown up for the old man's funeral. Which was something the revered senator's neighbors and friends might view as an unforgivable slight.

Clay tightened his fingers on the stem of the flute he still carried. At the first break in the conversation, he excused himself from the ranch owners and moved through the throng of bodies toward the far side of the room.

Dammit, he should have thought about that angle before. Maybe instead of thinking the kidnapper had a grudge against Sam Conner, he should also be looking for someone who might harbor ill feelings toward Kathryn for neglecting the old man.

Someone who'd combined their desire to take a slap at her with a need for a million dollars in cash.

If he needed a reminder that his instincts weren't to be trusted, this was it. He hadn't sensed the danger closing in on his parents, and they'd gotten kidnapped because of that. And died. Now, he was going to have to play catch-up and add the group of people he'd missed putting on the suspect list. People whom he should have already started running background and financial checks on.

The image of Matthew smiling up at him, a deputy's badge pinned to his T-shirt, assaulted Clay like sniper fire. He knew better than to let the image dig roots inside him, for if the unthinkable happened it would bloom with guilt. And join with the old nightmares about his parents that always left him with a dull, skittering sense of panic and damp palms.

No matter what Forbes said, *he* was the wrong man to entrust Matthew's life to.

"I hate these damn functions."

Jaw locked tight, Clay turned at the sound of Brad Jordan's voice. He noted the banker was wearing the same dark suit and gray tie he'd had on that morning. Now, though, the suit looked rumpled and the tie's knot was slightly askew.

Clay forced his shoulders to relax. Unclenched his jaw. Kathryn wasn't the only one who had to put on an act tonight.

"You hate fund-raisers?" he asked. "Or all social affairs?"

"The whole shooting match." Lifting a crystal tumbler of what looked like scotch, Brad took a long swallow. "Give me a football game, sturdy bleachers to sit on and a few ice-cold beers. That's heaven."

Clay raised a brow. "So, what got you here tonight?"

"My wife. Felicia drags me to as many of these things as she can. Says attending is good for our social image." Brad scowled. "Want to bet she got that line from her daddy?"

Clay flicked a look over the crowd, his gaze settling

on a tall, gray-haired man as lean as a lightning rod. Even in this social setting, Garner Smith's expression was grim, his eyes cheerless. It was well-known there was no love lost between Brad and his father-in-law.

"I'll pass on taking that bet," Clay said.

"Smart man," Brad murmured, then smiled at someone approaching from behind Clay. "I wasn't sure you'd be here tonight. Clay, you know my dad, right?"

"Our paths have crossed a few times," Clay said, offering a hand. Rich Jordan was a tall man with a thatch of blond hair shorn close along the sides. His face was bony, all jaw and cheekbones, with a big bumpy nose. In addition to a drink, Rich gripped his phone and kept sweeping his gaze around the crowd.

"Who are you looking for?" Brad asked.

"Arthur Kerr. I've got bad news about the booster club computers."

"What about them?"

"The tech called and said upgrading the system's gonna take two extra days."

Brad squeezed the bridge of his nose, as if he were trying to ease a sudden headache. "Why's that a problem, Dad? It's summer, it's not like there's any activity going on."

"We're gearing up to start our fall membership drive. I didn't think to print out a copy of our mailing list before the techs started the upgrade. Now, the whole thing's turned into a major pain in my ass."

Listening with half an ear to the Jordans, Clay went back to scanning the milling crowd. Some now held plates from the buffet set up in the dining room. Arthur Kerr had nudged Kathryn to the center of the huge room where she stood chatting with a group of civic leaders, one being Clay's uncle. Off and on, other guests directed looks her way, but he could spot no one who seemed to be watching her with an inordinate amount of interest.

Except for himself, he amended. If he didn't know about her emotional turmoil, the way her warm smile and easy demeanor appeared to have her melding with the people around her, he would have assumed the most important thing on her mind was talking up donations for the hospital wing. But he did know what she was dealing with, and while he watched her, he realized her inner strength drew him even more deeply than the physical appeal.

Which was a first for him. Though he'd had a couple of intense relationships during the past ten years, he'd never been interested enough to dig past the outer layer and learn what made a certain woman tick. Maybe that was because he'd never felt the hot, smooth sensation that just looking at Kat sent through him.

"Looks like Doc Silver's got his hands full tonight," Rich Jordan commented.

His son chuckled. "That woman's gonna eat him alive."

"Probably what he's hoping."

Pulling his attention from Kathryn, Clay shifted his gaze in the direction of the Jordans. His eyes narrowed when he caught sight of the veterinarian shooting a look of blatant invitation at the smoldering redhead latched to his right arm. With a sly smile on her face, she drew him through the open double doors out onto the patio.

After they disappeared from sight, Clay eased out a breath. Then another. The redhead was Shannon Burton, the reporter.

If Silver told her about Matthew, Clay had no doubt she'd pounce on what promised to be the hottest story of her career.

By this time tomorrow, news of Matthew's kidnapping could be running on every wire service known to man.

If that happened, Kathryn's son was as good as dead.

CHAPTER NINE

AT THE SAME TIME Clay moved outside to keep Reece Silver and Shannon Burton in sight, a white-haired, grandfatherly looking man motored his wheelchair through the sea of guests and snagged Kathryn's right hand.

After exchanging greetings, Howard Daily asked in a wispy halting voice, "Is that little boy of yours here tonight? Owen got a kick out of him when he picked you both up at the airport and drove you to the Cross C. Said your son's a real pistol."

"He is that," Kathryn agreed. She'd been asked about Matthew so many times, she felt as if a stone were lodged in her chest. "Matthew's not here tonight. He's visiting his father."

"Well, I'll have to meet him some other time." Howard rapped his free palm against the arm of the wheelchair. "I guess you heard a stroke put me in this contraption?"

"Yes." Kathryn leaned in closer to hear over the crowd's chatter. "Willa called me in California after you went into the hospital. I was so relieved when Owen picked me up at the airport and told me you were well on your way to recovery."

She flicked a look at her lawyer, standing a few protective inches behind his father's chair. Tall and broad-shouldered, Owen looked hard-edged and physical, his skin bronze against the pristine whiteness of his dress shirt. There was no missing the concern in his eyes as he gazed down at his father.

She gave a gentle squeeze to Howard's long, bony hand that felt as cold as winter and trembled against her palm. He was as tall as his son, but seated in the wheelchair his frame looked withered beneath his dark suit. A sad change from the robust man she remembered who had always slipped her lemon drops whenever business brought him to the Cross C.

"What Owen didn't tell me is that you've gotten even more handsome over the years," she murmured.

"The boy's just jealous." Howard pressed a kiss against her knuckles, the gleam in his blue eyes confirming his well-known talent for rakish banter hadn't been affected by the stroke. "I heard a rumor you were single again. Is that true?"

Kathryn arched a brow. "Yes."

"Run away with me," he urged. "*I* know how to treat a beautiful woman."

"Don't mind my dad." Although Owen's expression had turned sardonic, there was warmth in his voice. "He's incorrigible."

She nodded. "It's good to know some things never change."

For as long as she could remember, Howard Daily had been Sam's closest friend, confidant and attorney. But months before her grandfather died, he'd jerked all of his business from the Daily's law firm and transferred his legal affairs to a Dallas attorney. Kathryn was sure that, for Howard, the personal blow from Sam's action had been as great as the financial one. Less than a week later, he'd suffered the stroke.

She looked back at Owen, trying to read something in his face, but his expression was impenetrable. On the day he'd driven her and Matthew to the Cross C, she had wondered if Owen blamed Sam for his father's ill health. If so, had he decided to get revenge against the Conners by taking her son?

According to Willa, after Owen joined his father's firm he'd often accompanied Howard when he'd come to the Cross C to discuss legal business with Sam. Which meant Owen was familiar with the layout of the house. He'd heard Matthew ask about the outlaw tunnel. The day before the kidnapping, Owen had brought legal papers by the ranch. Willa had been sitting on the front porch swing, her lap filled with bowls of beans she was snapping so she'd asked Owen to leave the papers in the study. While alone in the house, he could have drugged the bottle of wine, then gone to the basement and unlocked the doors at each end of the tunnel.

Which was why Clay had put her attorney's name high up on the list of possible kidnapping suspects.

Kathryn's fingers toyed with the clasp on her beaded bag. She didn't want to think about the reasons why the names of so many of the people at the fund-raiser were on the suspect list. Not when it took all her control to engage them in uncountable lighthearted conversations while her nerves slowly shredded.

"Well, one thing's changed," Howard said. "I can't charm the girls the way I used to. You remember how

Felicia Jordan's always been an all-out flirt? Tonight, I couldn't even get her to give me a kiss on the cheek."

Kathryn's gaze tracked Howard's to the petite woman standing near one of the tables loaded with items donated for the silent auction. In high school, Felicia's ethereal looks had drawn males like a parched plant to water. Now, she was even more attractive. Her body, tanned, toned and sleek, looked perfect in the blue dress that dipped low in the front. Her hair, shorter and a richer honey-blond, framed and softened her sharp chin.

Felicia was currently involved in what appeared to be an intense conversation with the uniformed Layton County deputy whom Arthur Kerr had hired to keep an eye on the auction's proceeds. While Kathryn observed them, the deputy's smile shifted to that of a male physically aware of a female. The resulting expression wasn't quite predatory, but it was far from safe. Felicia must have thought so, too, since a blush rose high in her cheeks. Kathryn did a quick sweep of the room to see if Brad Jordan was watching the exchange between his wife and the deputy. Although she'd spoken to her banker earlier, he wasn't in sight now.

"Guess Felicia's too busy flirting with that lawman to pay attention to me," Howard mumbled.

"That's her loss," Kathryn said, then pressed a kiss to his parchment-pale cheek. "And you're doing just fine in the charm department. Why don't we get in line for the buffet?"

WHILE KATHRYN HELPED Howard fill a plate, Clay followed Reece Silver and Shannon Burton as they strolled across the wide expanse of gray slate that stretched the entire length of the back of the Kerr's enormous house.

Dusk had settled in, turning the sky a mix of pale blues and pinks. Twinkling white lights strung through the trees that bordered the expansive grounds and the lights in the landscaped flower beds had already winked on.

Tonight, Silver didn't bear much resemblance to the veterinarian who often wore worn denim and scuffed boots. His tall, powerful frame was clothed in a navy-blue suit, creamy shirt and designer tie. With his brown hair combed back from his narrow face, he had the look of wealth: suave and elegant. Very much an heir to the Silver family's telecommunication fortune.

Thing was, he wasn't an *heir*. Which was what Clay had learned during the call he'd received while waiting for Kathryn in the entry hall at the Cross C. According to the P.I. who Clay had running background and financial checks, the wealth in the Silver family belonged strictly to Silver's older brother, who inherited the whole ball of wax when their parents died. The doctor received a modest annual stipend, but it wasn't enough to touch the debt he'd chalked up establishing and maintaining his practice. Debt his brother wasn't likely to help with, since a personal feud had kept the two from speaking to each other in over five years.

Debt that a million dollars in cash would help knock down.

Clay narrowed his eyes. Silver hadn't landed on his suspect list solely because he had made enough visits to the Cross C to know the workings of the ranch like the back of his hand. The vet had admitted to possessing the same drug that lab tests had now confirmed was added to the bottle of wine Kathryn drank from the night Matthew was kidnapped. And it would have been nothing for Silver to jab a hypodermic needle into Abby's thigh to sedate the dachshund.

Clay conceded it might be coincidence that Silver and Johnny Sullivan had shown up at the house the following morning about the same time Kathryn had roused from the drug-induced sleep. Or, Silver could have made sure he and the foreman wound up there around that time supposedly to talk to her about the ailing mare. Convenient that Silver was there to suggest Kathryn call in a negotiator, whose job he admittedly knew was to ensure the ransom got paid with as much speed as possible.

None of that was proof Silver had snatched Matthew, Clay reminded himself. The doctor could be totally innocent.

But there wasn't anything innocent in the look he was sending Shannon Burton. And the way she had her centerfold's body pressed against Silver's told Clay the relationship was at the stage where sharing pillow talk was a distinct possibility. *Damn*. Why the hell did one of the few people who knew about Matthew's kidnapping have to be playing around with a reporter?

Clay snagged another glass of champagne off the tray of a passing waiter. He never thought he'd be grateful he had the town gossip's son working for him. But the fact that Eddie Woodson hadn't mentioned anything about Silver and Burton being an item gave Clay hope they hadn't been hooked up long enough to engage in intimate talk that might drift to the subject of kidnapping.

Either way, Clay needed to know what the reporter was privy to.

Positioning himself near the patio where guests danced to soft music provided by a small band, he waited until the couple came abreast of him, then he stepped forward. He extended his hand to Silver at the same time he nodded to Shannon.

"Hello, Doc. Shannon. Good to see you."

"You, too, Clay," Shannon murmured. The red dress that fit her body like a good paint job make her look as skinny as a snake. "I think this is the first time I've seen you at a social to-do."

"Uncle Les had to twist my arm to get me here."

"Uh-huh." She gave him a crafty smile. "You don't have to be coy, Clay. The whole town's talking about how you and Kathryn Conner have taken up with each other."

Clay gave a mental nod to Sheriff Boudry who'd predicted as much. "Guess there's no keeping secrets."

"Not from me," Shannon agreed. "I'll be interviewing Kathryn as soon as the photographer assigned to the story gets here. I've already added your name to the list of topics I plan to ask her about. Be sure to read my story in tomorrow's paper."

Nodding, Clay shifted his attention to Silver. "Doc, I need to have a quick word with you."

"All right. I'll get with you after Shannon and I dance."

"I'd appreciate it if we could talk now," Clay persisted. "It has to do with the business you and I discussed last night." Clay caught the flash of understanding in Silver's eyes before giving Shannon an apologetic smile. "I won't keep him long," he said and offered her the glass of champagne.

She accepted the drink, then smiled up at Silver. "You go ahead, Reece. I need to call and see what's holding up my photographer."

"You're sure you don't mind?" Reece asked.

She skimmed a red-painted fingernail down the lapel of his dark suit coat. "Only if you promise to make it up to me later."

"Count on it."

Clay watched Burton saunter off while pulling a phone from the small purse that dangled off one of her bare shoulders.

"What's happened?" the vet asked in a lowered voice.

"Follow me," Clay said and headed to a shadowy part of the yard at the far end of the house away from the party noise. There he turned, and faced Silver. Too much was at stake to beat around the bush. "Have you told Shannon about the kidnapping?"

The vet's dark eyebrows registered brief surprise. "No. I told you I wouldn't tell anyone."

"I know what you told me." Clay pushed back one flap of his suit coat and shoved a hand into the pocket of his slacks. "I also know that great intentions go down the drain when a man and a woman wind up in bed together. Things get mentioned that wouldn't otherwise get said. In your case, I'd hate for that to happen, especially if the woman you're whispering to is a reporter."

A muscle in the side of Silver's jaw clenched. "What happens between Shannon and me is none of your business."

"I agree. But what happens to Matthew Mason *is*. So, consider this a reminder that very few people know about the kidnapping. If word of it leaks, the leak won't be hard to find."

"If word gets out, it won't have been my doing," Silver said through gritted teeth.

"Good, because I'll make sure that anyone who talks, brags or *sells* the story about the kidnapping will be charged as an accomplice to murder, if that's how things turn out."

"Last night you as good as accused me of snatching the boy. Now, you threaten me with arrest if I mention the kidnapping to anyone. You're making me damn sorry I suggested Kathryn go to you for help."

"Understandable." Before Silver could turn away, Clay lifted a palm. "Bottom line is, I'm doing all I can to make sure that little boy stays alive."

"I've got that, Turner. Otherwise, I'd have already plowed my fist into your jaw."

Remaining in the shadows, Clay watched Silver stalk away. He didn't blame the vet for being pissed—he'd feel the same if someone got in his face the way he had Silver's. Too bad, Clay thought. Matthew would be in even more danger if Shannon Burton got wind that the son of Hollywood's hottest actor had been kidnapped.

A noise had Clay making an abrupt turn. He thought he and Silver had been the only ones near this shadowy section of the yard, but now he could hear voices, agitated whispering, coming from around the corner of the house.

He eased closer, not making any noise, trying to filter out the hushed voices from the soft dance music drifting on the air. As he moved, the front of a white van came into view. The van was parked on what apparently was a section of the driveway used by companies providing food and other services for evening.

"Sam Conner was a heartless prick," a woman hissed with snarling fury. "It's not right we have to work ourselves into the ground for the rest of our lives because of him. *It's not right*."

Clay peered around the corner, saw the woman's back. She was short and thick-waisted with frizzy blond hair anchored in a ponytail. She wore a white blouse and black slacks; a stream of smoke from the cigarette clenched in her right hand rose, forming a haze around the lights of the portico under which several vehicles were parked. Her hand shook with the anger that shimmered in her voice, making the cigarette tremble.

"It may not be right, but it's so," a man replied. "Olivia, you have to remember the senator didn't *force* me."

Although the woman blocked Clay's view of the man standing at the rear of the white van, he knew the voice belonged to Norman Adams. Earlier in the dining room, Clay had spotted the owner of Layton's newest café replenishing trays of food on the buffet table. And although he had never met Norman's wife, Clay had learned her name when Willa told him Norman and Olivia Adams had been hired numerous times to help prepare food and serve during Sam Conner's parties at the Cross C.

Which put the Adams on the list of kidnapping suspects.

"No, the bastard just dangled this too-good-to-be-true dream in front of your nose and you took the bait. *Without asking me.* I'm sick of your excuses, Norman," Olivia hissed. "Kathryn *owes* us for what her grandfather did. She's right inside. You tell her we want the money. Tonight."

"I can't just—"

"Tonight, Norman. *Or else.*"

Olivia turned and jerked open a door. She paused long enough to crush out her cigarette in quick, vicious little jabs against the side of the house before disappearing inside.

Clay now had an unobstructed view of Norman Adams. Dressed like his wife in a white shirt and black slacks, he held a cardboard box in his arms. His shoulders were slumped, his plain, unremarkable face a study in misery.

"Evening Norman," Clay said as he stepped around the corner.

Astonishment crossed Norman's face. Replaced by uneasiness. "Clay. I didn't know anyone was there."

Clay gave the man a benign smile. "Couldn't help but overhear you and your wife. Sounds like she's really upset."

"Yes. I need to get inside and calm her down."

Clay stepped in front of him, blocking his path. "Or else what?" He kept his voice low, conversational. "What will your wife do if you don't go to Kathryn for money tonight?"

"Nothing," Norman said, even as Clay watched nerves rush across his face. "Olivia was just blowing off steam."

"About what?"

"That's a private matter. Between Olivia and myself."

"Wrong answer, Norman. It involves Kathryn, too. She's a friend of mine, and the conversation I just overheard didn't sound at all friendly toward her."

"I…" Norman dipped his chin at the box clenched

in his arms. "I need to take these champagne glasses into the kitchen."

"The sooner you talk to me, the sooner you'll get them inside," Clay said, keeping his voice mild. "Tell me why your wife thinks Sam Conner was a heartless prick. And what it was he dangled in front of your nose."

With dull resignation in his eyes, Norman lowered the box to the driveway. "I invested money in a stock venture the senator recommended. The stock didn't…do well."

Clay frowned. Introverted Norman Adams didn't strike him as the type of guy whom Sam Conner would give investment advice to.

"Did the senator give you stock tips often?"

"No. Just that one time. And it was a fluke, really. Senator Conner stopped by the high school, and happened to walk by my classroom during my free hour. He came in to say hello. While we were talking he mentioned a stock investment he had just heard about. He seemed very excited about its potential."

"Did he invest in it, too?"

"The way he talked I assumed he had. I found out later I was wrong—he hadn't put any of his own money into the stock."

"Did he convince anyone else you know to invest?"

"Not that I'm aware of." Norman looked away, his jaw muscles flexing. "I knew there were no guarantees. It was my own fault I didn't investigate the stock fully before I took out a loan using my retirement savings as collateral. But everything Senator Conner touched seemed to turn to gold. Just look at the Cross C. And he talked like the stock was a sure thing."

"How much did you lose?"

"All the money I'd borrowed, and everything in my retirement fund. Olivia and I don't make a lot on our teacher salaries, and we needed another source of income to pay back the loan. My parents used to run a diner, so I know a lot about the business. Olivia's aunt owns the building where we opened the café, so we don't have to pay rent on the space." He shook his head. "I'm not trying to make excuses for what I did. It's my mess. I don't blame Senator Conner for it."

"But Olivia does," Clay said.

"I've tried to reason with her, but she won't listen."

"And now she wants you to hit up Kathryn for the money you lost."

"Yes. Which is something I refuse to do." Norman lifted the box. "I need to get these glasses inside. And make sure Olivia doesn't bother Kathryn."

"One more question." Clay had no idea if knowing the time-line on this mattered, but while a cop he'd learned that seemingly useless information sometimes became of prime importance somewhere down the line. "When did the senator first talk to you about the stock?"

"Last year. Not too long after Kathryn won her Emmy award, because I asked the senator to thank her for mentioning me in her acceptance speech. Now, if you'll excuse me?"

"In a minute." Clay thought back to the day he'd run into Kathryn and Matthew at the café. Norman had been as enthralled with Kathryn's presence as his customers had been. And his position behind the counter put him within earshot of hearing Matthew talk about the outlaw tunnel. Still, whoever took Matthew had to have been at the Cross C in order to drug the bottle of wine. If

Norman or Olivia had been there, Willa would have mentioned it.

Which was something Clay intended to confirm with the housekeeper as soon as he got Kathryn home.

For now, all he could do was try to protect her from unnecessary stress. "Let me give you some advice, Norman. Kathryn's got a lot on her mind and I doubt Olivia will accomplish her goal if she asks for money tonight."

"I intend to make sure my wife doesn't do that, as soon as you stop blocking my way to the door."

"Have a nice night." Sliding his hands into the pockets of his slacks, Clay stepped aside. First thing in the morning, he would hit up Sheriff Boudry for info on Norman and Olivia Adams.

When the door slammed shut, Clay stepped to the van, pulled open one of the rear doors. With the vehicle unsecured, he didn't for one minute think he would find Matthew inside. But a van with no rear windows was perfect for transporting a kidnap victim. And Clay wasn't about to pass up the opportunity to check for evidence.

"I'M SURE IT WAS difficult when your husband made no attempt to conceal his affair with his costar, Theresa O'Meara."

Kathryn kept her gaze locked on Shannon Burton's. Up to now, the reporter's questions had stayed on the subject of fund-raising for the hospital's new wing. The expression on Burton's flawless face was all business, but she couldn't quite conceal the crafty gleam the shift of topic had settled in her eyes.

"I don't comment on my personal life in interviews,

Miss Burton. If you have additional questions about the fund-raiser, I'll be happy to answer them."

Burton thumped the end of her pen against the small pad she'd jotted notes on. "Your grandfather commissioned me to write his biography. Are you aware of that?"

"No." Kathryn hesitated. She knew from the articles speculating about her absence from Sam's funeral that Burton was the type of reporter intent on creating a scandal if none existed and blowing it out of proportion if it did.

"It's a shame my grandfather passed away before you could complete the book."

"Oh, it's almost done. Even at the end when Sam was so weak, he continued recording tapes for me. The ones where he talked about you and your son are especially poignant."

Kathryn's fingers tightened on the glass of tonic water she'd traded an hour ago for a champagne flute. "Really?"

"Yes. Sam was so hurt when you severed ties with him," Shannon continued. "Then refused his requests to see his only great-grandchild. Especially the last one he made on his death bed."

Kathryn fought to keep her expression unreadable. Sam had never asked to meet Matthew. *Never*.

Shahnon angled her chin. "Lots of folks took exception to your not showing up at the funeral. Of course, I'm covering that in my book. But I want to give you a chance to comment on things. Explain what was so important you couldn't be here. Add your side of the story about your relationship with Sam."

Kathryn took a sip of tonic. She was tempted to tell Burton to go to hell. But although satisfying, such an action would cause undue scrutiny she couldn't afford.

"I don't discuss my personal life with reporters, Miss Burton. And I don't make exceptions."

"It would be a positive gesture to Sam's memory if you let me come to the Cross C. Take photos of you and your darling little boy for the book. That way you don't have to make a statement. All you and Matthew have to do is smile."

The memory of Matthew smiling up at her, laughing with her, flashed in Kathryn's brain. Was he somewhere alone in the dark, scared and crying for her? Was he still alive?

Fear for her son, intense and uncontrollable, started a trembling deep inside her. Sweat popped out on her flesh.

"Are you okay?" Shannon asked. "You suddenly went pale."

"I'm…fine."

"Glad to hear that," Clay said as he stepped beside Kathryn and slid an arm around her waist. "Since it's time to make good on your promise to dance with me."

Grateful for his sudden arrival, Kathryn leaned against his side while she drew back her composure. "Perfect timing," she said, forcing a smile. "Miss Burton and I are finished talking."

"Then you and I have a date on the patio." Clay lifted the drink from her hand and set it on a nearby table.

As he led Kathryn toward the open French doors, Shannon moved with them. "What about the photos of you and your son?"

Kathryn flicked her a look across her shoulder. "I'm sure your book will be a bestseller without them."

"She's writing a book?" Clay asked after Shannon gave up following them.

"About Sam." The knots in Kathryn's shoulders tightened. "I don't want to talk about it right now."

"All right."

The instant she and Clay stepped onto the patio, he drew her into his arms and began moving to the slow, dreamy music. "I take it the interview got a little tough," he said quietly.

Nodding, she gazed up at him. "Did you find out anything tonight?" She made sure her voice was low enough to escape being overheard by the other dancers. "See anything that might lead us to who took Matthew?"

"I've got some things to check out." His voice was low as well, his tone casual. "But nothing solid."

Kathryn fisted her hand against his shoulder. She needed to stay strong for Matthew, yet she could feel fingers of hopelessness plucking at her insides. "This is the second night he's been gone," she murmured while soft music drifted around them. "I'm so afraid for him."

"I know." Clay dipped his head. "You've done a good job tonight, Kat. I'd never know by looking at you what you're dealing with."

"I feel like there's something ripping inside me." Her voice cracked. "God, Clay."

His arm tightened around her waist; his fingers shifted, lacing with hers. "Try to relax for a few minutes. Just close your eyes and concentrate on the music. When you feel steadier, we'll take off."

Because her legs felt like glass ready to shatter, she leaned into him, resting her head against his shoulder.

While they swayed to the music, the familiarity of the curves pressed against him had Clay gritting his teeth. Beneath his hands, he felt the tightness begin to seep out of Kathryn, felt her relaxing. He remembered how it felt to have her lying beneath him. How it felt to have her come apart in his arms.

He wanted to go back to that time. Wanted a chance to undo all he'd done, to make different decisions. Smarter ones that would change the course of both his and Kat's lives.

A clutch of minutes passed while Kathryn became aware of the rock-solid feel of Clay's body, the firmness of his arm circling her waist, the brush of his thighs against hers.

He was all heat and hardness and musky male scent.

Her blood was now pounding so hard, it sounded like thunder in her ears.

It was the wrong response. A dangerous one. Clay might be the only man she could depend on right now, but she'd already been down that path. She wouldn't trust her heart to him again. Ever.

So, despite the reason they'd wound up on the dim recesses of the patio, she shouldn't be dancing with him. Shouldn't tremble each time his breath stirred the tendrils that had loosened from her chignon. Shouldn't give the wall she'd built around her emotions a chance to crack.

She lifted her head and met his gaze. The hunger in his dark eyes had heat flaring between her legs, spreading outward in soft, breath-stealing waves. While the music swelled inside her head, she felt her will to resist him ebb away.

And knew it was too late to stop the wall from cracking.

Every muscle inside her tensed. She didn't want this. Couldn't deal with it, not now. Not when her world was so close to falling apart.

She halted midstep, swayed slightly. "We need to find the Kerrs. Thank them for hosting the fund-raiser," she said to Clay's waiting look. Her voice was raw with emotion, but she couldn't help it. It was all she could do to hold back the tears that burned her eyes. "Then I want to go home."

"All right." Clay's arm slipped away from her waist, but he kept his fingers linked with hers. "Last I saw Arthur he was in the dining room, making sure everyone turned in a bid on the silent auction."

Kathryn stepped back. She pulled her hand from Clay's, desperate to shut herself off from him, from the emotions she could no longer control.

Gripping the beaded bag holding the phone that had remained silent all evening, she turned her back and began winding her way through the crowd.

CHAPTER TEN

FINGERS LINKED behind his head, Clay lay in bed, his gaze focused on the ceiling. Light from the full moon streamed through the windows, illuminating the bedroom in silver light and shadow. Every so often, his gaze flicked to the red digital numbers on the clock on the nightstand.

It was nearly two o'clock; fourteen minutes had passed since he heard Kathryn leave the bedroom next to his. The wooden floor had creaked twice when she passed by his closed door.

So far, she hadn't returned.

After another minute passed, he shoved back the sheet. Ignoring his shirt, he pulled on jeans and boots and stepped into the dark hallway.

Since Kathryn had left the door to her room open, he went inside and flicked on the light. The bed was made, so he doubted she'd even tried to sleep after they returned from the fund-raiser.

Her outward calm during the evening had been convincing. But she hadn't said a word on the drive back to the Cross C, just stared out at the dark landscape.

No one had to tell him her torturous thoughts were centered on Matthew. Wondering if she'd ever see him again. If she could have done something more to protect him.

Clay had suffered through those same questions and recriminations during his parents' kidnapping.

He moved down the hallway to Matthew's room. The bed was still unmade, toys scattered on the rug. Clay felt the silence all around him, as if the room had been frozen in time at the exact moment the kidnapper struck.

He was vaguely surprised not to find Kathryn there.

Nor was she anywhere on the second floor. Downstairs, he checked the living room, the study, then the dining room. The kitchen was dark, save for the wedge of light from the open door to the basement. Clay descended the wooden steps, the air turning cold when he reached the cement floor.

On the far side of the basement, he saw the door to the outlaw tunnel standing open. Beyond the door was a black, yawning abyss. He paused at the metal storage cabinet to grab the same flashlight he used when he searched the tunnel for clues. Still in the pocket of his jeans was the toy soldier he had found that day.

Stepping into the tunnel, Clay clicked on the flashlight and followed its beam along the hard-packed dirt floor. Toward its center, the tunnel's solid-rock walls narrowed, then widened again as Clay neared the far end. There, the air grew warmer and lost its musty smell.

He paused when he spotted Kathryn standing in the open doorway with her back to him, her body a dark silhouette against the moonlit night. When he inched closer, he saw she had her face buried in her hands. She made no sound, but the way her shoulders heaved there was no doubt she was crying.

Finally, he thought. As far as he knew, this was the first time she'd let go since she discovered Matthew missing. A good cry might help release some of the tension.

He angled the flashlight's beam toward the ground. "Kat?"

The sound of his voice had her pivoting to face him. She drew in air in broken gasps while using her fingertips to wipe the tears off her cheeks. "I didn't hear you."

"I'm sorry to intrude. I just wanted to make sure you're okay." Shoving his fingers through his hair, he realized how asinine his comment had been. She wouldn't be "okay" until she had her son back.

He stepped closer. She might want to be alone, but he couldn't just leave her here, crying. "We're going to get Matthew back."

"I shouldn't have brought him here." The flashlight's dim illumination darkened her eyes, shadowed her damp cheeks. "It was selfish of me."

"Selfish, how?"

"I wanted to erase all the bad memories of the Cross C. Make new ones with my son."

"What bad memories?"

"Of Sam." She leaned a shoulder against the doorjamb and stared out at the night sky. "They're all of Sam."

Clay frowned. Ten years ago, she seldom spoke about her grandfather.

"If it would help to talk, I'm willing to listen."

She pressed her fingertips against her eyelids and remained silent. Clay held his tongue. *Wait*, he thought. *Wait*. If she was going to say more, it wouldn't be because he pushed.

Finally she dropped her hand and met his gaze. "Sam hated me."

Layton was the typical small town where secrets didn't stay secret very long. All the summers Clay had spent working on his uncle's ranch, and the two years he'd lived there, he had never heard a derogatory word about Senator Conner. That wouldn't have been the case if anyone had even the vaguest suspicion his feelings for his granddaughter weren't loving.

Clay flicked off the flashlight as he moved to the doorway. He set the light at his feet, then rested his shoulder on the jamb opposite her. The full butterball moon illuminated the mouth of the tunnel in ghostly silver light. "Why did Sam hate you?"

"I don't know." She slid her hands into the pockets of her shorts, pulled them out again. "I was only a few months old when my parents died in the car wreck. My grandmother was already dead, so she wasn't around to insist he take me in. I think he did it because he would have lost votes if he hadn't."

"What about Willa? Was she working here then?"

"No, Sam hired her after my parents died. He basically gave me to Willa to raise."

While she spoke, Kathryn kept her eyes locked with Clay's. Devin was the only person to whom she'd told the truth about Sam.

She had no idea why she suddenly felt the need to tell Clay. She just did. The skepticism that had settled in his eyes told her he was going to take some convincing. Not a surprise—Sam had fooled everyone.

"Hard to believe, isn't it?" she asked quietly.

"All I've ever heard was that Sam doted on you."

Clay furrowed his brow. "But things aren't always as they seem."

"Sam never did anything without considering the political ramifications. He knew it would cost him votes if his true feelings for his only grandchild were known. So he acted like he cared about me whenever anyone else was around, including Willa."

"Kat, what are we talking about here? Did Sam abuse you? Sexually? Physically?"

She felt a chill flow over her, and knew she would never be free from the drag of the pain that lay in her past. Pain that came from not only her relationship with her grandfather, but with Clay. Two of the most important men in her life hadn't wanted her.

Devin at least had, for a time. The charismatic actor who'd strolled into her life had been exactly what a barely twenty-one-year-old Kathryn had needed. He'd offered excitement and a dazzling freedom from the past. A way to forget. And he'd *wanted* her. They'd married before she'd been able to catch her breath. Long before she'd come to terms with the excruciating miscarriage of her child with Clay Turner. But they were talking about Sam now. Only Sam.

"The abuse was mostly emotional. Whenever we were alone in the house and I walked into the same room, Sam would leave. When it was just the two of us together, he spoke to me only when he had to."

"You said the abuse was 'mostly emotional.' Did he ever hit you?"

Easing out a breath, she shoved an unsteady hand through her hair. She should have known the cop in

Clay would pick up on the word. "Remember the other night when Willa told you about my dog, T-Bone?"

"You said he got run over."

"That's what Sam told everyone. It was a lie. He killed T-Bone."

Clay stared at her for a long moment. "Tell me what happened."

"T-Bone was terrified of storms so whenever one blew in, he hid under my bed. Late one evening it started pouring. There was lightning, and thunder so loud it shook the whole house. I was standing at my bedroom window, watching the storm when I realized I wasn't alone. I hadn't heard footsteps, nothing. Until that minute I thought I was the only person in the house—Willa had gone to a meeting at church and Sam was in Austin at a political reception. But when I looked over my shoulder, there he was."

Kathryn kept his gaze on Clay's. The moonlight shadowing his face shifted as his expression hardened. "What did he do?"

"At first, he just stared at me with so much hatred in his eyes I broke into a sweat. That was the first time I'd been afraid of him. Really afraid. When he took a step closer, I smelled bourbon. It was as though he'd bathed in it." She fisted her hands against the memory. "I asked him why he wasn't in Austin. That's all I asked. 'Why aren't you in Austin?'"

"Go on," Clay prodded.

"He yelled that I had no right to *torment* him every day of his life like I had. Then he backhanded me. The next thing I knew I was on the floor. When Sam jerked me to my feet, I screamed. T-Bone lunged from under the bed, snarling, his teeth bared. Sam shoved me against a dresser and I fell. T-Bone went for Sam's throat, nearly knocked him down. I heard something snap. I lay on the floor, praying it was his wrist, not T-Bone's neck."

When Clay reached out as though to touch her cheek, she held her breath. While they'd danced, the slide of his fingers on her flesh and the iron strength in his arms were all that had kept her from losing control. Now, she felt cold on the inside. Hollow. She wanted him to touch her again. Wanted to press her body against his bare, muscled chest and absorb his heat.

When his fingers were only inches from her face, he let his hand drop. "God, Kat."

She turned her head, stared into the tunnel's black depths while she collected her thoughts.

"My prayer wasn't answered," she continued. "Sam dragged T-Bone's body outside, tossed him into the trunk of his car and sped off." She knew she was trembling, but couldn't help it. "I cried myself to sleep. The next morning, one of the hands found T-Bone out in the road. Everyone figured the storm had spooked him and he'd run into the path of a car. Johnny came to the house to tell me. I felt so sorry for him, standing in the front hall with his hat gripped in his hands and tears in his eyes."

"Why didn't you tell Johnny or Willa the truth?"

"The night before, Sam threatened that if I said one word about what happened to T-Bone he would fire Johnny and Willa, and I'd never see them again. They were the only real family I'd ever had. I couldn't risk losing them, so I kept quiet."

Clay's mouth thinned. "Guess that explains why you didn't come back for Sam's funeral."

"That's not why." Her voice quavered. "Willa took Sam's death hard, and I planned on coming to give her support. But just before I was scheduled to leave for the airport, Matthew started running a fever. His doctor couldn't discount the possibility he would lapse into the first stages of rejecting his kidney. I was frantic. Thank God it was a false alarm."

Clay hooked his thumbs in the front pockets of his jeans. "Shannon Burton wrote a series of articles in the *Layton Times* hammering you for missing Sam's funeral. She wouldn't have had the ammo to do that if you'd let the real reason be known for why you weren't here."

"I told Willa and Johnny. Also, my attorney. Now you. I don't want anyone else to know."

"Why?"

"Some parents won't let their children play with Matthew because they have the idiot notion the problem he has with his kidney is catching. I do what I can to protect him, but when other children won't play with him, he sees their rejection and it hurts. Using his health as the reason I didn't come to Sam's funeral would have just reminded everyone of his condition."

"And if Burton knew that, she'd put it in the book she's writing about Sam," Clay said. "Which would be an eternal reminder to people of Matthew's health."

"Yes." Kathryn gripped the phone clipped to the waistband of her shorts. "Burton said Sam recorded tapes about his life. He made sure to tell her how hurt he felt when I severed all ties with him. And turned a deaf ear to his pleas to meet Matthew. But Clay, Sam never asked to meet his great-grandson. Never."

She felt anger kindle inside her. "Even from the grave

Sam's using my son as a pawn. It wouldn't do any good for me to tell my side of the story. Not when everyone around here worships Sam's memory."

"I found out tonight that's not the case," Clay said.

Kathryn listened while he related the conversation he'd overheard between Norman and Olivia Adams, and then his own talk with her former English teacher. When Clay finished, she stared at him in disbelief. "Sam gave Norman Adams a stock tip?"

"Hard to believe?"

"Sam never had a kind word to say about Mr. Adams. Whenever I mentioned something that happened in English class, Sam would scoff and say I had a tedious wimp for a teacher."

"And years later, the senator makes a point to stop by Norman's classroom and give him a tip on what was supposed to be a hot stock," Clay said, his brow furrowed. "Kat, the day we saw each other at the café, Norman thanked you for mentioning him in your speech when you won the Emmy."

"He deserved my thanks. He taught me more about writing than anyone. And he made me believe I could be a success."

"Sam went to see Norman right after that."

Kathryn's throat tightened against an abrupt realization. "Do you think Sam did that as payback? Because I didn't mention *him* during my acceptance speech?"

"From what you've just told me about your grandfather, I'd say it's likely."

"Oh God," she said as a sick sureness settled inside her. "Sam would have considered my failure to share the spotlight with him as the equivalent of a slap in the face." Kathryn raked her fingertips across her forehead. "Those poor people. How much money did they lose on the stock?"

"Norman didn't say. But it wiped out his retirement account."

"Damn you, Sam," she whispered. "I'll talk to Norman. Figure out some way to reimburse him."

"It'd be best if you hold off on that until I have time to check out Norman and his wife."

"Aren't you already doing that since they worked here during the parties Sam hosted?"

"Yes, but I need to dig deeper. It's clear Olivia Adams wears the pants in the family. And from what I heard, she's fed up and will do whatever it takes to get money from you. Like you said, after she and Norman got into financial straits, they worked here off and on. That means both know the layout of the house. At the café, Matthew mentioned this tunnel. That could have given Norman ideas."

Kathryn's heart skipped a beat. "You think Norman and Olivia kidnapped Matthew?"

"All I know is they're desperate for money. I'll go see Boudry in the morning, find out what the sheriff knows about them, especially Olivia."

Kathryn flexed her hands into fists, unflexed them. "If they took Matthew, it's because of me." As she spoke, she began to tremble and her eyes filled with a fresh swell of tears that she was helpless to hold back. "I put my son in danger."

"No, it's not your fault, Kat. If Norman and Olivia took Matthew, Sam's the one who started those dominoes falling with the bogus stock tip."

"All I can think about is Matthew alone, somewhere in the dark." Her shoulders began to shake as tears flowed down her cheeks. "He must be so afraid. He could be hurt. Dying."

Although she wasn't aware he'd moved, Kathryn felt Clay touch her hair, smooth it back from her face. One of his hands came up to cup her cheek. His breath was whisper-soft against her flesh when he spoke. "You can't let yourself think that way, Kat. It doesn't do you or Matthew any good."

She stared up at Clay, his face unfocused through her tears. "Do you honestly believe that the kidnapper will call? That we'll get Matthew back? Alive?"

He pressed his lips against her temple. "I won't let myself believe anything else."

The words were simply said and touched her heart. What would she have done if Clay hadn't been there for her after the kidnapping? What if she didn't have his strength to rely on? She closed her eyes while his mouth moved with incredible warmth down her cheek to her throat and his arms slid around her waist.

He'd held her already tonight. Then, though, they'd been on a crowded dance floor and he'd had on a dress shirt and suit coat. Now, they stood in the moonlit tunnel where they'd once made passionate love, her thin tank top the only barrier between their upper bodies.

He was all heated flesh, hard muscle and seductive strength.

She was so tired, physically drained, emotionally exhausted that she needed to draw on his strength. Still, she knew it was vital she somehow pull herself together, find her own reserves of emotional energy to get her through this ordeal.

But when his mouth settled on hers, all thought of distancing herself faded. One of his hands threaded through her hair, the other pressed the small of her back, bringing her closer against his rock-hard arousal. And when his tongue touched her lips, she opened for him.

His familiar taste, his scent had memories that had been dammed up for a decade raging through her like a spring flood. The mindless pleasure she'd always felt with him was back, and she wanted to surrender to it.

As if she were drowning, she clutched at his shoulders, felt his muscles bunch beneath her palms. If circumstances hadn't thrown them together again, would she be standing here with this man? No, was the answer that echoed in her ears and in the heart that still bore scars from that long-ago summer. Not with Clay, not ever again.

Too much. It was all too much. It had been fifteen hours since the phone left by the kidnappers rang. The seconds ticked a deep, painful pounding in the well of her chest. She should be thinking only of Matthew. But here she was, kissing the man she had spent years mourning for, mourning for their child, until she thought she would die from it.

If she didn't get Matthew back, it would be the equivalent of dying.

She tugged her mouth from Clay's, stepped out of his arms. Her lungs were heaving, her blood pumping hot. "I can't deal with this," she said, her voice hoarse and raw. "Not now. Not ever again."

His dark gaze stayed on hers as he lifted a hand to cup

her chin. "The timing couldn't be worse," he said, his thumb tracing her bottom lip. "But I think we both have to agree that what was between us before is still there."

She closed her eyes. The way he'd softened his voice reminded her of how it felt to lie in his arms, he inside her. She also remembered what they'd had before hadn't equaled out. He'd felt lust; she'd been in love.

"So," he continued as his thumb stroked her lips, "after Matthew's home safe and sound, you and I need to deal with it." He nudged her chin up. "Look at me."

When she did, his eyes seemed as shadowed as the night that surrounded them. "Kat, there are things I need to say to you. I want to explain how I felt back then. And what's happened since."

She wanted to tell him she wasn't the same person she was all those years ago. Tell him they'd never be able to pretend the years away. That no matter how attracted they were to each other, she would never forget the stunned hurt she felt when he went back to Houston and left her behind. And that now she could never trust him enough to allow the chemistry that lingered between them to go any further. But her heart was aching and she suddenly found herself unable to voice the words.

"Ready to go upstairs?" he asked.

Nodding, she kept one hand clenched on the phone while he retrieved the flashlight, flicked it on. Then he closed and locked the tunnel's outer door.

The flashlight's long finger of light permeated the darkness around them as she and Clay made their silent way back to the basement.

CHAPTER ELEVEN

EYES NARROWED behind mirrored sunglasses, Deputy Vernon Lang rapped his knuckles against the front door of Sheriff Jim Guy Boudry's house. It was Saturday morning—the prime time to set up radar surveillance on the county's main road to snare speeders hotfooting it toward Dallas. Instead of sitting in his county cruiser upping his activity report, Vernon had just begun a week of unpaid disciplinary leave.

Granted, he'd forgotten about traffic court yesterday. His absence had resulted in tight-ass Judge Preftakes dismissing all tickets Vernon had issued over the past week. *That* meant the county lost revenue from the fines Preftakes would have assessed. And the judge made sure Sheriff Boudry heard about it.

"Lang, the general fund took a hit because of your irresponsibility," Boudry said yesterday afternoon when he ordered Vernon to his office.

The sheriff slid a memo across his desk that stated Vernon's forgetfulness had earned him one week of unpaid leave. Before dismissing him, Boudry leaned back in his swivel chair, a knowing look on his leathery face. "Son, I sure hope whatever woman you were with when you should have been in court was worth it."

Gritting his teeth, Vernon rapped again on Boudry's door. Felicia Smith Jordan was worth *anything*. *Everything*. But his getting slapped with a week without pay wasn't going to impress her, even if their latest rendezvous at her daddy's lake house was the reason he'd been a no-show in court. And his screwing up damn sure wouldn't convince her he was a better man than her shiftless husband, Brad.

He had plans. They included making Felicia his, and amassing enough political pull to get elected to Boudry's job. That wasn't going to happen with a disciplinary memo in his file.

So, here Vernon was, ready to plead his case. Apologize in hopes Boudry would rethink his punishment. In Vernon's mind, spending the next week manning a desk or even doing a graveyard stint in dispatch would be better than time off.

He rapped again, his scowl deepening when the door remained closed. The sheriff's cruiser was parked in the driveway. Everyone in Layton knew that Boudry considered himself always on-call so anytime he went anywhere, he drove the cruiser. Which meant he was home. Why the hell didn't he answer the door?

Vernon descended the porch steps into morning sunlight intense enough to melt the skin off his bones. When he'd first hired onto the department, one of the other deputies had mentioned that the sheriff spent a lot of his time in the workshop behind his house. Wouldn't hurt to check there.

Vernon spotted the tree-shaded metal storage shed the instant he stepped into the backyard. Since the door to the small building was propped open, he started across the lawn, the lush, green grass muffling his footsteps.

When he neared the workshop, Boudry's three-packs-a-day voice drifted out on the hot air. "Sounds like Sam Conner did one hell of a job on Norman Adams and his wife."

"A huge job," a deep voice replied. "Olivia is determined to force Kathryn into paying what Norman lost when he took the bait on the senator's lousy stock tip."

"And you're thinking a way to apply that force would be to kidnap Kathryn's son," Boudry commented.

"Yes, but that doesn't prove they're the ones who snatched Matthew. I'm here to check to see if you know of any place they might have available where they could keep a small boy."

"Not offhand. They live out past Layton's city limits near one of my wife's cousins. I'll drive out that way. Drop in and say hello to Norman and Olivia and have a look at whatever structures they have on their property."

"Appreciate it, Sheriff."

Crouching at one side of the workshop's open door, Vernon shoved his sunglasses higher up the bridge of his nose. He didn't recognize the voice of the man Boudry was talking to, and there was no other vehicle parked nearby that might give him a clue. But Felicia had told him all about Kathryn Conner Mason and Vernon knew she and the movie star she'd divorced had a son named Matthew. So, the boy had been kidnapped, and the sheriff knew about it. Why, then, wasn't everyone on the department working double-overtime to search for the boy?

The men's voices lowered, and all Vernon could hear was muffled conversation. He leaned in closer.

"…ransom's ready," the unidentified speaker said. "I hope to God they call Kathryn today and tell her where to deliver the money. She can't take much more of this."

"Understandable. It sounds like you've got things under control, Clay. I'll let you know what I find out when I drop in on Norman and Olivia."

Clay, Vernon thought as he crept back toward the house. Last night at the fund-raiser, he'd spotted Kathryn Conner Mason on the dance floor with Clay Turner. If body language was any indication, the ex-cop considered her more than just a casual acquaintance.

So, her kid had gotten snatched. And for whatever reason, the kidnapping was being kept off law enforcement's radar.

But not his.

Vernon's mind went to work, analyzing, assessing. If he saved the son of that rich heartthrob actor from some kidnapper's clutches, he'd not only be on the front page of the *Layton Times,* he'd make the cover of every magazine in the country. *In the world.* Felicia would damn well be impressed.

Not to mention every voter in Layton County.

Vernon slid back into his car, started the engine and coasted out of Boudry's driveway. Having the following week off now seemed like a godsend. It saved him from having to make up an excuse for why he needed to take personal leave.

All he had to do now was find a prime spot near Cross C land and wait. When Kathryn Conner Mason left to make the ransom drop, he'd keep her company.

THREE DAYS, Kathryn thought. Her son had been gone three days. The feeling that the kidnapping couldn't have happened, that she was trapped in a nightmare and would soon wake up and find Matthew safe beside her had worn off long ago. Now that reality had set in, it was a constant mental battle not to let herself believe that her agonizing fears would soon be confirmed and replaced with equally torturous grief.

She'd already lost one child. Clay's child. Even though she had loved the baby growing inside her, it had been a part of her for only a short time. She had loved, nurtured and cherished Matthew for years. She couldn't even imagine what sort of dark hell her life would become if she lost him.

And, because the waiting was driving her crazy, she forced herself to keep busy. That's why she'd spent the morning sitting in the study, at Sam's big mahogany desk going through folders she pulled out of the desk's drawers.

Most of the files contained invoices, letters and documents pertaining to the Cross C's operations. Over time, she would study that information, learn what it took to run the ranch. The last file she plucked from the drawer brimmed with letters from constituents that had been mailed to the Cross C instead of the senator's office in Austin. Kathryn set the file aside. Clay had asked her to save all of Sam's personal correspondence so he could go through it.

With the drawer empty, she leaned back in the leather swivel chair and stared at the dark eye of her computer's monitor. When she moved her office equipment in days ago, she'd envisioned herself working at the desk, dividing her time between running the Cross C and writing her latest screenplay. Matthew's kidnapping had changed everything. She had neither the emotional fortitude nor the desire to do either.

She wanted her son back. Alive and well. *Please God*.

The sudden shattering of glass had Kathryn bolting out of the chair as if she'd been shot out of a canon. She raced into the hallway where she found Pilar, kneeling beside the drop-leaf table, a puddle of water and a dozen yellow roses spread around her. With trembling hands, the maid gathered up the remnants of what had been Kathryn's grandmother's crystal vase, placing them in the lap of the white apron that covered her long, black dress.

"Pilar, are you okay?"

The maid turned her head, tears glistening in her dark eyes. "I am so sorry." Her voice trembled with the same force as her hands as she continued collecting the glass shards.

Kathryn gave an anxious glance up and down the hallway to make sure Abby wasn't near and in danger of cutting her paws. The dachshund wasn't in sight.

"Señorita Conner, forgive me. It was an accident. I'm so clumsy." Pilar's words ended on a sob.

Crouching, Kathryn laid a hand on the woman's scarecrow-thin arm. "Pilar, I know you didn't break the vase on purpose."

"You must take the money to replace it out of my wages." Her shoulders heaved. "I have to clean up this mess."

"Don't worry about the vase." Kathryn slid a palm down the woman's long, black braid. "What has you so upset?"

"I have a sick friend. Very sick."

"I'm sure Willa will adjust your schedule so you can take off to tend your friend."

"No. I must stay here and work. I'm supposed to be here."

She shot up so suddenly Kathryn had to brace a palm on the floor to keep her balance. "I will get a rag to clean up this mess." Scrubbing tears off her face, Pilar scurried away.

Kathryn looked back at the water, the roses and the remaining glass shards. Any other time she would accept Pilar's explanation of being upset over her sick friend. But times were far from normal. And Pilar had unsupervised access to the house, the wine cabinet, the tunnel. She'd known Willa would be gone the night Matthew was kidnapped. And the morning after, Pilar had been off, to take Antonio to the dentist.

An appointment which Clay had confirmed she'd made months ago.

Kathryn rose, making a mental note to tell Clay about Pilar's overwrought behavior.

She heard the squeal of an incoming fax as she stepped back into the study. The machine had been busy all morning, spitting out background and financial information compiled by the P.I. Clay knew. Clay had called after his meeting with Sheriff Boudry to check in and say he needed to stop by the Double Starr to touch base with his uncle about their ranch's operation.

Kathryn was halfway to the credenza where the fax machine sat when something in the bottom of the desk's empty file drawer caught her eye. At first glance, it looked like a torn corner off a piece of paper. But when she leaned to retrieve it, the drawer's entire wooden bottom came up with it.

A false bottom, she realized as she clutched the edge of the envelope that had been hidden under the extra piece of wood. Reaching back inside the drawer, she retrieved a small black jeweler's box that had been secreted with the envelope.

She settled onto the leather chair and opened the velvet-covered box. The cluster of diamonds blazing across a gold band took her breath away.

Forehead furrowed, she opened the envelope. Inside was a single piece of stationery with the Cross C brand embossed at its top.

Lauren—
Years ago when I buried my dear wife, I thought the possibility of my loving again had died along with her. You've shown me I was wrong. I love you, Lauren. You've brought gentleness and laughter back into the life of a man who believed he had no time for either emotion. Even if I lose this election, it will have been worth it, because it brought us together.
I want to share my life with you. I want you to be my wife. Say yes.
Sam

Her stomach clenched in disbelief, Kathryn stared numbly at the letter. There was no mistaking Sam's distinctive script. Yet, how could such endearing, love-filled words come from the man who had shown her nothing but loathing all her life? Loving words and promises for the future—a future with her mother. Kathryn stared at the ring, ablaze with diamonds. *Her mother*.

Her grandfather had been in love with her mother!

Kathryn considered heading for the kitchen to talk to Willa, but dismissed the idea. Sam hadn't hired Willa and her husband until after Kathryn's parents died. Willa had helped clean out their apartment and put the family photographs in an album for Kathryn. Those snapshots were the source of the housekeeper's remarks about Kathryn's strong resemblance to her mother.

Kathryn knew only one person who had worked at the Cross C during the time frame Sam must have written the letter. She rose, made sure both her own and the kidnapper's phones were clipped to the waistband of her jeans, then headed outside.

The July air was a soup of heat and humidity. Wishing she'd grabbed her sunglasses, she reached back to tug the band ponytailing her hair a little higher while she walked the length of the curved driveway, then cut around the paddock where several horses grazed. The closer she got to the stables, the air grew heavier with the scent of horseflesh and fresh hay.

Moments later, she passed beneath the stable's high double doors and walked the long, shaded corridor lined with stalls. All were empty, with fresh hay layering the floor. This time of day the horses were out in either the paddock or one of the pastures.

One end of the expansive structure was sectioned off to form living quarters for the unmarried hands. In close proximity were the tack room and small office Johnny Sullivan used.

She found the foreman working at his ancient

wooden desk eternally awash with paper. The stained Stetson Johnny had worn for years sat on top of one of the piles.

When he looked up and saw her, the weathered lines in his face crinkled into a tobacco-stained smile. Just as fast, the smile disappeared. "Do you have news about our boy?"

"No." Shutting the door, Kathryn sat on the metal chair beside the desk. "I keep praying that any minute the kidnapper will call and tell me how to get Matthew back." She closed her eyes against a shudder. "Whoever has him *has* to call."

"They will." Leaning in, Johnny patted her knee with a callused hand. He smelled faintly of horseflesh and sweat. "And when our boy comes home he'll be as right as rain."

Nodding, Kathryn pulled in a deep breath. "Johnny, I need to ask you some questions. About the relationship Sam had with my mother."

Something flickered in the old man's eyes. "I don't expect I know much about that."

"But you can tell me something, right?"

"I mind my own business. Never have been one to gossip."

"You're the only person I know who worked here before my mother and father died. Just now I was cleaning out a drawer in Sam's desk and found a ring and a letter he wrote to my mother, a love letter." She shook her head. "I had no idea they'd been involved. I'm just trying to find out what happened between them. Please, Johnny, tell me what you know."

Regarding her, he tapped arthritic knuckles against the arms of his chair. "Well, I expect that since all parties involved have passed on, my talkin' about 'em don't matter much."

"Not to them."

"Sam hired your momma right out of college to work on one of his early campaigns. After time, he started bringin' her here whenever he came home from Austin. One day they wanted to go out ridin' so I was saddlin' their horses when your daddy drove up. Travis said he'd managed to take the weekend off from medical school and was home for a visit. Sam was real happy to see his boy. He was always braggin' about how Travis was the first Conner to get through college. That meant a lot to Sam."

"Did my mother and father already know each other?"

"No, Sam introduced 'em that day. An old bachelor like me don't know much about romance, but I remember thinkin' there was some sort of spark between Travis and Lauren. I figured if I seen it, Sam did, too. But it was real close to the end of his campaign, so I guess he had all that on his mind."

"In the photo album I have, there are pictures of my parents on their wedding day. They eloped."

"On election day. I don't expect your grandpa took much joy in winnin' when on the inside he must have been hurtin' like nobody's business."

"And bitter, I imagine."

"Probably, though he never spoke of it to me." Johnny frowned. "'Bout a year later I was up at the house, goin' over the ranch's books with Sam when your daddy walked into the study. Your momma was right behind him, holding you in her arms. Said they wanted to introduce Sam to his new granddaughter."

"What happened then?"

"I went to the kitchen and poured myself a cup of coffee, thinkin' Sam and I would finish up our business after he got done with your parents. I should have got myself out of the house right then 'cuz it didn't take no time for the yelling to start. Thought the roof was gonna' come off."

"Could you hear what was being said?"

"No. And right when I was gettin' ready to skedaddle out the back door, your momma brought you into the kitchen. She was crying and you was screaming your head off—guess all the noise scared you. She handed you to me and sat at the table, sobbing her eyes out. Finally Travis came in. His face was red, he was shaking. He didn't say a word, just bundled both of you up and left. That was the last time…"

Johnny shook his head. "Two miles down the road, a drunk driver hit their car head-on. The sheriff came to tell Sam his son and daughter-in-law were dead. They took you to the hospital, but you'd been strapped in one of those baby seats, and just got scratched up. Sam went to the hospital to get you. I expect that was one of the hardest things he had to do, what with reporters all over the place. There was pictures in the paper the next morning of the wrecked cars, and one of Sam carrying you out of the hospital, tears in his eyes."

Kathryn set her jaw. No one had been more media savvy than Sam—he would have known how to leave the hospital without the media seeing him. Instead he'd carried her out into a mass of reporters, the seemingly grieving senator taking in his orphaned granddaughter. From day one he'd used her as a public relations tool.

"That was a real sad time, but havin' you livin' here

was a comfort." Again, Johnny patted Kathryn's knee. "The older you got, the more you came to look like your pretty momma. Now you're her spittin' image."

"So I've been told," Kathryn said and looked away, emotion wedged in her chest. All the hatred Sam had felt for her was finally explained. And understood. He had taken her to raise to score political points. By his own actions, he'd sentenced himself to perform a lifelong public pretense of loving a granddaughter whose very existence must have sickened him.

And the older she got, the more she grew into the image of the woman who had betrayed him with his own son.

"I hope I haven't upset you by tellin' you all that," Johnny said. "Lord knows you've got enough on your mind right now."

"You helped me understand some things that no one else could. Things I needed to know." Reaching out, she gripped the foreman's rough-as-a-cob hand. "Thank you, Johnny."

"You don't have to thank me for just talkin' to you."

"Not just for that." She kissed his stubby cheek. "For loving me, too."

CLAY STOOD in what had been Sam Conner's study, scanning the pages the fax machine had spit out while he'd been at the Double Starr, helping his uncle deal with business that couldn't wait.

The P.I. had now checked the financials of everyone on the list Clay had sent him. Credit cards, debit cards and checking accounts had been run. With a few exceptions, most people seemed to be living within their means.

And no one had past arrests that might foreshadow a leaning toward criminal behavior.

Damn, he had hoped the checks would unearth the scent of a trail that might lead to Matthew. Instead Clay had run into a dead-end.

Time was running out for Kathryn's son. Clay felt that as sure as he felt his own heart pound in his chest.

He laid the fax pages on the only corner of the big desk that wasn't stacked with file folders. The desk's deep file drawer was open and empty. As he stared down at the drawer, he frowned at the extra piece of wood angled inside it.

The sound of the front door opening registered in his brain seconds before the door slammed like a bullet. By the time Clay made it into the hallway, Kathryn had already pounded halfway up the staircase. She was dressed in snug jeans, a red T-shirt and black boots with her dark hair pulled back in a ponytail. He saw the emotion in her brisk movements, but her stiff shoulders and clenched fists didn't translate into despair or sorrow. Anger was more like it. Hot, furious anger.

What the hell had happened? he wondered. And while he watched her, every single thought of her shot straight to his glands. Ten years ago, it had been rare for the young head-strong woman he'd taken as a lover to let her temper loose, but it had been wicked when she did. And oh so intriguing for a man whose blood ran hot for her.

Both then and now.

He started up the stairs after her while a possessive hunger tightened his gut. For the hundredth time, he damned himself for not making her his all those years ago.

By the time he reached the top of the stairs, she was

out of sight. He strode down the hallway toward her bedroom and stepped through the open door.

The room's textured stucco walls, pine-washed furniture and loomed Indian rugs in rich shades of teal and maroon registered in his brain the instant before she heaved a book over her shoulder.

Because his reflexes were good, he dodged it by inches. "What the hell?"

Her head whipped around at the sound of his voice. "I'm sorry. I didn't know you were there." She took a step toward him, her voice tight. "Have you heard back from Sheriff Boudry? Did he find out anything that might lead to Matthew when he drove out to where Norman and Olivia Adams live?"

"Boudry called a few minutes ago. He didn't see anything suspicious." And because Clay had given his word not to keep anything from her, he added, "There's nothing to go on in the background and financial checks the P.I. sent."

She threw up her hands. "So, all we can do is wait for whoever has Matthew to call. Just stand around and wait."

He heard more than just desperate worry in her voice. The anger that had propelled her up the staircase was there, too. And glinting in her eyes was ripe and ready temper. *What was going on?*

"We wait," he agreed, then glanced down. It hadn't been a book, but a photo album she lobbed across her shoulder. It had landed open, and he did a double-take at the snapshot of a smiling, dark-haired woman wearing a white suit and holding a bouquet while she stood on the steps of some courthouse. It took him an instant to realize the woman wasn't Kathryn. *Her mother.*

"Are you tossing around stuff just for the hell of it?" he asked while scooping the album off the floor. "Or is there a particular reason you sent this airborne?"

"Oh, I've got a reason."

Kathryn knew her words had spewed like water through a sluice gate, but she couldn't help it. She remained in front of the bookcase she'd ripped the album out of, her breath shuddering as she tried—and failed—to calm it. Her temper was horrible when unlocked. And right now the lid was off.

"A damn good reason." She jerked off the band holding back her hair and flung it at the bed. "I found a letter hidden in Sam's desk that he wrote to my mother. A love letter."

Clay's brows snapped up. "They were involved?"

"Sam wanted to marry her. Then my mother left him for his son. My father. The woman Sam loved didn't want him, so in turn he made her child's life miserable. *My life*."

Clay lifted a hand, let it drop. "He had no right to treat you that way."

"Damn straight." Her jaw ached from having her teeth clamped together so tight. "When I was little, every night in my prayers I asked God to make my grandfather love me. I just wanted him to love me." The memory sent hurt rippling through her and she turned toward the wall where a mirror in an antique frame hung. Her reflection stared back at her, her face flushed, her eyes glinting with emotion. "All those years I thought there was something wrong with me. That it was *my* fault Sam hated me. But it wasn't." She swept a trembling hand toward the mirror before turning back toward Clay. "I just happened to look like the woman who'd broken his cold, black heart."

Through a haze of anger, she watched Clay step to the bed and lay the album on the end of the mattress.

"Kat, I wish I could change things for you." His expression was somber, the scar on his right cheek and temple a pale thread in his tanned flesh. "If I could, I'd go back in time and plow my fist into the bastard's face."

"If *I* could, I'd go back and do that myself," she snapped. "It's clear now what Sam meant the night he came home drunk and killed T-Bone. That I had no right to *torment* him every day of his life like I had." Her voice was low and vibrating with fury. "All he had to do was look at me and it brought all his suffering back. *Poor Sam.*"

Kathryn whipped around toward the nearest window that provided a view of the ranch, the endless land and sky. All the hurt from her past bubbled inside her like lava, heating her blood, her anger.

"I had no clue I was pregnant when you left to go back to work in Houston." Behind her, she heard Clay move closer, then out of the corner of her eye saw him shift into view. He had his eyes locked on her face, watching her with intensity.

"I'd been tired and sick for weeks and I thought I'd caught some bug so I went to see Doc Hennessy. He was Sam's buddy, and after I left his office, he called Sam. My grandfather knew I was pregnant almost before I did."

Pivoting, she met Clay's grim gaze. She'd spent years holding everything in, damming up the memories that even a decade later ripped at her heart. The dam was now broken.

"I had just hung up from telling you I was pregnant when Sam stalked into my bedroom. He was seething, his face beet-red. He said I was mistaken if I thought he'd get trapped into raising another unwanted brat."

As if by reflex, she pressed her palm against her abdomen. "I told him after the way he'd treated me I didn't want my baby near him. That you were driving up from Houston, and we'd make our own arrangements for our child. Sam sneered. He said by the time you got here there wouldn't be any baby because Doc Hennessy was waiting for us at his office."

Clay took a quick step closer, his eyes narrowed. "Sam was going to force you to have an abortion?"

Kathryn nodded, tears in her eyes. "Yes. I told him I was eighteen and he couldn't force me to do anything. He grabbed me, said he'd strap me to Doc's table and scrape the bastard out of me himself if that's what it took."

"Jeez, Kat."

When Clay reached out to touch her, she drew back. She didn't want to be soothed, she wanted to smash something. "Don't." She wrapped her arms around her waist. "I need to get this out. I feel like I'll explode if I don't talk this out."

A muscle bunched in Clay's jaw. "What happened next?"

"I could see in Sam's face he intended to get me to the doctor, no matter what it took. So I slammed my fist into his chest. When he staggered backward, I ran. I only had a few seconds lead and I could hear him, his footsteps hammering behind me. He was almost on top of me when I reached the stairs. A voice kept screaming in my head that if I could just make it to my car I'd be safe. I could drive away and save my baby."

"Did he push you?" Clay's eyes were as hard as his voice. "Kat, did the son of a bitch push you down the stairs?"

"No, before he got to me I lost my balance and fell." She knew if her arms got any tighter around her waist they'd stop all circulation. "I'll never forget lying at the bottom of the stairs, pain stabbing at my head, my belly. My vision doubled, tripled, but for an instant everything came into focus. That's when I saw Sam standing over me. Smiling."

Clay's mouth thinned and there was murder in his eyes. "Why didn't you tell me this when I got to the hospital? I'd have made sure Sam Conner never got near you again."

"You came there because of the baby. The baby no longer existed. You left me behind, Clay. I was hurt and humiliated and the last thing I wanted was to involve you in something that wasn't any of your concern."

"Not my concern? That was my child, too."

"Which is why I called to tell you I was pregnant," Kathryn shot back, then closed her eyes, fighting for control. "You had every right to leave me, Clay. You'd always told me your true feelings. I was just too starry-eyed to let myself believe I couldn't change them. That I'd be the one woman who'd make you want something you didn't."

"Yeah, I told you the truth," he agreed. "But I left things out. Things I should have told you. Things I need to tell—"

"It doesn't matter." She cut him off with a slice of one hand through the air while all the pent-up frustration rolled through her in one powerful surge. "I've let what happened with Sam, with you, matter for too long. I won't let it anymore."

When she started to turn away, Clay locked his hands on her upper arms, held her still. "Dammit, what happened between us does matter. It *all* matters."

"Maybe to you. But I don't want it to matter to me anymore. So it won't. Get it?"

She could smell his aftershave, pine and spice and underneath the bone-melting scent that was him: her former lover. The thought of the dark, sultry nights when she lay in his arms inhaling his scent while sweat slicked her flesh and their pulses beat as one made her feel as if she were plugged into a two-twenty line. He'd been all that mattered then.

Now, his brown eyes burned down into hers and she felt the power in his fingers when they flexed on her arms. Just the feel of his hands on her flesh called to her to step closer the way she had done so often during that long, hot summer. And, God knew she wanted to. She *needed* to.

"Yeah, I get it," he said. "You don't want to hear what I have to say. You don't want what happened between us to matter. How about telling me what you *do* you want?"

"To forget." She fisted her hands against his shoulders, but couldn't force herself to push from his hold that called forth warmth and wetness, comfort and thrill. "The pain, the hurt. The humiliation. I just want to forget. All of it."

"Including me?"

She almost blurted a knee-jerk "yes," but staring up into his grim face, she saw emotion simmering in his dark eyes. In truth, she wanted to remember how it felt when he held her, how the passion that seared between them could wipe away all reason, all thought. Remember how when they were together he made her forget the rest of the world, forget her responsibilities. Made her even forget the darkness. She wanted that again, that release from having to think. To hurt.

"There are things about you I could never forget." She smoothed her hand along his broad shoulder to the side of his throat.

"Like?"

"This." She went up on tiptoe and locked her lips against his.

Need rolled through Clay like a train at midnight. Even as he pulled his head back to break the kiss, he struggled to hold on to control. "Kat, what are you doing?"

"That should be obvious."

His fingers flexed against her upper arms. "It's obvious you're pissed off and upset and cruising on straight emotion. Until things settle down, you ought to take a step back."

"Are you telling me you don't want me?"

He dipped his head. "I want you more than I want to take my next breath. But I want whatever we do to be done for the right reasons."

"I'm tired, Clay. Of thinking. Hurting." She shook her hair back, her voice a raspy whisper. "I need this. I need you. Isn't that reason enough?"

"Dammit, I don't think—"

"Don't. Don't think." She moved closer, rolled her hips against him, settling her softness against his hardness. "Just feel."

With her body pressed against him and her scent clouding his lungs, *feel* was all he was capable of.

"Hell," he ground out, then jerked her up on her toes. Her dark eyes were the last thing he saw as he closed his own eyes and captured her mouth with his.

CHAPTER TWELVE

His mouth fused with Kathryn's, Clay locked one arm around her while he speared his free hand through her hair. Then he deepened the kiss with all the fire and all the fierceness he'd held back since fate propelled her into his life a second time.

Okay, so she didn't want to *think*—fine with him! He was as rock-hard as a teenager cruising on hormones and he intended to ravish her, take her, have his fill of her until even her own name was wiped out of her head.

And while they were at it, they would make new memories to overshadow the pain-riddled ones from their past. Memories that would matter to both of them.

He wanted to matter to her like he once had. Wanted her to love him again. He didn't care if it took him years to whittle away at her until she gave him all of herself. He'd had that once and been too brainless to know what it meant. But he'd learned how it felt to be lost. Completely lost. Everything gone. He had thought that about Kathryn but now he had a shot at reclaiming the woman he should have held on to all those years ago. Dammit, he wasn't going to let her go this time.

Greedy for more, he clenched his hand tighter in her thick, black hair and hardened his kiss.

With her focus on the unyielding mouth that ravaged hers, all Kathryn could do was hang on tight when Clay slid one arm beneath her bottom, boosted her up and headed across the bedroom. Heat saturated her as though a furnace door had been thrown open and the roaring blaze threatened to envelope her flesh.

Clay was that furnace.

Beneath the demands of his mouth her blood pounded in her veins, between her legs; her pulses throbbed like primitive music. Time seemed to turn elastic and for this one moment, there were no thoughts of pain or grief, no thoughts of anything beyond searing need.

Need that could only be sated by rough and frenzied joining.

Driven, she locked her legs around his hips and yanked until the tail of his shirt came free of his jeans. She fumbled open the buttons, shoved the shirt off his arms, then swept her palms across his flesh. She remembered the hard jut of shoulder blades, the taper from broad chest to narrow waist and iron-hard stomach. Remembered, too, the salty taste of his warm, smooth skin. Wanting that taste again, she tore her mouth from his and sank her teeth into his shoulder.

"Lord," he groaned while his hand kneaded her bottom through her jeans.

She felt the jolt when he kicked the door shut; heard the snick when he set the lock. Striding toward the bed, he yanked up the hem of her T-shirt, dragged it over her head and tossed it aside. The crazed need throbbing between her thighs had her fighting to unbuckle his belt, open the top snap.

He'd barely tumbled her backward onto the mattress

when he tugged her cell phone, then the one the kidnapper had left off her waistband.

She grabbed for his arm. "Clay, no!" she panted. "The phone—"

"It'll be here on the nightstand." His voice had gone low and husky. "If it rings, we'll hear it."

Seconds later, he had her boots off and her jeans peeled down her long, endless legs. He lowered onto the edge of the mattress, thrust his hand inside her panties and curled his fingers up into her wet depths while his palm rode her.

"I want you," he whispered a hot inch from her ear while he dragged down one strap of her bra. "For the rest of my life, I want you." Then his mouth was on her hard nipple, nipping, suckling. A fresh wave of heat stormed through her system and her body began vibrating like a string already plucked.

His fingers moved inside her, against her, his mouth fed at her breast. Every nerve in her body sizzled with desire; she panted against the rough, raw need clawing inside her as urgently as her nails clawed at his shoulders.

He drove her with his hand, his mouth. Her breathing grew labored, punctuated by half gasps and low moans. Sensation slid over sensation; she arched under his touch and shuddered. And nearly wept as spasms of pleasure whipped through her.

When he pulled away, she reached for him. Needing him, wanting him. "Clay."

"I'm not going anywhere."

His eyes never left her as he tore off his boots, his remaining clothing. Then he was back, wedging himself between her thighs, his muscles hot and tight, his entire body taut with anticipation. He stripped off her bra, her panties and caught the lemony scent of her perfume, mingling with the hot scents of their own bodies.

Tearing open the condom he'd dug from his billfold he sheathed himself while blood roared in his head, in his heart, in his loins. His breathing grew harsh as his fingers caressed her breasts, stroking the swollen nipples back into erection. Then his hands slid down her flat belly to her loins where she was wet and tender and tight. He could count every beat of her pulse.

She arched when he entered her with possessive force, and moaned his name. Only his.

Right. The word echoed in Clay's ears as his hands sought hers, their fingers locking into fists. For the first time in ten years, everything inside him clicked into focus. His world felt right. *She* made it right.

"Look at me, Kat. Look at me."

Her eyelids fluttered open. Their gazes locked, he moved inside her while her hips pumped beneath him, urging him on. Every shudder of her body drove him closer to his own jagged threshold.

He watched her blue eyes turn smoky while the need for release ripped at his gut. Gritting his teeth, he strained to hold on to control until he felt her muscles clench around him.

Panting hard, he buried his face in her hair and ground into her. Her nails dug into his back. She tightened around him and dragged him over the brink.

HOURS LATER, screams woke him.

Dazed, Clay gulped in deep breaths of the cool dark air while he fought his way out of the nightmare. His flesh slicked with sweat, he lay unmoving until the worst of the grinding nausea faded and the tremors passed.

Beside him, Kathryn shifted in sleep.

He held his breath until she stilled. After their first frenzied mating, their lovemaking had transformed into slow, heated caresses which had continued off and on for hours until they both surrendered to sleep. Clay figured this was the first real rest she'd had since the kidnapping, and he didn't want to risk waking her.

When his system leveled he rose, pulled on his jeans and moved toward the closest window, the loomed rug soft beneath his bare feet. The hazy light of dawn hung just above the horizon, a graying so fragile it scarcely penetrated the glass.

He scrubbed a hand over his stubbled jaw, his fingers skimming the scar on his right cheek. He had gotten past the death wish that had haunted him those first few days after he woke in the hospital and learned his parents had been kidnapped by the rebels who'd shot him. But always after, when he suffered through the nightmare of hearing his mother's terrified screams and his father's panicked shouts, Clay cursed the doctors who had saved him.

But save him they had and he accepted now that it was his fate to deal with the nightmare for the rest of his life. And for the rest of his life, he wanted the woman sleeping soundly a few feet away.

That wasn't going to happen if she didn't trust him. Trust him not to leave her again.

Why the hell had he ever left her? And how was he going to make her believe he never would again?

"Clay?"

He turned. Enough hazy light came through the

window for him to see that she was on her side, propped up on one elbow, the white sheet a ghostly drape across her curves.

"I didn't mean to wake you," he said.

"You didn't." Wedging the sheet under her arms, she scooted up, propping her back against the bank of pillows. Then she reached for one of the two cell phones on the nightstand. She flipped open its lid, checked the display, then closed her eyes. "It was a dream," she said, her voice a half whisper.

"What was?"

"I thought Matthew was back. That the bastard who has him called and gave him back to me." She dragged in a breath, closed the phone's lid and replaced it on the nightstand. "It was just a dream."

Clay moved to the bed, settled on the mattress. "We'll get him back, Kat." Her hair was a gorgeous mess, and he tucked an errant wave behind her right ear. "You can't give up hope."

"Every day Matthew's gone makes it seem more impossible I'll ever see him again." She gnawed her bottom lip. "This is the fourth day he's been gone. *Four days*."

"We can hope it'll be the last day," Clay said quietly. "That we'll have him back by tonight."

"God, I hope so." Her gaze returned to the cell phone. "How long…?"

"How long, what?"

"How long did the rebels hold your parents before…?"

"The Colombian military moved in and they died in the crossfire," he finished for her. "Three months."

Her eyes whipped back to him. "I had no idea it had been that long." She squeezed his arm, then just as quickly moved her hand away. "That must have been horrible for you."

Skittish, he thought. They'd touched each other in every way imaginable last night, but now she wouldn't maintain contact. And she made sure the sheet stayed wedged beneath her arms.

"It was hell." He reached for her hand, threaded his fingers through hers. "What made things worse was knowing my parents might not have even been in harm's way if I'd done things differently where you're concerned."

"Where *I'm* concerned?" A crease formed between her dark eyebrows. "I don't understand."

"There's a lot you don't understand. I've been trying to tell you, but so far you haven't let me. Kat, I need to tell you about how I felt back then."

He watched her close in, shut off. "I know how you felt."

"Not hardly." When she tried to slip her hand from his, he tightened his hold. He wasn't going to let her get away again.

"Yesterday, after you found out the truth about Sam, you had to get it out," he said levelly. "You said you had to talk about it or you'd explode. That's how I feel. I need you to hear me out."

Kathryn shifted against the bank of pillows. He wanted to talk, she thought. Okay, she'd listen, but that didn't mean she intended to lower the wall she'd built around her heart where he was concerned. Just because they'd spent the past night setting the sheets on fire didn't mean anything had changed. They'd set a lot of fires ten years ago and he'd still walked away.

"I'm listening."

"Before I took you to bed the first time, I told you I didn't want strings. No commitment. I meant that. I was used to moving from one woman to the next without repercussions, and that's the way I liked things." He raised a shoulder. "Every time my mother said she and Dad would retire from the State Department and move back home as soon as I got married and gave them a grandchild, I sidestepped it. Told her they were way too young to be grandparents.

"That's the way things were until the end of the summer you and I spent together. By the time I had to leave and report back to work, I was in love with you."

Kathryn stared at him, too stunned to think. But in a finger snap of time she forced her mind to begin working again. "If that were true, why didn't you tell me? Why didn't you take me to Houston with you like I asked you to?"

"I didn't tell you because what I felt scared me."

She tossed her head. "Men like you don't know what scared is."

"Men like me?" The bitterness, lodged deep for years, swirled into his throat. "Let me tell you about the man I was. I had a comfortable life, a job I loved and I didn't answer to anyone but myself. I didn't want anything or anyone screwing that up, including a woman. Including *you*. So I told myself to take things slow. To go back to Houston and put some space between us. Wait and see if I didn't come to my senses."

He grazed his thumb over the pulse point in her wrist. "I finally did, about the same time you called to tell me you were pregnant. By then I'd gotten it through my thick head that I was in love with you and no amount of time was going to change that. I'd made up my mind to tell you."

"But you didn't," she got out in a thick whisper. "You didn't say anything when I called."

"Because I wanted to tell you in person. Ask you to marry me in person. I figured we had all the time in the world and a couple more hours wouldn't make a difference." He tightened his grip on her hand. "I couldn't have been more wrong. By the time I got here, you'd lost the baby. And when you looked at me from that hospital bed there wasn't any love in your eyes anymore. All I saw was hurt and derision. You didn't want me around, and I didn't blame you."

Kathryn could still feel the hurt that had rippled through her as she lay battered and bruised in the hospital. At that point, she'd had nothing left but her pride and she wasn't going to let him see how much his leaving had hurt her.

Clay eased out a breath. "I went back to Houston and tried to put you out of my mind. I got pretty good at that, especially after I read about you marrying Devin Mason. Later, the State Department transferred me to Colombia, which worked out great since Dad was the number two man at the U.S. Embassy in Bogota and Mom worked as the ambassador's executive assistant. The day of the kidnap, I was driving them to a diplomatic reception when rebels ambushed our car."

Clay swiped a stiff finger along the scar that ran from his cheek to his temple. "I didn't sense the danger closing in, and I should have. Should have *known* something was wrong."

His words might have been calm, but Kathryn heard

the undertone of self-derision in his voice. "How could you have possibly known?"

"Instinct. A cop's sixth sense. Something akin to the early-warning system that had saved my butt a couple of times over the years. That morning it failed me, and the rebels caught me off guard. Shot me. The last memory I have of my parents is hearing my mother scream and my father shout a warning. Three months later, they were dead."

"I'm sorry." Her voice caught on the words. "Clay, I'm so sorry."

"Me, too." He shoved a hand through his hair. "That was two years ago, and not a day has gone by that I haven't wondered what would have happened if I'd faced my feelings for you sooner. If I had, I would have taken you to Houston. You wouldn't have fallen and lost the baby. My parents would have moved home to be near their grandchild. They wouldn't have been kidnapped. Murdered."

Kathryn heard more than regret in his voice. There was also guilt. She didn't want to risk getting closer to him emotionally, but she had to try to help him the way he'd helped her since Matthew's abduction.

"After Matthew was taken," she began, "and I told you he would still be safe with me if only I'd had an alarm installed or hired a security service, you said the more I hammered myself with 'what ifs,' the more the guilt would eat at me, until it consumed me. The same thing applies to your situation, Clay. You can't dwell on the 'what if's.'"

"Easier said than done." His thumb stroked her knuckles. "One thing I learned was that you were the one woman for me. The only woman. Over the years, anyone else I got halfway close to was only a substitute. You were a ghost who haunted me every waking minute, who faded away every time I tried to reach out and touch. I never thought I'd see you again, sure never believed you'd come back to Layton to stay. But you are back, and I don't want to lose you again. I love you, Kat."

She felt tears welling up in her eyes. How many nights had she lain alone, unable to stop herself from loving him, from fantasizing about him, wishing he would say the very words he'd just said? Words that now scared the hell out of her.

Okay, so maybe he had loved her before, but not enough to stick around or to take her with him when he left. She had no guarantee he wouldn't take off again someday. And it wasn't just her own heart she had to think about this time, it was Matthew's, too. If—when— she got him back, she couldn't chance letting Clay become so important to Matthew that a hole would be left if he walked away.

The prospect of having her son hurt was too big a risk to take. As was letting herself love Clay again.

"I can't—"

He pressed a fingertip to her lips. "You can't think about this right now, I understand." He clenched his jaw for an instant, then visibly relaxed it. "I wanted to tell you everything because I learned the hard way there can be repercussions when you don't grab opportunities when they present themselves. That's what I'm doing, Kat. I want you. I want Matthew." He smoothed a palm down her hair. "I want to *matter* to you like I did before. The only reason I'd ever leave you again is if you told me to."

She opened her mouth, unsure of what to say.

Then the kidnapper's cell phone rang.

Kathryn's stomach lurched. Her mouth went dry. With fear for her child clawing inside her, she reached for the phone.

CHAPTER THIRTEEN

BEFORE KATHRYN could answer the phone, Clay laid his hand over hers. His touch was firm, steady. "This is a negotiation, Kat. He's going to try to scare you. Intimidate you. You have to stay strong for Matthew. Demand proof of life."

She nodded. Her heart was pounding so hard she could feel her pulse throbbing under her skin. She turned her hand beneath Clay's, linked her fingers with his and held on tight.

She flicked on the phone. "Hello?"

"You got the money?"

"Yes."

"All of it?"

The voice sounded more robotic than human. Kathryn couldn't even tell if it belonged to a man or a woman. The pitch was low, but sexless. She felt the knots in her stomach tighten.

"I have one million dollars in cash ready to give to you, in exchange for my son's safe return." She kept her eyes locked on Clay's steady brown gaze. Over and over, he had rehearsed her on what to say during this call. "Let me talk to Matthew—"

"No."

"I want assurances my son is alive." She tried to force bravado into her voice. "I need to know you've given him the antirejection medicine you took from the cabinet in his bathroom. I want to talk to Matthew. I *need* to talk to him. Otherwise, you don't get the money."

"You want me to hang up? I do, you'll spend the rest of your life wondering what the hell happened to your kid."

"Don't hang up." She felt her body begin to quake against the bed pillows banked behind her. "I need to talk to my child. Surely you understand why. Please."

"What I understand is you're trying to take control here. Not going to happen."

"If you let me talk to Matthew, you'll get the money. One million dollars in cash." Kathryn felt like a steel belt was tightening around her chest, making her breath hitch. "I don't care who you are. I don't care why you did this. I just want my son back alive."

"Then shut up and stop wasting my time. Put the cash in that shiny red SUV of yours and take the main highway out of Layton toward Dallas."

"Dallas?"

"We're watching your every move." The robotic voice was as hard as packed earth. "You want to get your kid back alive and in one piece, come alone."

"I will." Kathryn squeezed Clay's hand tighter. "I'll be alone. I just need to know for sure that Matthew is unharmed."

"Kid's fine. You'll get proof of that when I'm ready to give it to you. Not before."

"And you'll get your money after I have that proof." Her voice quavered. "Where in Dallas—"

The phone went dead.

Her hand was sweating, shaking when she pulled the phone from her ear. She stared down at the phone as if it'd just materialized in her palm.

"Kat?"

She looked at Clay. "He hung up. He wouldn't let me talk to Matthew. That must mean he can't talk."

"No, that's not what it means." Clay tightened his grip on her hand. "Kat, you've got to hold yourself together. We talked about something like this happening. Remember?"

"Yes." Kathryn swallowed hard. It wasn't just Clay who'd warned her the kidnapper might not let her speak to Matthew. During one of her phone conversations with the negotiator Quentin Forbes, he also predicated that possibility. *A typical kidnapper's ploy to incite desperation*, Forbes had called it.

It was working, she thought.

"Tell me what he said," Clay prodded quietly. "I need to know his *exact* words."

Struggling to control her roiling emotions, she repeated the conversation.

"All right," Clay said when she was done. "Tell me about the voice. Did you recognize it?"

"No, it sounded like a robot's. It could have been a he or a she. Young or old."

"Meaning, it's someone you'd recognize. Why else bother with the disguise?"

"I don't care about that," she shot back. She tugged her hand from Clay's, tossed back the sheet and headed for the chest of drawers on the far side of the bedroom. She didn't care that she was naked. Didn't care about anything but getting Matthew back.

"He, she…*it* wouldn't even let me hear my baby's voice." Kathryn jerked open a series of drawers, then slammed each shut after snatching up underwear, jeans and a T-shirt. "If Matthew were able to talk, why wouldn't they put him on the phone?"

"It would have been better if you could have heard his voice," Clay conceded while she jerked on her clothes. "But that didn't happen, and trying to logic out why won't get us anywhere. We have to move to the next step."

"Which is Dallas," she said. "What if he calls when I get there and tells me to drop the money someplace, then leave? Just leave."

"You tell him no, not without proof of life."

"That's easy to say, isn't it?" She walked to the door of the adjoining bathroom, then paused and glanced back across her shoulder. "It's easy to agree to demand proof of life when the bastard's voice isn't in my ear, threatening my baby. It isn't so easy when he's talking to me, saying I might never see Matthew again."

"I know, Kat," Clay said levelly while he pulled on his T-shirt. "I know just how hard it is not to cave in to those type of demands."

Her gaze slid to the scar on his right cheek, and her heart clenched for all he'd lost at the hands of another group of kidnappers. Yes, he knew the risks all too well.

He snagged his boots and socks off the floor. "I'll go downstairs to the study and get the gym bag with the ransom out of the safe. I need to activate the GPS chip I hid in the pack of bills, and run a diagnostic check on it. My P.I. pal also supplied me with a small fiber-optic camera that I want you to wear in case this guy shows himself."

"Do you think he will?"

"No. Doesn't mean I'm not going to cover all the bases. It'll only take a couple of minutes to get the equipment ready before we leave for Dallas."

Kathryn blinked. "Not *we*, me. He told me to come alone."

"I know what he told you." Boots and socks dangling from one hand, Clay walked toward her. "I'll fold down the back seats in the SUV and hunker down on the floor. He won't see me."

"What if he does?" Fear of what all could go wrong bubbled up her throat, sounded in her voice. "He'll *kill* Matthew if he knows I'm not alone."

"The kidnapper won't know that. But here's what he *does* know. In less than half an hour you'll be heading east out of Layton with a million dollars in cash. Alone, you're the equivalent of an armored car without the armor and armed guards. Think how easy it would be to run you off the road and take the money. If you're still alive after that, maybe the kidnapper will wait a few days or weeks or months, then demand a second ransom for Matthew. Or maybe one million dollars is enough money to set the kidnapper up for the rest of his life and you won't hear from him again. Ever."

Kathryn felt the blood drain from her face. "I… hadn't thought of that. Any of that."

"That's why I'm here." When Clay cupped a palm against her cheek, she drew in the warmth, the steadiness. "We'll get Matthew back, Kat. We just have to beat the bastard who's got him at his own game."

THE CELL PHONE RANG again when they were an hour out of Layton.

"Steady," Clay said when he saw Kathryn's shoulders stiffen. He'd positioned himself with the gym bag bulging with cash behind the passenger seat in the SUV's rear compartment where he had a good view of her profile as she drove. So far, she was holding her own.

He listened to her answer the phone, then give their location. A moment later she asked, "You'll give me proof that Matthew's alive then?"

"Same robotic voice?" Clay asked after she clicked the phone off.

"Yes."

"What did he say?"

"There's a diner about five miles up the road. I have to stop and buy a *USA Today* out of the newspaper rack. Instead of the top paper, I take out the bottom one."

"All right." Clay hoped to hell she'd find a recent photograph showing Matthew alive instead of some bloody body part.

Setting his jaw against the thought, he switched on the handheld unit with a screen that afforded him a realtime view of whatever direction Kathryn looked in, complements of the tiny fiber optic lens clipped to one earpiece of her sunglasses. The unit Clay held also served as the "base station" for the GPS tracking device hidden in the ransom.

"Kat, when we get to the diner, don't talk to me. Someone might be posted there to watch you and we can't chance them seeing you talking, and figure out you aren't alone. After you park, take your time getting to the newspaper rack while you do a slow scan of the parking lot. This unit will record everything the camera on your sunglasses sees. I want a good view of every car and every person in the diner's parking lot."

"Okay."

Kathryn's heart picked up speed minutes later when she turned into the diner's parking lot, gravel and grit popping beneath the SUV's tires. While growing up, she must have driven by this place hundreds of times without ever paying attention to it. Now, she noted the building was old, a simple cube-shape with dry-as-dust shingle siding and smudged windows that spanned the front. The parking lot was packed with cars, a sure sign the food was good, because atmosphere wasn't a draw.

Clay had already dropped a couple of quarters on the console, so after she parked she scooped them up, along with the cell phone and shoved open the SUV's door. She walked slowly, scanning the lot until she spotted several newspaper racks crowded side by side on the front sidewalk. She slid the quarters into the *USA Today* rack, raised the lid and tugged out the bottom newspaper.

Shoving her sunglasses higher up the bridge of her nose, she forced herself to maintain a slow pace on her way back to the SUV. Her legs were like jelly by the time she slid behind the wheel. She locked the door and opened the paper. An envelope dropped onto her lap.

Her hands were shaking so badly it took her two tries to get the flap open. Her heart twisted and her lungs burned when she pulled out the single photograph that showed Matthew sitting on a grimy mattress, one thin shoulder propped against what looked like a stone wall. He was wearing the same pajamas she'd put on him the night he was kidnapped. His face was streaked with dirt; his eyes were open, but there was a glassy look to them. Clenched in one of his small hands was the front page of yesterday's *Layton Times*. As of yesterday, Matthew had still been alive.

"Oh God, my poor baby." Hot tears ran down Kathryn's cheeks. She couldn't imagine what he'd been through. What he was going through. How desperately afraid he must be.

"He's alive, Kat." Clay's voice was a soft murmur from the SUV's rear section, reminding her he could view the photograph through the camera on her glasses. "We're close to getting him back," Clay continued. "Once we do, you can fall apart."

Kathryn jolted when the cell phone rang. She grabbed it, barked a too-quick hello.

"You have the newspaper yet?" the robotic voice asked.

"Yes."

"Then you got your proof. Now I want my money. Drive back to Layton."

"Where in—"

The call ended.

AN HOUR LATER, Kathryn followed the directions from Robot Voice and approached the chain-link gate on the West side of Layton High School's football stadium. A chain that had probably been secured by a padlock hung loose, clanking against the metal gate when she pulled it open. With the gym bag full of money looped over one shoulder, her movements were off balance, her pace uneven as she walked between rows of bleachers. Her insides felt hollow, scooped out. She wanted this to be over. She wanted her son back.

Please God.

When she stepped onto the playing field, the July sun beat down with blazing intensity. The heat was relentless, the humidity oppressive. Mindful that Clay remained hidden in the back of her SUV while monitoring everything within her view, she turned her head as she walked toward the middle of the field, making sure the lens hooked to her sunglasses scanned both sides of the stadium and the opposite end zone.

She saw no one lurking on or under the bleachers. Detected zero movement up in the small press box. Heard nothing but the faint swish of traffic a few blocks away. It seemed she was totally alone, yet the hairs on the back of her neck stood on end, and her instincts called out a warning she was being watched.

As ordered, Kathryn shoved the gym bag under the first row of bleachers at the east end of the fifty-yard line. In her mind's eye, she saw the minute GPS chip Clay had hidden in one of the bundles of bills, could almost feel its signal pulsing on the hot air.

Sweat trickled down her spine at the prospect of the kidnapper spotting the chip. But it was a risk she had agreed with Clay they should take. As long as she had possession of the ransom, she maintained a measure of control over her son's fate. By leaving the money here and walking away, she lost all control. If something went wrong, if Matthew was harmed in any way, she would spend the rest of her life hunting the bastard who took her child. At this point, the GPS chip was her only means to do that.

She turned slowly, her gaze doing a final sweep of the stadium before she began retracing her steps toward the gate.

While she walked, she wiped her sweaty palms down her jeaned thighs. Robot Voice had assured her Matthew would be released immediately after she left the ransom at the stadium. Although Kathryn would like to believe her son might now magically appear, she knew that wasn't the case. Clay had made sure she understood that the most dangerous, delicate stage of any kidnap was the actual handing over of the ransom. Because it was then, at the moment of collection, that someone, somehow, had to step out of the shadows…and a kidnapper came to his watering hole with more caution than any beast in the jungle.

The gym bag might remain hidden beneath the bleachers until nightfall when the kidnapper had the cover of darkness to shield him.

Robot Voice had ordered her to drive back to the Cross C and wait for the call that would tell her where to pick up Matthew.

Please God, Kathryn prayed. *Please keep my baby safe. Don't let anything go wrong.*

LYING ON HIS BELLY beneath the trees lining the rise over the high school stadium, Deputy Vernon Lang adjusted the focus on his binoculars. He'd been following Kathryn Conner Mason since she left the Cross C. In the two hours since she deposited the bulging duffel bag somewhere inside the stadium and drove off, not a soul had appeared.

Until now.

Through his binoculars, Vernon tracked the piece-of-crap tan Chevy with dents down both sides that blasted into the parking lot.

The man who scrambled out of the car was medium height, solidly built, dressed in worn jeans and a wrinkled work shirt. Although a ratty straw Stetson dipped low on his forehead, Vernon could see enough of his face to peg the guy as a Mexican.

A *nervous* one, Vernon decided, watching the subject's gaze dart from one point to another around the empty parking lot. Apparently deciding the coast was clear, the man fast-walked toward the gate, jerked it open, then disappeared inside the stadium.

With the subject out of sight, Vernon dug a pen out of his shirt pocket and scribbled the Chevy's tag number on his left palm. He'd parked his own car on the far side of the rise, and the minute he got back to it he would call dispatch and run the tag.

Less than five minutes later, the Mex charged back into sight, the bag Kathryn Conner Mason had left slung over one arm.

"Got your ransom," Vernon murmured, his mouth curving behind the binoculars. Already he imagined his picture on the cover of every Hollywood magazine and tabloid, proclaiming him a hero for rescuing the kidnapped son of Devin Mason and his screenwriter ex. Once that happened, Felicia would see his real worth. Realize he was a much better man than that bastard, Brad Jordan.

In the Mex's haste to get back to the Chevy, he dropped his keys. When he leaned to retrieve them, the bag shifted, sending him into a stagger. He finally reached the car, shoved the bag across the seat and scrambled inside after it.

Vernon was halfway to his own car when he heard the Chevy's engine grind to life.

THE INSTANT HE HEARD the beep, Clay grabbed the handheld tracking unit off the dash of his pickup. Finally the gym bag containing the ransom was on the move.

He thought of Kat, no doubt pacing the wax off the floors at home waiting for news. She hadn't wanted to go to the Cross C after leaving the money at the stadium but the kidnapper had ordered her to wait at home for a call that would tell her where she could pick up Matthew.

Watching the blip move on the handheld's display, Clay sent up a silent prayer that Kathryn wasn't destined to face the same nightmarish ending as he when the Colombian military's rescue attempt of his parents went so horribly wrong.

He shoved his pickup into gear and pulled out of the grocery store parking lot where he'd sat for the past hour and a half. The store was one mile from the stadium, and with the GPS tracker there was no risk of him having to show himself to whoever had retrieved the ransom.

He just hoped to hell the kidnapper didn't hole up somewhere and start counting each bill. If he did, chances were he'd find the tracking chip. But it was a risk Kathryn had agreed was necessary—if Matthew wasn't getting his daily antirejection pill, the boy's time was running out. Clay sensed that as surely as if there were a metronome ticking in his head. In his gut.

Keeping one eye on the handheld's screen, he headed in the direction the blip was going. Then frowned when it did a sudden change in course and picked up speed. Seconds later, the readout on the tracker clocked the vehicle at eighty miles an hour.

Clay's chest tightened at the possibility Matthew was in that speeding car. It wasn't unheard of for a kidnapper to have the victim with him when he picked up the ransom. If the police all of a sudden closed in, holding a gun to his helpless victim's head might be the suspect's sole hope of avoiding capture.

The blip changed course again.

Heading for the interstate, Clay theorized, and stepped on the gas. He didn't need to see the vehicle to track it but he didn't want to let it get too much of a lead on him.

Three miles down the road, the blip suddenly halted. It pulsed twice like a heartbeat on the screen, then disappeared.

"What the hell?" Clay ground out. No way had the kidnapper had time yet to find the tracking chip among all the bundles of bills and destroy it. Still, there could be an accomplice in the car counting the cash while his partner drove.

Clay tightened his grip on the steering wheel and made a hard turn at the nearest intersection. His only option was to head to the location where the chip transmitted its final signal.

The instant he came out of the turn, he saw black, churning smoke.

When his pickup topped the next rise, panic gripped him by the throat. Parked on the shoulder was a bottle-green sports car, a tall man with a phone plastered against his ear stood in the vee of the open driver's door. Yards beyond that, a tan car with its interior engulfed in flames had crashed into a bridge abutment near the interstate ramp. Smoke billowed skyward, folding in over itself as it rose.

Clay hit the brake and his pickup skidded to a halt on the road's shoulder. The man spun around. He wasn't in uniform, but Clay recognized him as the deputy who'd worked security at the hospital fund-raiser. *Lang*, Clay thought, then realized it was the same deputy the sheriff had received a call about.

Clay shoved out his door, raced toward the burning vehicle.

He got six yards away before the heat seared his skin. Acrid smoke filled his lungs. No way could he get close enough to try to save whoever was in the car.

God, don't let Matthew be inside.

"Turner, stay back!" Lang barked and grabbed Clay's shoulder. "Fire department's on the way. The gas tank on the car might explode any minute. There's nothing we can do for whoever's in that inferno."

Clay whipped around, jerking from the deputy's hold. "What the hell happened?"

"I was tailing the guy, keeping my distance. Something must have spooked him because he just took off like a bat out of hell. Turned too sharp to make the ramp, lost control and smashed into the bridge."

Clay narrowed his eyes. "Why were you tailing him?"

Lang's eyes went flat and unreadable. "If I'm aware of a crime, I do something about it."

"What crime?"

"The guy driving the Chevy retrieved the ransom from the stadium."

"*The ransom?*" Jaw locked tight, Clay stared at Lang in disbelief. "What do you know about a ransom?"

"I overheard you and Boudry talking about Matthew Mason getting kidnapped. I'm a cop, I hear about a crime, I do something about it. I wanted to help find the boy. Get him back to his mother." Lang showed Clay a tag number inked on his palm. "From the look of things, the abduction was an inside job. The Chevy checks to Nilo Graciano. He works at the Cross C. So does his wife, Pilar. You know them?"

"Yeah." His throat knotted, Clay pictured the ranch hand whom he'd last seen inside the house two nights ago to repair Willa's leaking kitchen sink.

There had been nothing about the encounter with Nilo Graciano that had set off Clay's radar.

Just as his instincts hadn't sounded a warning before rebels ambushed the car he was driving, then dragged his parents away while he lay in a pool of blood.

Clay felt physically, almost uncontrollably sick. He'd known from the beginning he was the wrong man for this job, but he'd let Quentin Forbes talk him into taking it. And Kat. How could he have said no to the woman whose memory had haunted him for so long?

Dammit, despite all that he *should* have said no. He was an *ex-cop* because he couldn't trust his own instincts. For him to take on the responsibility of trying to save an innocent little boy had been utter foolishness.

Foolishness that might have just cost Matthew his life.

Clay stared at the Chevy, his eyes watering from the smoke, the dampness joining the river of sweat already rolling down his face. A living wall of black smoke billowed. Scarlet tongues of flames, writhing and churning, engulfed the vehicle's interior, giving him a glimpse into hell.

A mix of rage and dread roared through him as he looked back at the deputy. "Was Matthew Mason in the car?"

"I don't know," Lang replied. "The fire started on impact. I couldn't get close enough to see."

From a distance, the shriek of sirens joined the roar of the fire. Seconds later, the Chevy's gas tank erupted in a thunderous explosion.

CHAPTER FOURTEEN

WHEN WILLA WALKED into the living room, Kathryn looked up from the leather sofa where she'd settled with Abby on her lap. Kathryn glanced at the clock ticking softly on the mantel over the massive fireplace and realized she'd been staring over an hour at the list of people who might have had something to do with Matthew's kidnapping. Just sitting there, staring.

"I wish Clay would call with news," Willa said. Dressed in her usual sedate dress and apron, gray hair in a tidy bun, the housekeeper drifted to one of the windows that looked out on the shady front porch.

"I keeping thinking the phone will ring any minute," Kathryn said. "Either phone." She'd lost count of how many times since she returned home from delivering the ransom that she'd checked to make sure the kidnapper's cell phone was still hooked to the waist of her jeans. She shifted her gaze to her own phone which she'd laid on the coffee table, willing it to ring.

When it didn't, she sighed. "Clay promised to let me know if he had news." While she spoke, she stroked Abby's smooth, glossy coat. "He said the kidnapper might not pick up the money until after dark."

"That's hours away." Lines of concern fanned from the corners of Willa's eyes, her mouth. "Hours."

"I know." With the strain of waiting gnawing at her nerves like termites, Kathryn shifted the doxie off her lap then rose and moved to Willa's side. Outside, the early afternoon sun beat down with such intensity that heat rose in fluid sheets from the long driveway, distorting the distance.

How much longer? Kathryn wondered. How much longer would she have to wait for Matthew to come home?

"I've stared at that list for what seems like an eternity," she said, gesturing toward the table.

"There are so many names, people who we've known for years and years. Who we consider friends."

Kathryn slid her arm around the waist of the woman who'd raised her. "It's like that nursery rhyme Matthew loves, about the butcher, the baker and the candlestick maker. Only my list has the banker, the English teacher, the lawyer and the veterinarian. Even now it's hard to imagine any of them being behind the kidnapping."

Willa pressed a kiss to her cheek. "How about I make you lunch? And fresh lemonade."

Just the thought of food made Kathryn's already nervous stomach roil. "I'll pass on lunch. But lemonade sounds good."

While Willa headed for the kitchen, Kathryn remained at the window, staring out past the front porch at the long driveway. She knew she could dial Clay's cell, but he'd assured her he would call if he had news. Any news.

And he had promised he wouldn't keep anything about Matthew from her. Good or bad.

She squinted when sunlight reflected off the

windows of a vehicle coming at a fast clip from the access road that led to the stables. When it turned up the driveway and steered toward the house, she realized it was Clay's pickup. Coming from that direction, he must have entered Cross C property using the west entrance, usually reserved for heavy farm equipment and live-stock trailers. Why would he do that, when coming in that way added time and distance to his drive?

On the heels of that thought came a surge of ice that rimmed Kathryn's belly and frosted its way up to her throat. Something was wrong—if Clay had good news, he would have called. Bad news was something he would deliver in person.

She raced toward the front door, tore it open, then ran across the porch and down the steps into the heat and blinding sunlight. She reached the pickup at the same instant Clay crammed it into Park and shoved out of the door.

Beneath the brim of his Stetson, his face was as calm as carved stone, but there was a grimness in his eyes that tightened her chest.

"What's happened?" Her brain cataloged the acrid stench of smoke that clung to his clothes. "What's happened to Matthew?"

He grabbed her arms. "Let's go inside. We'll talk there."

"No." His voice was so gentle it made her lungs burn. As did the tremor she felt in his hands. "Tell me what happened."

He looked away, dragged in a breath. "The ransom got picked up from the stadium about two hours after you left it there." He shifted his gaze back to her. "By Nilo Graciano."

"Nilo?" she asked, her thoughts reeling with shock. "Pilar's husband?"

"Yes."

Kathryn looked across her shoulder toward the stables. She saw Reece Silver's black pickup parked near the open doors. Out of view was the house the Gracianos lived in with their son, Antonio. "Nilo and Pilar kidnapped Matthew?" She whipped her gaze back to Clay. "If you know they took my baby, *where is he?*"

"Pilar claims they didn't take him. Sheriff Boudry just picked her up at home. He's driving her to the station for more questioning."

"What about Nilo? If he had collected the ransom, he must have Matthew."

"Nilo's dead."

Shock hit Kathryn like a slap in the face. "I... *How?*"

"Let's go inside." Clay tightened his grip on her arms. "You need to sit down."

"No!" She jerked away while fear tore at her. "Dammit, you tell me here. *Now.* Tell me what happened to my son."

"I don't know, not for sure." Clay raised a hand, palm up, let it drop. "Yesterday, the second time I went to talk to Boudry, one of his deputies—Vernon Lang— eavesdropped on our conversation. Lang claims he only wanted to 'help' find Matthew, so he set up his own unauthorized surveillance on the Cross C. When he saw you drive away this morning, he figured you might be on your way to make the ransom drop so he tailed you."

"A *cop* followed us?" *We have your son. We will kill him if you contact the police.* The kidnapper's words pounded in Kathryn's brain. "Lang followed us to the diner? The stadium?"

Clay nodded. "When he saw you carry the bag into the stadium and come out without it, he knew his hunch was right. So he waited there. A couple of hours after you left, Graciano picked up the ransom. When he drove off, Lang tailed him.

"Graciano maybe spotted Lang. Or something else spooked him. Either way, Graciano started driving like a crazed man. He missed the ramp to the interstate. Crashed into a bridge abutment. His car caught fire, then exploded."

"Was Matthew…" The stench of smoke from Clay's clothes took on a new meaning. A horrible, unimaginable one. Her hands shook so badly that she balled them into fists to try to control the tremors. "Did he… Did he have Matthew with him?"

"I don't know. I tried to get to the car but the fire was too intense. We won't know if anyone else was with Graciano until the lab finishes processing it."

"Oh, God. Oh, God." Kathryn's chest was so tight, she felt as if someone had banded steel around it. "Where…is the car? I want to be there. *Have* to be there."

"The state crime lab picked it up. They're transporting it on a flatbed trailer to Dallas so the techs can go through it. I don't know where in Dallas. It'll take hours before we know how many bodies are inside."

"Why? Why can't they just look inside and know?"

Clay's mouth tightened. "The fire was intense. Some of what was in the car, including bone, would have incinerated to ash. Anything made of synthetics and plastic like the seats, dashboard, carpet is melted into globs. Sometimes X-rays have to be taken to try to determine what's inside the globs."

Trying to hold back the bile rising in her throat, Kathryn pressed a palm over her mouth.

"One of Boudry's deputies followed the flatbed to the lab," Clay continued. "He'll call the sheriff as soon as he knows something. And Boudry will call me."

Clay nudged up the brim of his Stetson before continuing. "The sheriff and a couple of deputies came onto the Cross C using the west entrance so they could approach the Gracianos' house from the rear. Boudry let me tag along and watch while they searched the house. I was hoping we'd find Matthew there, that I could bring him home to you. Kat—"

When Clay reached for her again, she stumbled back. "Don't."

He let his hands drop, fisted them. "Pilar swears they didn't take Matthew. She claims that two days ago, Nilo drove into Layton, and on his way home he heard a phone ring. He opened the glove box and found a disposable cell he'd never seen before. He answered it. The caller said he knew Nilo was using a stolen identity and in the country illegally. That if he didn't keep the phone with him and do what they said when they called, they'd turn him over to immigration and it would be years before he would see his family again. Pilar claims the disposable phone rang again this morning. The voice ordered Nilo to pick up a bag hidden under the bleachers at the stadium. After he did that, he'd get another call, telling him where to take the bag."

"Do you believe her? Do you believe Pilar's story?"

"It's credible, but right now there's no proof. If there was a phone in Nilo's car, the fire destroyed it. The lab might find traces of it, but that'll take time." Again, Clay reached for her. "Let's go in—"

"No." Kathryn batted his hands away. She was crying now, fast, choking sobs brought on by a mix of fear and grief and razor-sharp condemnation. "You said…we should go to…Sheriff Boudry. That it would be…okay to tell him…about Matthew."

She saw the flash of emotion in Clay's eyes, recognized it as raw anguish. But she didn't care how he felt. *Couldn't care*, not while her own pain boiled inside her like acid. "You said going to Boudry was the right thing to do."

"I thought it was," he shot back.

"You thought wrong!" She was gasping, choking on her tears as if invisible hands had clenched around her throat. What if Matthew had been in the car the deputy tailed? What if her child had burned alive? The possibility of that plunged a hot blade through her heart.

Clay took a step toward her. "If you won't go inside with me, let me get Willa."

"No! I can't go in that house right now. I can't *breathe* in there." She looked at the stables through a haze of tears. During her youth, horses had been her haven, her means of escaping Sam's hatred. She had to get away. Go where she could think. Breathe.

Instinctively she started that way, her legs barely supporting her.

"Kat, where—"

She whipped around. She refused to acknowledge the torment in Clay's eyes. Blocked out the knowledge he had gone to Boudry only after getting her permission.

"I can't be with you right now." Her body, her voice, trembled with the words. "I can't be with *anyone*. I have to think. I need to ride and think."

TEN MINUTES LATER, Clay stood on the house's front porch, his gaze locked on the distant stables. Reece Silver stood at the rear of his massive black pickup, pulling open various compartments in which he stored supplies used in his veterinary practice.

Just then, Kathryn rode out of the stable's wide doors, lashing her chestnut mare, Dakota, into a full gallop. If she saw Reece raise a hand to get her attention, she ignored it.

At the first fence they came to, the sleek animal launched gracefully into the air, crossing the white-washed rails with little effort. Then Kathryn, hatless, her dark hair flying, veered the mare toward the north. Its hurtling hooves sent up clouds of dust before horse and rider disappeared over the rise.

Standing beside Clay, Willa dabbed a tissue at her eyes. "I don't like her going off by herself. It isn't good for that child to be alone right now."

"I couldn't get her to stay," he managed to say after a moment, the words emerging in a harsh whisper.

The instant Kathryn had raced off toward the stables, he called Willa out on the porch and briefed her about what had happened to Nilo and the ransom money. And possibly Matthew. Knowing that Kat wouldn't turn to him for comfort when she got back home, Clay wanted the housekeeper prepared.

"Do you think Pilar was telling the truth?" Willa asked, her voice trembling. "That neither she nor Nilo knew anything about the kidnapping? And Matthew wasn't in the car with Nilo?"

"My gut says Pilar was being truthful." Clay hoped to hell she was, anyway.

"I'll hold on to that and pray you're right." Willa

shook her head. "Poor Nilo. And Pilar." The woman's tear-filled eyes suddenly widened and her lips parted. "What about Antonio? That sweet little boy has just lost his father. His mother's being questioned by the police. Someone needs to see to him."

Guilt balled in Clay's throat. The fact that Antonio's father had burned alive was one more brick on his back. "Boudry had a deputy drive Antonio to his grand-mother's house."

"Thank goodness. That's one less worry."

"Yeah." Clay shifted his gaze back to the horizon while fighting an instinctive urge to go after Kathryn. He had the sick feeling he hadn't just lost sight of her. He had *lost* her. This time for good.

She was the one person who mattered most to him, yet he seemed destined to forever hurt her.

You said going to Boudry was the right thing to do.

He had thought so. Had never counted on some half-assed deputy setting up his own surveillance of the ransom drop site. And screwing things up so thoroughly.

"Lord, I forgot about Brad Jordan."

Willa's comment had Clay looking toward the driveway. "You have an appointment with Brad?" Clay asked, watching the banker's pristine midnight-blue Jaguar approach the house.

"He called yesterday to see if we could go over some household receipts today. I forgot about him coming."

"Despite what happened to Nilo, the kidnapping isn't public knowledge. Not yet, anyway. I don't want you to mention anything to Brad."

"I won't." Squaring her shoulders, Willa mopped quickly at her eyes then stuffed her tissues into the pocket on her apron. "I'll give him the receipts and a slice of apple pie, then send him on his way. Just like I always do."

"Sounds like a plan."

Clay knew he couldn't stand around and wait for the lab to call with word of how many bodies they'd found in the remains of the car. He had to *do* something. Since the location of the ransom drop had raised questions in his mind, he intended to keep occupied by focusing on getting answers.

By now, word of the fiery wreck would have spread across Layton. People would know he'd been a witness, so his presence at the sheriff's office shouldn't raise alarms.

"Mrs. McKenzie, I'm going into Layton to talk to Sheriff Boudry. The minute Kathryn gets back, I'd appreciate a call."

"All right." Willa patted his arm. "You've done everything you can to help keep Matthew safe. I know that, and so does Kathryn. And I expect it's time you start calling me Willa."

"Thanks." Despite the guilt eating a ragged hole in his gut, he forced his mouth to curve. "Willa."

Heading off the porch, he nodded to Brad, then slid into his pickup.

It wasn't until Clay was alone that he started to shake.

"NILO GRACIANO was a pawn," Clay said while pacing Sheriff Jim Guy Boudry's tidy office. By then, the tremors had eased and forcing his brain into cop mode made Clay feel somewhat steadier.

"The kidnapper didn't want to risk collecting the

ransom himself," he continued. "We already know the bastard who took Matthew has inside knowledge of the Cross C. Maybe he checked out employees, chatted them up, kept his ears open until he found dirt on one of them. That was Graciano. Easy enough to blackmail an illegal into picking up a bag when the alternative is being separated from his wife and child."

Boudry leaned back in his chair. "Now that I've interviewed Pilar, I tend to agree with you," the sheriff commented in his sandpaper-rough voice. "It goes in her favor we didn't find any trace of Matthew Mason when we searched her house. Even so, I'm holding her as a material witness. She's so upset over her husband that I had the doc sedate her. I'll hit her with more questions in the morning, but I just don't think she's a lead that's going anywhere."

"How about working one that might?" Clay asked.

"Which is?"

"The stadium. Why choose the stadium as the ransom drop?"

"It's summer, school's out. Nobody around."

"True." Clay continued pacing, hands jammed in the back pockets of his jeans. With the door to the small office closed, he glanced out the panel of glass set into the wall facing the squad room. Several uniformed deputies sat at gray metal desks, writing reports or talking on the phone. On the opposite side of the room, a female dispatcher in civilian clothing worked the radio. Her long hair was the same glossy ebony as Kathryn's.

Clay felt the knots in his gut tighten. The more he tried to focus on the case, the more guilt ate at him. He had gotten Kat to trust him again and now he might be responsible for her losing the person she loved most in the world. Her child.

He looked at his watch. Wished he knew how long the lab would take until they knew if Matthew had been in that car.

"I've got a deputy at the lab," Boudry reminded him, as if reading Clay's thoughts. "He's under orders to call me the minute they know."

Clay turned. "Waiting's hell."

"Yeah." Boudry raised a palm. "I figure talking about the case might help make it seem like time hasn't slowed to a crawl."

Nodding, Clay forced his thoughts back to the case. "About the stadium, why did the bastard choose it for the ransom drop when he could have picked someplace away from town that's more isolated? What does the stadium give him that he needs?"

"I figure you've already got an answer, so you tell me."

"Kathryn said the entire time she was inside, she felt like she was being watched," Clay answered. "I had a camera on her, and I've viewed the recording a couple of times. As far as I can tell, she was the only person there."

"My deputies went over every inch of the stadium. Except for the chain on the gate being cut and the padlock missing, there's nothing to indicate someone else had even been inside."

"I don't think the kidnapper was inside. But I damn well think he was watching."

"Planted some sort of surveillance equipment?"

"No, he would have had to retrieve it and that's a chance he couldn't take." Clay grabbed his handheld unit that he'd left beside his Stetson in one of the visitor chairs. "Right before Kathryn reached the fifty-yard line, she looked up and did a slow scan of the press box."

Clay paused while Boudry tugged a pair of glasses from the pocket of his denim shirt and slid them on. "There are cameras installed on the roof at the center and both ends of the press box," Clay continued, angling the unit's display to give the sheriff a clear view. "I imagine they're used to tape games so the coach can critique each play. What I need to know is if the cameras can be activated by someone off-site."

"They can," Boudry said, peering at the unit's display. "I know that because my two grandsons played high school football. A couple of dads with kids on the team traveled for a living and weren't always in town to attend the games. They got the booster club to buy a system where anyone with a password can go online and watch the football games in real time."

Clay felt a ripple at the tip of his consciousness. "The booster club?"

"Right. That ring a bell with you?"

"At the hospital fund-raiser, I heard Rich Jordan complain to his son, Brad, about the booster club's computers. Upgrading the system was going to take extra time, and Rich was pissed."

"His one claim to fame is his work in the booster club. Well, that and his son being the quarterback when the football team won the state championship fifteen years ago."

"Sounds like Rich Jordan is deep into sports. A lot of people who are bet on games. Does he?"

"He's been known to organize betting pools." Boudry pursed his mouth. "It's an interesting coincidence, you overhearing Rich talking about the booster club's computer system, which includes the stadium, then the ransom drop taking place there."

"What are the odds?" Clay murmured. He felt an adrenaline rush whoosh up his spine, the same unmistakable tingle he'd felt often while a cop when an investigation moved off high-center. "Rich Jordan didn't run in the same circles as Sam Conner, so he was never invited to dinner parties at the Cross C. Meaning, Rich isn't familiar with the layout of the house."

"But his son is," Boudry said.

"Very. In fact, right before I left the Cross C, Brad showed up to go over receipts with Willa." Clay stroked the scar on his right cheek. "The first time the kidnapper's cell phone rang, Kathryn was at the bank in Brad's office."

"Was Brad with her?"

"Yes. She asked him for privacy to take the call so he left the office. She answered, but the caller never said a word."

"So, maybe Brad isn't involved in the kidnapping, but his daddy is," Boudry theorized. "Mrs. Mason's a celebrity, and because of the terms in Sam Conner's will, Brad oversees the Cross C's finances. He might have bragged to folks about how he gets to rub elbows with a famous, beautiful woman. Could be he told the wrong person about how things operate at the Cross C."

"What does Rich Jordan do for a living?" Clay asked.

"He's a regional distributor for an auto parts company based in Dallas." Boudry retrieved a notepad and began jotting. "I'll run a check on Rich to see what shape his finances are in."

"Can't hurt," Clay said. "Do you know what it

takes for a parent to log onto the stadium's network to watch a game?"

"Anyone who makes a donation to the booster club gets a password. That's all they need to go online and watch what's called a 'live Webcast' of any event in the stadium."

"Any event, including a ransom drop," Clay said. He needed a lead, *now*. Was he seeing one that didn't exist? It didn't matter. This was all he had, so he would follow it.

"Sheriff, we need to find out if anyone logged onto the stadium's computer system today. And, if so, who."

KATHRYN WASN'T SURE how far she rode while the dry wind bore sharp bullets of grit that hit her skin, her eyes, her teeth. She didn't care. She had booted Dakota on relentlessly while they passed barns and sheds at mind-numbing speed, jumping fences at near-disaster rate, riding hell bent she didn't know where.

And when the enormity of all that had happened caught up with her, she jerked back on the reins so suddenly Dakota reared up, front legs churning. Then Kathryn slid out of the saddle and sat on the hard-packed ground, staring into the distance while her mind became a jumbled collection of images: Matthew, his brown eyes brightly alive, exploding into her bedroom every morning as if fuel propelled. Matthew squealing with delight while he and Abby wrestled on the living room rug. Matthew wrapping his small arms around her own neck and giving her a smacking kiss on the mouth. Matthew, pale and still with a spiderweb of tubes and monitors around him as he lay in a hospital bed awaiting the kidney transplant.

While she sat, staring into the distance, fear and helplessness overwhelmed her. The fear locked her in a suffocating void, while the helplessness—the awful knowing she might have caused her son's death—wrapped her in a straightjacket of pain.

Now, tears rolled down her cheeks. Rough, dry sobs stuck in her throat. She knew she had to call Devin. He was Matthew's father; she *had* to tell him it was possible their son was dead.

She reached for her cell phone, realized the only one clipped to the waist of her jeans was the one the kidnapper had left in Matthew's bedroom. Her own phone was on the coffee table beside the list of suspects.

Kathryn eased out a trembling breath. She would have to wait until she got back to the Cross C to put a call through to the movie set in Tibet. Maybe by then she would be able to say the words that even now seemed unthinkable.

Matthew possibly dead, because *she* had let Clay go to the sheriff. Her son maybe burned alive, and it was all her fault.

Hers, not Clay's. Devin wasn't the only person she needed to talk to, Kathryn knew. She'd tossed all the blame onto Clay's shoulders when they both knew he never would have gone to Boudry without her okay.

Guilt sat in her stomach like a huge, jagged rock. For the rest of her life she would see the pain her accusing words put in Clay's eyes. She had to get back on Dakota, ride to the Cross C and tell Clay that no matter what had happened to Matthew, he wasn't to blame.

She scrubbed the tears off her cheeks and pushed herself up stiffly. Her legs were still weak and trembling. Had been since Clay's awful words sunk in.

For the first time she was aware of the dark line of storm clouds on the horizon. Greedy fingers of wind slapped her hair against her cheek as she walked to where Dakota stood patiently, propped on one hip, resting a rear leg.

Kathryn gathered the reins, rubbed the mare's glossy neck. "Gave you a workout today, didn't I girl?" she crooned.

Along with the mare's soft nicker came the distant sound of an engine. Kathryn looked across her shoulder. And spotted a gray car in the distance, barreling across the pasture.

She glanced around, trying to get her bearings. How far had she ridden? she wondered. She had no idea. No idea who's land she was now on. All she knew for sure was that when she'd left Cross C property she had reined Dakota toward the north.

She watched the car barreling across the flat pastureland that was broken by a thick grouping of gnarled trees and underbrush. So, where had the car come from? The trees? If so, why? A sedan wasn't the type of vehicle used for farm work. Or even by an owner checking on his property.

Just as the car disappeared from sight, she felt a prickling along the length of her spine. A deep, intuitive disquiet swept through her. She couldn't explain why, but she had to see what, if anything, was in or around those trees.

Gripping the reins, she swung into the saddle.

By the time Dakota neared the trees, thunder bellowed, bursting through the gathering clouds. Kathryn leaned forward over the mare's neck, straining to see through the thick shadows beneath the trees.

And then she remembered Sam's age-old rule that every saddlebag on the Cross C had to contain a flashlight. She hoped Johnny had continued that policy.

Twisting in the saddle, Kathryn jerked on the saddlebag's leather strap as the howling wind tore at her hair. Her fingers had just curved around the barrel of a flashlight when Dakota snorted and sidestepped nervously.

"Steady, girl," Kathryn said, tightening her hand on the reins.

The next instant, something hard slammed into Kathryn's back. With a shriek, she pitched out of the saddle. Small rocks bit into her palms and knees when she hit the ground.

She had time only to shake her head before a hand grabbed her by the back of her hair. With brute force, the hand slammed her forehead into the hard-packed dirt.

CHAPTER FIFTEEN

"WHAT DO YOU MEAN my password was used?" Rich Jordan asked. "Nothing went on at the stadium today. Why would I log onto the system when there's nothing to watch?"

With one shoulder braced against the wall of the interview room, Clay studied the man sitting at the scarred table across from Boudry. Dressed in a plaid shirt, faded Levi's and scuffed boots, Rich Jordan looked as big and rangy as he had at the hospital fundraiser. But being brought in for questioning had transformed his bony face into a landscape of gray gauntness.

"Something *did* go on at the stadium," Boudry countered. "Something that would have given you reason to fire up your computer for a live Webcast."

Rich flicked an uneasy look at Clay. "You're not a cop, so I don't know why you're here. But since you are, how about telling me what's going on?"

"I'm an observer," Clay said, his words almost obliterated by a blast of thunder that shook the walls of the windowless room. "Sheriff Boudry is who you need to talk to."

"I *am* talking." Sarcasm dripped from the man's voice like acid. "Problem is, I'm not getting any answers."

"I didn't invite you here to ask questions, Rich. I need you to answer them."

"I don't call getting pulled over by a deputy an invitation." Jordan stabbed fingers through his close-clipped blond hair. "It's more like harassment."

"You didn't have to come in," Boudry said easily. "You're not under arrest."

"Then why'd you read me the Miranda?"

"To preserve your rights," the sheriff explained.

And to ensure everything you say is admissible in court, Clay added silently while rain pounded the roof like angry fists.

He checked his watch and frowned. Four hours had passed since he left the Cross C. Four hours with no word from the deputy waiting at the Dallas lab for word of how many bodies had burned in Nilo Graciano's car. Four hours, during which he'd checked in several times with Willa to find out if Kat had returned from her ride.

So far, she hadn't.

Clay knew if Kat had been too far from the Cross C to make it back before the rain set in, she would have found shelter for her and Dakota. His thoughts drifted back ten years to the night a hard, driving rain kept him and Kat in the outlaw tunnel. They'd waited out the storm in each other's arms.

With the accusation he'd seen in her eyes today filling him with a throbbing sense of loss and regret, he harbored no hope of a future with her. Not when he had failed her so totally.

"So, where were you coming from when my deputy pulled you over?" Boudry's question wrenched Clay's attention back to Jordan.

"My wife and I are thinking about building a house. I was looking for land to buy west of Layton."

"Find any?"

"Not yet."

Boudry tapped a stubby finger against the table. "Rich, if you were just messing around on your computer and logged onto the stadium's system by mistake, it's no big deal. Just tell me."

"Look, my computer got fried last night when some bug got past my virus checker. According to the tech I took it to this morning, I have to replace the hard drive."

Boudry shrugged. "You only have the one computer?"

"Yeah." Rich shifted in his chair. "I've got a laptop that belongs to the company I work for."

"Did you use the laptop today?"

"To check e-mail. Touch base with my accounts."

"What about gambling?"

Rich frowned at the change in subject. "What about it?"

"You're into sports. All sports. You ever bet on games?"

"Yeah, sure. Who doesn't?"

"How often do you win?"

"Not nearly enough."

"Your employer's in Dallas. You're there a lot. You ever place bets with the bookies there?"

"I've been known to."

Clay studied Jordan. The man's financials had come back showing a less than stellar income level, but he wasn't in hock up to his eyeballs, either. He paid his mortgage and utilities on time, and his credit cards weren't maxed out. Since his outward nervousness didn't increase at the mention of gambling, Clay suspected Rich Jordan's betting habits were in control.

"So," Boudry continued, "you didn't use your password to log onto the stadium's system today?"

"Ask me a question I haven't already answered."

"Okay, Rich, who else knows your password?"

A look crossed Jordan's face, a quick shadow, and Clay recognized it, had seen it numerous times during his law enforcement career: Jordan knew something. He wiped the expression away, tried a vague look while he scratched his chin. "I don't recall that anyone else knows my password."

"Well, then I'm going to have to hold you."

"*Hold me?* What's the charge?"

"Vandalism," Boudry replied. "Someone cut the lock off the stadium gate and used your password to log onto the computer system, all around the same time today. I have to figure the events are somehow connected."

"*I* didn't log onto the stadium's computer."

"Someone did, using your password. You claim no one else knows it. You want to rethink that?"

A muscle worked in Jordan's jaw. "I want my lawyer."

"We'll get him over here," Boudry said as he stood. "May take him a while on account of the storm. You just sit tight."

Clay followed Boudry into the hall. The sheriff turned and said, "I think he told the truth, except for knowing who else has his password."

"I agree," Clay said. "You figure it's his son?"

"Yeah. The password is eleven. That's the jersey number Brad wore when he was the high school's quarterback." Boudry pursed his mouth. "This wouldn't be the first time a parent covered for his kid."

Clay's cell phone rang. He tugged it out of his pocket and answered.

"Clay, it's Willa." The housekeeper's voice sounded strained, like a wire snapped tight.

His fingers clenched on the phone. "Is Kathryn home?"

"Not yet. I called the stables, just to make sure she wasn't waiting out the storm down there. Johnny hasn't seen her since she rode off this afternoon."

"Did you try her cell?"

"She left it here. Clay, she knows not to ride during a storm. Knows to find shelter from the lightning and just wait it out. That's probably what she's doing." Willa's voice quavered. "But she was so upset when she left. As soon as the rain lets up, Johnny and some of the hands are going out looking for her."

Clay's throat constricted. "I'm heading back now. Tell Johnny I'll coordinate things with him as soon as I get there."

"I will. Clay, I know you said you would call..." Willa paused when her voice died.

He closed his eyes, felt the same unsteadiness he heard in Willa's voice churning inside him. "We're still waiting to hear from the lab."

After ending the call, he briefed Boudry.

"Want me to send a deputy with you to look for Mrs. Mason?"

Clay shook his head. "No, she could be waiting out the storm somewhere. And we still don't know if Matthew was in that car. If he wasn't, the kidnapper might be watching the Cross C., figuring out how and when to demand a replacement ransom. It'd be best not to have cops around the ranch right now."

"Makes sense. In the meantime, I'll call a contact I've got at the Dallas P.D. He works Vice and has a line on some of the gambling syndicates there. If either Rich or Brad—or both—have big debts, that'd be solid motive for the kidnapping."

"Let me know what you find."

Just then, Boudry's cell rang. He pulled it out of his pocket, checked the display, then motioned for Clay to wait.

"This call is from the deputy I sent to the lab," the sheriff said. "I imagine we're about to find out how many bodies burned in Graciano's car."

KATHRYN CAME TO slowly, her head throbbing, her brain fuzzy. Once or twice she nearly surfaced, only to drop into the grayness again. Time had no meaning apart from her coming and going through a heavy drumming that filled the verge of consciousness.

The air around her felt cool; the musty scent of dirt filled her lungs. Then came the realization she was lying facedown, nose pressed against hard-packed earth. Her back throbbed, and a firestorm of pain raged in her head.

She lay motionless, her thoughts coming clearer and clearer. She'd been digging a flashlight out of the saddlebag so she could investigate the stand of gnarled trees when something slammed against her spine. Knocked her off Dakota's back. Then fingers dug into her hair and rammed her forehead against the ground.

She forced her eyes open. Her vision grayed, then focused. She was in some sort of room that had stone walls. Murky light came from a portable lantern that sat in a corner.

She rolled onto her back, and groaned from the effort. Overhead was a plank ceiling with joists spanning the walls. To her right were wooden stairs that jutted up a short distance to a slanting door. *A cellar*, she realized. She was in a cellar. Who had put her here? *Why?*

She pushed into a sitting position and nearly passed out again. Lifting a hand to her forehead, she winced when her fingers grazed an egg-size knot. Dried blood had caked over her right eye. Her head buzzed. Sweat rolled down her face. Better to wait to check the door until she felt steadier, she decided. She turned her head and squinted at the section of the cellar that the light barely reached.

The shadow against the far wall could be a pile of rubble, clothing maybe.

Maybe not.

Using the wall for support, she pushed to her feet. The room whirled. Her legs trembled and gave out; with a startled gasp she fell hard onto the floor, dizzy and sick. Her stomach heaved, forcing bile up her throat.

She lay sweating and shivering until the worst of the nausea subsided. She had one doozie of a concussion, she decided. With no strength in her legs, she began to crawl. Dirt and grit ground into her palms.

When she neared the wall, her heart shot into her throat. Matthew, dressed in the camouflage pajamas she'd put on him four nights ago, lay on a dirt-streaked twin mattress. His back was to her, his head resting on a soiled pillow. Beside the mattress sat an unopened water bottle and a sack sporting a fast-food restaurant's logo.

"Matthew!"

He was as still as death. Kathryn's throat went dry. "Matty…" she whispered. "Oh, my God, Matty!"

She placed a trembling hand against his neck. His

skin felt warm, his pulse strong. Her heart dropped back into her chest and started beating again.

She slipped her fingers beneath the waistband of his pajamas and palpitated his transplanted kidney as his doctor had taught her to do. The kidney felt firm to her touch; its shape and texture seemed normal. As far as she could tell in the dim light, his color was good.

"Matthew." She shook him gently. "Baby, wake up."

He stirred and moaned softly, but didn't wake. Not normal behavior. Drugged, she thought. He'd been drugged.

Tears coursing down her cheeks, her entire body trembling, Kathryn rolled him onto his back and unbuttoned his pajama top. His skin felt cool, not feverish, which would have been the case if his body had begun rejecting the kidney.

Physically he seemed fine. She closed her eyes. The vicious pain in her head, in her back, didn't matter anymore. All that mattered was that Matthew was alive. Alive and well.

She scooted onto the mattress, propped her shoulders against the wall and gathered him close. Rocking him, she sat in silence, overwhelmed.

Thank God. Thank God, whoever kidnapped him had given him his antirejection medicine.

Her gratitude quickly transformed into a knot of seething anger even as she gently smoothed Matthew's silky blond hair. She would never be so grateful that she would forget what had been done to her child. Of how frightened he must have been, all alone, locked in this dank cellar.

Nor would she forget the terror she'd lived through

over the past four days. Whoever had taken Matthew had kept him healthy because it was the kidnapper's one guarantee of collecting the ransom.

"Greedy bastard," she hissed under her breath. And now, he had her. She was well aware there was no ransom waiting to be collected. By now, the kidnapper would know that, too.

Shifting Matthew's weight, she fumbled her fingers across her waistband. The cell phone was gone. She'd left her own on the coffee table when she'd seen Clay drive up.

Clay. Did he know yet that Matthew had not died in the fire with Nilo Graciano? Was Clay even aware she hadn't returned from her ride?

She checked the time and date on her watch. A couple of hours had passed since she'd been knocked out.

It was dark outside—she could see moonlight seeping in under the cellar door. Surely Clay knew by now she hadn't come home. A dull throb settled in her belly. Despite what she had said to him this afternoon, despite the blame she had wrongly flung at him, he would come for her.

Leaning her head back against the wall, she centered her thoughts on Clay. For so long she had thought of him solely as a man who made a study of romance and seduction. Even now, the years-old bittersweet ache rose in her heart, as fresh as yesterday.

But she had learned there was so much more to him. She'd seen it in his concern over Matthew, in the way Clay had shifted her own emotional burden onto his shoulders. In the guilt and grief he carried over the deaths of his parents. And for the child they had both lost long ago.

Could things work between her and Clay this time? Was she willing to take that risk, to give him the second chance he had asked her for that morning?

I don't want to lose you again. I love you, Kat.

For a split second, she imagined she could feel Clay's heart beating in time with her own. She didn't have to wonder if he would walk through hell to find her and Matthew. She knew. Knew that Clay wouldn't give up until he found them because he was a good man with a warm, caring heart. A heart that was now hers for the taking.

A pang of longing swelled in her chest, making it hard to breathe. Being around Clay, being *with* him, had always felt so right.

It still did.

This thing between them didn't want to die, and maybe she shouldn't let it. Maybe she should take a risk on the man she had never been able to exorcize from her heart and her thoughts.

She looked back at the staircase, at the moonlight seeping under the door. First, though, it was up to her to get her child out of harm's way.

THE RELIEF CLAY FELT after Boudry's deputy reported that only Nilo Graciano had died in the fiery car dissipated when Johnny Sullivan called his cell. "Dakota came back without Kathryn."

"Where are you?"

"At the stables. I drove back when Trampas called me about the mare. Wanted to check her myself."

"I'm on my way." His jaw clamped tight, Clay whipped his pickup into a U-turn, its headlights sweeping over the knee-high prairie grass in the pasture he was currently searching.

Fifteen minutes later, he parked in front of the stables. The rain had ended a couple of hours ago and now the night air was still as death and heavy with humidity.

Passing beneath the stable's high double doors, the scents of horseflesh and fresh hay filled Clay's lungs as he walked along a corridor lined with stalls. Along with the occasional nicker of a horse, he heard crickets chirping from the vast stores of grain.

Dakota's stall was halfway down the corridor. As if expecting him, the mare stood with her head out over the bottom half of the door, ears pricked up in curiosity.

"Hi, girl," Clay said, stroking the lopsided blaze that ran down Dakota's muzzle. The mare nickered and tossed her head.

"There you are," Johnny said, stepping into view at the far end of the corridor. "I was just double-checking with Trampas to make sure he didn't see what direction Dakota came back to the Cross C from. He didn't." His weathered face taut with worry, the foreman fondled the mare's muzzle. "Trampas said she was just grazing in our farthest north pasture when he spotted her."

"There's no telling how long she'd been there," Clay said.

"Sure isn't," Johnny agreed. "I checked her good… doesn't look like she's got any injuries from tumblin' into a ravine or anything like that."

Meaning, Clay thought, it didn't look like a riding accident was the reason Kathryn hadn't come back with her horse. He pulled off his Stetson, scraped the back of his hand across his sweat-soaked forehead, and cursed himself for not going after her when she'd ridden away that afternoon.

"Willa told me Kathryn left her phone up at the house," Johnny said. "Otherwise I'd have tried to call it."

Clay's thoughts shot back to the instant Kathryn raced out of the house when he drove up. She'd had the kidnapper's cell phone clipped to her waistband. Ordinarily he wouldn't risk calling the phone in case the kidnapper had some way of monitoring its calls. But Kathryn was an expert rider, and Dakota coming back without her meant something had gone wrong.

Very wrong.

Clay jerked out his billfold, retrieved the slip of paper he'd written the phone's number on, then punched it in on his own cell phone.

The sudden ringing coming from the saddlebags looped over the stall's rails had Dakota sidestepping nervously. Johnny soothed the mare while Clay yanked open the saddlebag.

Dread curled in his stomach when he pulled out the cell phone Kathryn had kept with her religiously since Matthew's kidnapping.

Clay saw his own phone number on the display. And the icon signifying that a text message was in the phone's inbox.

The air stopped pumping into his lungs when he read the message.

We've got the mother now. Two million in cash for her and the kid. Have the money ready by tomorrow afternoon or they both die.

"What's it say?" Johnny asked.

Clay's free hand closed into a fist. "The bastard who took Matthew also has Kathryn." He heard the low edge of fury in his voice, felt the sweat roll down his back.

"Lord help us," Johnny said and wiped a trembling hand over his stubbled jaw.

Staring at the text message, Clay eased out a breath. He hoped to hell the kidnapper had Matthew and Kathryn in the same place, so she at least knew her son hadn't died in the fire.

"I've had some of the hands out for the past couple of hours, combin' every inch of the Cross C for Kathryn," Johnny said. "Nobody's had any luck. You want us to start searchin' the neighboring properties?"

"Yes." Clay slid the phone into his shirt pocket. "Just don't mention to any of the hands that Kathryn's been kidnapped. All they need to know is she didn't come back on Dakota."

"All right." Johnny stroked the mare's neck one last time, then headed toward his small office at the rear of the stables.

Clay turned in the opposite direction. Kat would be all right, he told himself. She was strong. She was a fighter. She would protect Matthew as best she could. And she would hang on until *he* found her.

If it was the last thing he did, he would find her and Matthew.

Jaw set, he dialed Boudry's number. Clay wanted to know what the sheriff had found out about Rich Jordan and his son, Brad.

KATHRYN GAVE one last shove on the cellar's wooden door. Nothing. The damn lock wasn't going to give. She might as well try to push a mountain out of her way.

She used the sleeve of her T-shirt to mop the sweat off her forehead, and winced when she hit the egg-size lump. Her arms ached, her head pounded and her back felt as though it might break.

Glancing across her shoulder, she gave a wishful look at the unopened water bottle beside the fast-food sack. Her throat was parched, but she didn't dare take a drink. Matthew had not yet awakened from his drugged sleep and she had no way of knowing his true physical state. Even if his kidney was functioning, he'd spent four days in this hole. He might be dehydrated and need every drop of water for himself.

She eased her aching body down the wooden steps. There was only one way in and out of the cellar, and the door was it. Since she couldn't open it, she had to figure out some way for her and Matthew to escape when the bastard who'd locked them here showed up.

At that instant, Matthew stirred.

She rushed across the hard-packed floor and knelt beside the mattress.

"Matthew?"

He expelled a soft moan as he woke slowly, groggily. Even after he opened his eyes it took him several minutes to focus on her face.

"Matthew?"

"Mommy?" he asked in a frightened, confused voice.

"Yes, Matty, it's me."

"Mommy!" He lunged clumsily onto her lap; his arms surrounded her neck in a stranglehold.

"I'm here." Her voice hitched as tears filled her eyes. "Sweetheart, I'm here." She hugged him in a tight grip. "Are you okay?"

When he didn't answer, she asked, "Matthew, are you sick?"

He hesitated, then shook his head against her cheek.

She arched her head back to examine his face, inwardly cursing the dim light. "I know how scared you must have been, all alone here. But I'm with you now, Matty, and I need you to talk to me. Tell me how you feel."

He rubbed his eyes with his fists. "I'm...sleepy, Mommy. I want...to go home."

His movements were slow, his voice slurred, confirming her suspicions that he'd been drugged.

"I want to go home, too. Do you know who brought you here?"

He nodded against her shoulder. "The man."

"What man? Do you know his name?"

"No, he wears a mask. He gives me my pill every morning, just like you do."

"Okay, that's good." Feeling a measure of relief, Kathryn used her booted foot to slide the water bottle within her reach. As she twisted the lid, she heard its seal snap. "Here, sweetheart."

After taking several generous gulps, Matthew snuggled deeper into her arms. "You won't go away, will you, Mommy?"

"No, Matty. I won't leave you." The bastard would have to kill her first, she silently vowed.

She allowed herself a small, blessed sip of water, then placed the bottle beside the fast-food sack. "Does the man give you any medicine other than your morning pill?" she asked.

"No."

Kathryn placed a soft kiss against his hair. Since she'd broken the seal on the water bottle, she figured its contents were untainted.

The food was another matter. She had checked the bag and found two peanut butter and jelly sandwiches inside. It would be easy to grind up sleeping pills and add the drug to the sandwiches. Despite her gnawing hunger, the food would have to remain untouched.

"Matthew, do you remember when the man came into the house and took you out of your bedroom?"

"I was asleep and he woke me up. He said we were going to the outlaw tunnel and if I made any noise he would hurt you 'n Abby." His mouth quivered. "Mommy, Abby was in my room and wouldn't wake up. Is she okay?"

Kathryn fought to control her fury as she cupped her child's dirty, tear-streaked face and planted a kiss on the end of his nose. "The man gave Abby something to make her go to sleep, but she's fine now. And she's been moping around because she misses you. So does Grandma Willa."

"I miss her, too." He rubbed his nose with the back of his hand. "Mommy, why are you here?" he asked, his grimy face set in serious earnestness.

Kathryn hesitated while she stroked her hand up and down his back. "The same man who took you put me here. But I want to go home, too, so I have a plan on how we can get out."

"If we run away, will he hurt us?"

"Not if we're careful." Kathryn settled her chin on top of her son's head while her plan of escape solidified in her mind. It was risky. And she doubted both her and Matthew could get away. But it would be enough if only Matthew did.

She hugged her son closer and swallowed hard. "Matty, I want you to listen to my plan very carefully. I'm going to get us out of here and I need your help. You have to be brave. You have to be a big boy."

"I *am* a big boy, Mommy."

"That's right, you are." Kathryn's throat tightened at his solemn gaze. She ran her tongue across her dry lips, and tried not to think about how much could go wrong.

CHAPTER SIXTEEN

LYING ON THE CELLAR floor near the mattress, Kathryn listened to the sound of an engine approaching, then shutting off. She flinched at the slamming of a car door. Moments later, the lock on the cellar's door clicked and the door swung open.

Eyes closed, nerves snapping, she lay unmoving in the dim light, her cheek against the floor, the dry smell of dirt in her nose. Matthew was stretched out on the mattress, his face buried in the pillow. Enough time had passed since he woke up that the drug had totally worn off and he was alert.

Like her, he was playing possum.

She sent up a silent prayer that his bravery would last long enough to get him to safety.

Fresh, revitalizing air swept in through the open door. Through her lashes, she saw a flashlight's beam sweep across the floor. For what seemed like an eternity there was no sound from the doorway. She realized the man was standing there with his flashlight aimed, watching. Waiting.

Hollow echoes sounded when he advanced down the wooden steps, his booted feet halting inches from where she lay on her side. Her fingernails dug into her palms.

From outside came the rush of wind whipping through trees, making her think the cellar was part of a house hidden in the stand of gnarled trees she'd seen earlier.

The air stirred against her face. The man, she realized with relief, had left the door open. He had lowered his guard because he'd found her and Matthew as expected—drugged from having eaten the sandwiches. She had heightened his sense of security by wadding up the empty sack and leaving it in view of the door. The food was hidden under the mattress.

Kathryn sensed him leaning over her. Thank God he couldn't hear the slow rise of the hairs on the back of her neck.

He waited. Listened. Sweat pooled on her palms. Then he moved away, walking in a slow circle around her. His boot-steps halted. He circled her again. Stopped. Waited. Listened.

Without warning, fingertips grazed her cheek. Swallowing back a scream, she managed to remain still. She knew in her heart Matthew couldn't pass the same chilling scrutiny.

She would have to make her move soon.

With apparent satisfaction that the drug had done its work on her, the man turned and moved toward the mattress.

Barely breathing, she watched the kidnapper. In the glow from the flashlight's beam, she could tell he was dressed all in black and had a dark ski mask pulled over his head. She strained to find something familiar about him, something she could identify him by, but the light was too dim.

He crouched beside the mattress. Raised his hand and reached for Matthew.

Kathryn lunged up, aimed the toe of her boot at the bastard's skull and kicked. Her ankle absorbed a jarring impact; he cursed and spun her way as he began an awkward, teetering rise.

"Don't touch him!" she snapped, and kicked again. The blow landed square against his temple. His solid form landed on the dirt floor with a heavy thud.

"Now, Matthew!" she shouted. "Run!"

Matthew bolted up the stairs and out the door like a shot. Kathryn followed his small, fleeing form, pausing long enough to slam the door behind her. Enough moonlight shone through the trees for her to see the shiny silver hasp on the door, but there was no lock hanging from it.

Probably has it in his pocket. She had wanted to trap the bastard in his own prison, but searching for something to cram through the hasp would waste valuable seconds.

Turning, she grabbed Matthew's hand and they raced toward the car parked nearby.

She jerked on the driver's door. It wouldn't budge.

"Plan B," she whispered, and snatched Matthew into her arms. Blessing the moonlight, she ran, dodging limbs, stumbling over rocks. Dry leaves and twigs snapped under her feet.

Behind her, she heard the rattle of the hinge. The loud bang as the cellar door exploded open.

Icy terror twisted in her heart. The kicks she'd delivered to the man's head hadn't been debilitating enough.

Plan C, she told herself as she raced out of the stand of trees into flat pastureland. She checked the moon, got her bearings, then settled Matthew on his feet.

"Okay, honey, it's time to run like I said you might have to." She gripped his right arm. "Keep the moon on this side of you." Then she pointed in the direction she and Dakota had approached from earlier. "Go that way until you find the first fence. Follow the fence line, Matty, and you'll get to a road."

He gripped her hand; fear had turned his eyes as big as saucers. "Mommy, I don't wanna go. I wanna go with you."

The pleading in his voice ripped at her heart. "We have to split up, remember?" She tapped the plastic badge that he'd insisted on wearing to bed four nights ago. "You're a deputy sheriff and a brave boy. You can do this." She kissed his cheek. "If you get home before me, tell Grandma Willa and Mr. Turner everything we talked about, okay?"

"Okay."

She gave him a hard hug. "I love you, Matty," she whispered, and watched his small form race away.

It was all she could do to turn and run in the opposite direction. Away from her child.

Using herself as bait to keep the bastard away from Matthew was the only way she knew to keep him safe. She had to make enough noise to ensure whoever the masked man was followed her.

So she fled, plowing through knee-high grass that was still wet from the storm. In the moonlight she could make out shadowy shapes and forms. Lungs heaving, her chest burning, she stumbled down a ravine and into muck stirred up by the rain. Mud splattered up onto her jeans.

The wind rose, whipping at her like hands grasping at

flesh. She raced on, tripping over rocks while mud sucked at her boots and tall grass grabbed wetly at her legs.

At first, she thought the pounding in her ears was the frantic beat of her heart. Too late she realized it was the hammering of the man's feet closing the distance between them.

Winded, her breath tearing out of her lungs, she glanced across her shoulder. The flashlight's beam rushed toward her like a headlight on a speeding train.

What felt like two hundred pounds of bulk slammed into her, sending her sprawling sideways onto rocks. Pain shot up her right thigh. Hands flailing, feet kicking, she fought the strong hands that clamped onto her arms. When he jerked her onto her back and pressed the sole of his boot against her throat, she stopped struggling.

She gasped for breath while the stars overhead spun.

"I ought to kill you here," he snarled, and increased the pressure on her neck.

She lay still, knowing it would take scant prodding for him to lean in with his full weight and crush her throat. She closed her eyes. Even if she could scream for help, she wouldn't. If she screamed, Matthew might hear. He would falter, wouldn't stay hidden in the dark, might not creep along the fence line as she'd instructed. She pictured her son's sweet, innocent face. *Be safe,* she prayed. *Dear God, keep him safe.*

Suddenly, the man's boot lifted off her throat. She coughed, gasping for air. He hooked one foot under her shoulder, rolling her sideways, forcing her to her knees. The pain in her thigh was so intense she closed her eyes against a white blur. Nausea gripped her. A pool of warmth spread down her leg.

He grabbed her arm. "Where's the kid?"

"Gone." Balling her hands into fists, she hit him under his chin as hard as she could. Even as he staggered backward, his hand stayed locked on her arm, dragging her with him.

She lunged, stabbing fingers at his eyes. He twisted his head; she grabbed the mask, trying to yank his face back around. When he ducked her next jab, the mask slid off in her hand.

Staring at Brad Jordan, she gave a startled cry.

"Stupid thing to do, Kathryn," he spat, then slammed his fist against the side of her head.

Half-conscious, equilibrium gone, she had the floating sensation of being dragged across rocks, mud, grass and leaves. It might have been hours or only minutes that passed until Brad lifted her and dumped her onto a hard surface. The trunk of his car, she realized when her fingers brushed against carpet.

His breathing was heavy and labored as he dug his fingers into her injured thigh. "Yell for Matthew!"

She moaned against white-hot pain, and felt her blood seep into the carpet beneath her.

"Call him!"

"No." The word passed across her lips in a whimper.

When she heard dry leaves and twigs crunch beneath Brad's retreating footsteps, she wondered if she had time to crawl out of the trunk. But when she raised her head, nausea swept over her. Everything began to spin.

She heard a door on the car open. Minutes later, it slammed shut.

Brad's image swam fuzzily into view. "If you hadn't called the cops, this would have been all over by now."

His voice sounded like chipped glass. "You'd have the kid home and I'd have the money. That's all I wanted, money. God knows you and that pretty-boy ex of yours have mountains of it."

She saw Brad's free hand raise, glimpsed the syringe a second before she felt the hard jab of the needle in her thigh.

"While I'm hunting Matthew, you think about how you screwed everything up. You think about how this is *all your fault.*"

Already she could feel the drug he'd pumped into her taking effect. "Leave…Matthew…alone."

"Not a chance."

She stared hazily up into eyes filled with hatred, then the trunk lid slammed down and everything went black.

BRAD JORDAN'S LEGS shook so badly he barely made it into the driver's seat of the going-to-rust gray sedan he'd bought for five hundred bucks. Breathing like a bellows, he stripped off his latex gloves, leaned his head back and pressed the heels of his palms against his eyes.

What the hell was he going to do now?

The ransom was burned to ashes, the kid was on the lam and Miss Hollywood was locked in the trunk.

Just thinking about the enforcer from the Dallas sports gambling syndicate had white-hot fear burning through Brad's belly. The man with a bull-like body and empty eyes was a sadist, a *punisher,* known for using power tools when dispensing living-hell payback. Brad didn't have to wonder what would happen to him if he didn't pay *in full* the half million in gambling debts he owed the syndicate.

Worse, though, he had spotted the enforcer yesterday,

sitting at the bus stop across the street from the sitter's house where he'd dropped off his two daughters. The man had made sure Brad saw him, even gave him a pleasant nod when Brad drove by the bus stop. He had gotten the message: if he didn't pay up, they could get to his kids anywhere, anytime.

He fumbled two antianxiety meds into his mouth, wrenched open one of the water bottles he'd brought to stock the cellar and gulped down the pills. The bottle slipped from his trembling hand and landed in his crotch, spilling water across his lap.

He snatched up the bottle, lobbed it out of the car's open window.

Enraged and out of options, he smacked the steering wheel with the palms of his hands. How the hell was we supposed to know what to do next? He didn't kidnap people every day. He was a banker, a bean counter. Thinking on his feet wasn't his strong suit.

Embezzlement was, and siphoning money from the bank to pay his debt would have been child's play. But his bastard of a father-in-law owned the bank and wouldn't have trusted even God to oversee the funds. So Garner Smith had frequent and comprehensive audits done on every account. One of the auditors had even let it slip to Brad that the old man told him to keep especially close eyes on the accounts managed by his son-in-law.

If Garner caught him juggling the books, he'd fire him and tell his daughter. Felicia would dump him. Take their daughters and leave.

He would lose *everything*.

Lord, he hadn't meant to get so far into debt. Hadn't intended to put his family at risk. He had needed money to set everything right again.

So, desperate circumstances had forced him to bag Kathryn's kid and hold him for ransom. Now, though, Matthew was gone and he had Kathryn in the car's trunk.

Brad scrubbed a hand over his face and realized his stomach was clenched so tight he could barely breathe. *Not good*. Not when he needed to think. To plan.

He stared out the windshield, watching the dark shapes of the trees move in the wind while he forced his mind to work.

Maybe looking for Matthew wasn't the smart thing to do. After all, he hadn't seen his face, so he couldn't ID him.

Kathryn was another matter.

He'd already demanded a second ransom. All he had to do was figure out where to keep her until he got his hands on the money.

He glanced at the abandoned house that looked even more decrepit with the moonlight ghosting through the trees. The rain had left the ground muddy, so Matthew could conceivably leave a trail that would lead the cops back to the cellar. Getting the hell away from this place was number one on Brad's to-do list.

Figuring where to go was second. By now, the tranquilizer he'd stolen out of Doc Silver's pickup had knocked Kathryn out. He'd used what little had been left in the vial, and he hoped it was enough to keep her unconscious for hours.

So, he had some time, Brad reasoned. All he needed now was a little luck, a quick ransom and he would be home free.

After that, Miss Hollywood would be expendable goods.

THE DAWN LIGHT was finally streaking faintly above the horizon. Throughout the night Clay had steered his pickup along muddy roads and high-grass pastures. He knew it'd been futile to search for Kathryn and Matthew in the dark, but waiting for the sun to come up would have driven him stark-raving mad.

So, he drove. And saw nothing in the headlights but pasture land, an occasional stock pond, wide-eyed cows and barbed wire fence.

Twice during the night, he talked to Boudry. The sheriff was still waiting to hear from the Dallas Vice cop who'd promised to hit up his contacts to see if either Rich or Brad Jordan's names came up as heavy hitters with bookies in Big D.

Boudry had also cruised by Brad and Felicia Jordan's house. Neither of the couple's Jaguars had been parked in the driveway, and no one answered the sheriff's knock on the door. Rich Jordan—in jail until a judge set bail for him this morning—claimed he had no idea where Brad and Felicia had gone.

Clay stifled a yawn as his pickup topped the next rise. The morning was dawning sparkling and clear. The air coming in through the open window was already on the high side of warm and he knew in a couple of hours the July heat would be stifling.

He checked his watch. Johnny Sullivan had agreed to meet him at the Cross C in half an hour to go over a map of the areas that had been searched. Then there was the matter of Devin Mason.

After getting the second ransom text message, Clay had put a call through to Kathryn's ex. Following a terse exchange, the actor agreed to wire the second ransom to a Dallas Bank. Then Mason announced he was leaving the movie set in his private jet and heading for Texas.

Clay scrubbed a hand over his bristled jaw. He didn't blame Mason—if Matthew had been his own son, nothing could have kept him away after the unforgivable screw-up with the first ransom delivery. And now with Kathryn in the kidnapper's clutches, too…

Clay forced away the thought. He couldn't think about what she and Matthew might be going through. He needed to concentrate on finding them. *He had to find them.*

Intending to make a U-turn, he gave a last glance out the window at the nearby barbed wire fence that seemed to stretch for miles. Movement near one of the posts had his spine going stiff.

He slammed on the brakes, crammed the pickup into Park and shoved out the door. It could have been a calf he'd seen moving in the high grass, he reasoned. Or some other animal. Which made him glad he'd gone by the Double Starr and picked up his 9mm Sig Sauer that was holstered at the small of his back.

The high grass grabbing at his jeaned legs, he approached the fence, one hand on the Sig's butt.

Clay's heart dropped to his knees and trembled there, leaving a raw, ragged hole in his chest. If he hadn't glimpsed the grass move, he'd have missed the small figure clad in dirty camouflage pajamas huddled beside the fence post.

Although the muffled whimpering Clay heard tempted him to rush over and snatch Matthew into his arms, he held himself back. He had no idea what the boy had been through.

No idea why he was out here, seemingly alone.

Clay crouched a few feet away and nudged up the brim of his Stetson. "Hey, Matthew, I'm Clay Turner. We met at the café when you were with your mother. Do you remember me?"

The boy nodded while tears rolled down his dirt-streaked cheeks. His blond hair stuck up in spikes and his mouth quivered. "Mommy told me to find the road. I can't...find it."

"Well, I don't think you're too far off course." It amazed Clay how calm his own voice sounded with his throat having gone so tight. Where the hell was Kathryn? He held out a hand. "I bet between the two of us, we can find that road."

In a flash, Matthew rushed to him, throwing his arms around Clay's neck. Clinging like a burr, the boy sobbed harder.

Clay wrapped him in his arms. Matthew's pajamas were damp and muddy and he was trembling. "Let's get you into my truck. I've got a jacket that'll warm you up."

Inside the truck, Clay kept one arm clenched around the boy's small frame while grabbing his jean jacket off the back seat. He draped the denim around Matthew like a blanket.

"Mommy." Twisting his head, Matthew gave a frantic look out the windshield. "Have you seen my mommy?"

"Not yet." Feeling a sinking feeling in his stomach, Clay swept his gaze over the landscape. "Was she with you?"

"Until we ran away from the bad man."

"Do you know the bad man's name?"

"No." Matthew tucked his head back against Clay's neck. "He wore a black mask."

Clay needed to hear what had happened, but first he had to assess Matthew's condition. Find out if he was in danger of rejecting his transplanted kidney.

"Did the man give you your medicine?"

"Every morning."

"Okay." Clay grabbed the water bottle he'd tossed into his truck when he picked up his Sig and twisted open the cap. "How about some water? Then you can tell me what happened."

Matthew took a choked breath, nodded and took the bottle in his mud-streaked hands. While he drank, Clay did a quick survey.

The boy's pajamas—with a plastic deputy's badge pinned to one side—looked like they'd been rolled in dirt. His face and hands were equally filthy. Somewhere along the line he had lost his right slipper. Clay winced at the bloody, grime-laden cut on Matthew's heel. Still, his color looked good and his eyes, though red from crying, seemed clear of physical pain.

It was fear for his mother that Clay saw when Matthew looked up at him through tear-spiked lashes.

"Were you and your mommy together when you ran away from the man?"

"At first," Matthew said and sniffled. Although tears still brimmed in his brown eyes, he seemed to be settling. "But Mommy ran the other way so he couldn't catch us together. She said she might not run as fast as me so if I got home before her I was supposed to tell Grandma Willa and you what happened."

Clay's hands faltered as he stroked the boy's back. If Kat had made it to safety, he would have gotten a call. "You did exactly what you were supposed to do, just like a good deputy. Do you know where you were before you ran away?"

"In a cellar. Mommy said the bad man put something in the sandwiches to make us sleepy. But we fooled him and just pretended to take a nap. When he came back, Mommy kicked him in the head and we ran outside. I saw a car, and big trees."

Clay glanced at the spot near the fence where he'd found Matthew. Already there was enough sunlight to follow the boy's tracks. And maybe, just maybe, they would lead him to Kat.

He needed to get to Kat.

And Matthew had to get checked by a doctor.

"How about I give your grandma Willa a call? I know she and Johnny are going to want to come here and see you."

"Will they bring Mommy?"

"Not yet." His heart a tight knot in his chest, Clay stroked the boy's tousled blond hair. "While you're with Grandma Willa and Johnny, I'll go look for your mommy. How does that sound?"

Matthew stared up at him with big, solemn eyes, his chin trembling. "You have to find her."

Knowing Kat had used herself as bait to give her son a chance to escape had Clay fighting for control to speak calmly. "I promise I'll do my best," he said, and hugged Matthew tighter.

Pulling out his cell phone, Clay placed a call to Johnny and briefed him. After giving the foreman his location, Clay told him to get Willa and bring her to meet them.

Clay ended the call and sat unmoving, snuggling Matthew's slight weight against him, letting his heat protect the boy from the chill. And all the while ice pumped through Clay's veins. Kat was in trouble. Big trouble.

Ten years ago, he'd deserted her. Now she needed him again and he was damned if he was going to desert her a second time. He would do whatever it took to find her.

Find her, and bring her home.

CHAPTER SEVENTEEN

BRAD JORDAN was in a zone now, so deep in, so far past scared that he had found a little quiet. And with that quiet came the ability to think.

So, while debating where to go, he had instinctively steered the piece-of-crap gray sedan toward his father-in-law's lake house. Which he should have thought of right after things went to hell.

The nearest neighbors were two miles away. A large storage shed sat at the back edge of the property. He only needed to keep Kathryn alive a short time, and the shed was the perfect place to stash her.

Brad steered off the main road and headed up the private lane. The roof of the three-story structure came into view first. Garner Smith had spared no expense when he had the contemporary masterpiece built on the sloped, wooded lot. Made of cedar and glass, the house afforded a spectacular view of the sparkling lake at its rear.

But it was the view Brad got of the driveway that had him spitting a vicious curse.

Felicia's red Jaguar was parked there. Beside it sat a green sports car that Brad recognized as belonging to Vernon Lang.

Cold fury bubbled up inside Brad. He'd seen Felicia

talking to the deputy at the fund-raiser, saw Lang look at *his wife* as if he owned her.

So, maybe Lang did, Brad realized, seeing as how there was only one explanation he could come up with for why their cars were parked here. How ironic was it that Lang was the cop who caused Graciano and the ransom to burn to a crisp?

After *that* huge complication, Brad had needed time to deal with things. So, he called Felicia and told her he was driving to Dallas with his dad and they would spend last night there.

Brad clenched his hands on the wheel. The minute Felicia hung up, she'd probably dumped their daughters on her parents, then set up an overnight assignation with the cop.

Adapt, Brad told himself as he struggled for control. *Adapt and improve.* A plan was only as strong as it was flexible.

His thoughts churning, he parked behind Felicia's Jag and climbed out. Not wanting to alert the lovers to his presence just yet, he left his car door open slightly.

He'd heard rumors that Lang was ambitious, with little principle about how he achieved his goals. Which, Brad decided, would make it easy to set up things to look like Lang was behind the kidnappings.

As Brad moved toward Lang's car, he spared a glance at the house, and felt betrayal rip through him. In his heart he'd known the only time Felicia ever considered him her equal was when he was the star quarterback and she was head cheerleader. The instant they got married and she figured out his bank salary wasn't up to her standards, she went to her daddy.

Instead of giving him a raise, Garner Smith bought them a house, cars, clothes. And he put anything with a deed or title in Felicia's name. Garner even gave her a monthly allowance, which Brad couldn't get his hands on. That money could have helped pay off his gambling debts, gotten him out of the hole he was in.

Gotten his life back on track. He'd just wanted to get his life back!

But now his whole world was crashing in on him. Clearly the loyalty and love he'd felt for Felicia all these years didn't mean a damn to her. Fine, he decided, as that love transformed into loathing that flowed through his veins, liquid and cold, like mercury. It was every man for himself now. And the insurance policy on his wife would pay his debts as well as ransom money would.

AFTER JOHNNY and Willa's tearful reunion with Matthew, they bundled him off to Layton where Dr. Teasdale waited for them.

It took Clay a little over half an hour to follow Matthew's tracks to the stand of old oaks in the center of an overgrown pasture. From a distance, it was impossible to see the abandoned house sitting amid the trees.

After calling Boudry, Clay searched the cellar. Since the house was boarded up tight, he then scouted around beneath the trees. He spotted a water bottle that didn't appear to have been out in the elements long. Planning to give it to Boudry to be dusted for prints, Clay slid a stick into its neck and carried it to his pickup. Just then, his cell phone rang.

"I found out a couple of things," Boudry said in his

smoker's rasp. "First, the people who owned the property the abandoned farmhouse sits on defaulted on payments a couple of years ago. Layton National Bank now holds the title."

"A direct connection to Brad Jordan," Clay said.

"That it is," Boudry agreed. "Second, I just now heard back from the Dallas Vice cop. He says Brad is in debt up to his eyeballs to one of the betting syndicates. Word is, the clock is ticking on his deadline to pay up."

"Add to that Brad's day-to-day knowledge of what goes on at the Cross C, and it doesn't leave much doubt Brad's our guy."

"Agreed," Boudry said. "I called the bank, but he hasn't shown up for work, and no one's heard from him. I'm sending a deputy to his house, but if Brad has Kathryn Mason, I doubt that's where he's got her."

Clay's free hand balled into a fist. He had to find Kat. He wouldn't accept a dead end now; he simply wouldn't. If she was still alive—and he would not let himself think anything else—he knew she wouldn't give up. She would hang on, and not by a thread, but by her teeth. She was a fighter; if she had any strength left in her, she would try to escape.

"The son of a bitch has to be desperate," Clay said, frustration honing his voice to an edge. "To save his own hide, he has to collect the second ransom. He can't do that unless Kathryn's alive. We have to figure out where he'll hide her."

"It just hit me that his daddy-in-law owns a house at that private lake west of Layton," Boudry said. "I'll head that way, but from where you are, you can get there faster."

"I'll meet you there."

Clay was in his pickup and tromping on the gas even before Boudry finished giving directions to the lake house.

WITH HIS PLAN now gelled in his brain, Brad peered into the window of Vernon Lang's locked car. There, behind the front seat, was the deputy's uniform belt with a holstered automatic.

Perfect. Things would go smoother not having to deal with a gun-wielding cop.

Brad headed for the house, giving scant thought to Kathryn, lying drugged in the trunk of his car.

Using his key, he unlocked the front door and eased his way into air-conditioned comfort.

He could hear the faint murmur of voices coming from overhead as he crept along the entryway, his soft-soled shoes silent against the wide-planked floor. He moved past Native American wall hangings, and the Frederic Remington bronzes of horses and riders positioned on massive side tables. A huge oil painting of Felicia and her late mother posed like a queen and a princess was propped on the thick slab of cedar that formed the mantel. The wall-size fireplace was built of rock and wide enough to roast an entire longhorn in.

Brad veered to an antique credenza and opened the top drawer. He retrieved the automatic Garner insisted on keeping to shoot "varmints" that got too close to the house. Brad eased the loaded magazine into the automatic. Then he tugged his shirttail out of his jeans and jabbed the pistol into his back waistband.

Taking a deep breath, he headed up the staircase. He

watched plenty of cop shows, so he knew all about ballistic tests and trajectory.

For his plan to work, he needed to separate Lang and Felicia for a short time. Force wouldn't do it, not when he had to get the deputy downstairs with no signs of struggle. Because when the cops showed up, he intended for them to find Lang, Kathryn and Felicia in the living room, all dead from gunshot wounds.

He would claim that when he arrived at the lake house, he'd heard through the open front door Lang admit to the women that he'd kidnapped Matthew Mason. But everything went to hell when Kathryn stumbled onto the abandoned farmhouse.

Brad figured the cops would conclude that, after Matthew escaped, Lang brought Kathryn to the remote lake house where he and Felicia often met for a tryst. But Felicia showed up without warning and tried to help Kathryn escape. Lang shot them both, seconds before Brad rushed in, trying to save them. Just as Lang was about to shoot *him*, Brad grabbed his father-in-law's gun out of the credenza and killed Lang in self-defense. Case closed.

By the time he reached the third floor, Brad had gotten himself into full-fledged outraged husband mode. Turning the corner, he stalked down the hallway, shouting his wife's name.

IT WAS THE JOLTS that first roused Kathryn. While she fought to remain conscious, she had felt the entire vehicle buck beneath her, tires straining for traction as Brad sped who knew where.

Each jolt, every turn, breathed life into the pain that

burned in her injured right thigh and pounded in her head. The astringent smell of gasoline had her stomach tilting nastily.

Do not get sick, she told herself. Not while she was locked in this dark, stifling trunk.

Over time her mind grew clearer, and she realized the car had stopped moving. The gasoline fumes weren't as strong. Brad had parked somewhere. She had no idea if he was even still in the car.

Although her arms felt like lead, she forced them to lift. Her groping fingers felt the closed lid of the trunk a foot from her face. She tried to shove it open, but it wouldn't budge. She fumbled for the trunk's latch, attempted to get it to snap open to no avail.

Claustrophobia squeezed at her chest, engulfing her in fear that sank into her bones. A sob caught in her throat; sweat drenched her body.

Frantic, she lashed out with her hands and feet, beating at her metal tomb. All that did was transform the pain in her thigh and head from breathtaking to hideous.

Tears flooded her eyes, tears of horror. Of hopelessness. Light-headed, on the verge of passing out, she struggled to breathe. In and out. One breath at a time.

She couldn't let herself black out again. Couldn't give in to the pain. Or the fear. She had to get out of this damn sweatbox and find Matthew. Had Brad hunted him down last night? Or had Matty stayed hidden and found someone to help him? Had he made his way home to Willa? To Clay?

Oh, God, Clay. Trembling, Kathryn gulped in hot air while she forced herself to lie still and collect her thoughts. She knew in her heart Clay was looking for her. All she had to do was hang on. He would find her. Eventually.

Still, it was possible the person who opened the trunk wouldn't be Clay, but Brad. The dirty bastard intended to kill her. If she was going to die, she wanted a shot at taking him with her.

She eased onto her injured side. Lashing out with her good leg, Kathryn kicked at the taillight. If she could knock it out, she could maybe have enough light to figure out how to work the latch and get the trunk open.

And just in case someone other than Brad was around, she started screaming for help.

THE INSTANT FELICIA Jordan heard her husband bellowing her name, she rolled off Vernon, and snatched her snow-white robe from the end of the bed. She had its silk belt lashed tight by the time Brad shoved open the door.

His gaze swept over the rumpled bed, then zeroed-in on her. "You going to try to lie your way out of this?"

She took in her husband's reddened face and dark, disheveled hair. Since he looked like a human rocket ready to take off, she decided not to go on the defensive.

"No sense in trying to lie when the proof's right in front of you." She was aware of Vernon behind her, easing off the mattress, snatching up his jeans.

Brad sent a screw-you sneer Lang's way. "It's a little late to put on your goddamn pants, Deputy."

Vernon zipped up, then stepped to Felicia's side. "Looks like the three of us have some talking to do."

Felicia set her jaw. Not ten minutes ago, Vernon had been screwing her blind while telling her *again* how she should leave Brad and marry him. She knew good and well that Vernon was happy they'd been caught.

In truth, she didn't know how she felt. She'd stopped loving Brad a long time ago, but her girls adored their daddy and she hadn't wanted to rock the boat.

Brad stalked into the bedroom, his tall, wiry body reminding her of the high school quarterback she'd been hot for so long ago. "The three of us don't have anything to discuss," he said to Vernon, even as he kept his hot gaze locked with hers. "I want to talk to my wife. Baby, tell your friend to go downstairs," Brad murmured. "He and I can have a discussion after you and I are done up here."

Felicia turned toward Vernon. Despite her best intentions, he seemed to have somehow burrowed his way into her heart. "You'd better wait downstairs."

"If that's what you want." He shrugged into his shirt, then picked up his boots. "You're sure you'll be okay, darlin'?"

Felicia jammed her hands into the pockets on her robe. "I'm sure." Despite the unsettling look in Brad's eyes, she'd always been able to handle him. No reason today would be any different.

She watched Vernon step toward the door, then pause and give Brad a steady look. "I'll wait for you downstairs, Jordan."

"Close the door on your way out," Brad said.

When the door closed behind Vernon, Felicia squared her shoulders. "I'm sorry, Brad, about you finding Vernon and me together like this. But I don't think you'll argue that you and I have grown apart over the years."

"You're right," Brad said, and took a step forward. "I don't intend to argue with you at all."

The quick fist he delivered to her jaw rolled Felicia's eyes back in her head. Everything went dark before she hit the floor.

YES! VERNON THOUGHT as he jogged down the staircase. He didn't feel at all bad about Brad Jordan finding him in bed with Felicia. Well, maybe he felt guilty that Felicia was upstairs having to deal one-on-one with the loser, but their marriage had breathed its last long ago, and Vernon wanted the sexy blonde for himself.

After today, there'd be no more sneaking around for him and Felicia. No more meeting here on the sly. They could walk hand in hand down Layton's Main Street and no one would have reason to say a thing.

Sweet.

Vernon shoved open the front door and stepped out onto the porch. He settled onto one of the wrought-iron chairs and pulled on his boots.

"Help me!"

He sprang out of the chair, thinking the scream had been Felicia's. He had his hand on the doorknob when a frantic pounding sounded from behind him.

"Help me!"

Vernon snatched his backup .22 out of his boot and headed toward the driveway.

"Help!"

His gaze zeroed in on the trunk of the gray sedan parked behind Felicia's red Jaguar. *Brad's car?*

When Vernon saw that the driver's door was ajar,

he pulled it open, fumbled around until he found the trunk latch.

Gun aimed, he reached for the trunk's lid at the same time it popped open.

Thinking the muffled footsteps she'd heard had been Brad's, Kathryn braced to defend herself. But the tall, broad-shouldered man looking as shocked as she felt at seeing he wasn't Brad. In a flash of seconds, she recognized him as the deputy she'd seen talking to Felicia Jordan at the hospital fund-raiser. He had a gun gripped in his right hand, aimed at the ground.

"Help me." She tried to push herself up, but her injured leg was too weak to support her weight. "He's going to kill me."

"Who is?"

"Brad Jordan. He kidnapped my son. Then me." The trembling words bubbled up her throat. "I don't know where my son is."

"Let's get you out of there," the deputy said. He wrapped a hard-as-steel arm around her waist and lifted her out of the trunk with seeming ease.

The instant he settled her on her feet, Kathryn heard the distinctive blast of gunfire. The deputy crumpled, pulling her to the ground with him.

She looked up in time to see Brad Jordan, eyes wild, face flushed, racing down the porch steps toward her, gun aimed.

"You bitch!" he screamed. "You ruined everything."

Kathryn grabbed the deputy's gun and scuttled under the rear of the car. From that perspective, she could see only Brad's legs advancing on her. Aiming, she squeezed the trigger.

He jerked and staggered back a step. "Not good enough, Miss Hollywood," he said and continued forward, his left leg dragging now.

She attempted to fire again, but the automatic's trigger was already all the way back. *Jammed*, she realized with a skitter of panic.

Brad dropped to his knees and peered under the car. She saw the hatred in his eyes as he aimed. "Can't miss at this range."

Kathryn flinched when the shot blasted though the air. She waited, expecting to feel the pain from the bullet ripping through her.

Then blood sprouted in the center of Brad's forehead. He did a slow fall sideways, his eyes open, staring at her.

She had to swallow, couldn't. Fear had dried up every bit of the saliva in her mouth.

"Kat, stay where you are!"

Her head jerked toward the sound of Clay's voice. He pounded up the driveway toward the car, the gun clenched in his hand aimed at Brad.

When he reached the banker's still form, Clay kicked the gun out of Brad's hand. Then he leaned and pressed two fingers against his throat. "Dead," he said.

Lungs heaving, Kathryn scooted from beneath the car. "The deputy's shot," she said needlessly since Clay already had a hand pressed to the wound on the man's upper back.

"Vernon!"

The woman's scream had both Kathryn and Clay looking toward the house. Felicia Jordan dashed down the porch steps, the hem of her silk robe billowing around her bare feet. She sprinted past her husband's body and dropped to her knees beside the deputy. Her manicured hands shoved Clay's aside and she pressed her palms against the wound. "Oh, God, Vernon baby!"

The sound of a car's engine nearly drowned out Felicia's quavering voice. Kathryn saw the sheriff's logo on the door as the car skidded to a halt.

Sweat running down his face, his breath coming fast, Clay crouched beside her and grasped her upper arms. "Damn, Kat." His voice was tight and raw as his grim gaze ran over her, settling on her right thigh where her jeans were ripped and blood-soaked. "I need to get you to the hospital."

She gripped his arms. "Matthew." Her voice shook. "Clay, do you know where Matthew is?"

"He's okay." Moving carefully as though she might break, Clay eased an arm around her back and pressed his lips to her hair. "I found him this morning. He seemed fine, other than being scared. Johnny and Willa took him to Doc Teasdale."

Relief burned through Kathryn. "Thank God." All of her strength gone, she leaned against Clay, savoring his warmth. "Thank God."

The world seemed to revolve in slow motion as she watched Sheriff Boudry dash toward his fallen deputy. Heard his gruff voice bark orders into his handheld radio.

"Ambulance is on the way," he said, then turned his attention to the wounded man.

The nightmare was over, Kathryn thought while shudders racked her. Matthew was alive. Her baby was alive.

Burying her face against Clay's shoulder, she burst into tears.

CHAPTER EIGHTEEN

VISITING HOURS were nearly over by the time Clay strode off the elevator and into the hospital's dim hallway that smelled vaguely of antiseptic and pine cleaner. He checked the room number sign, then turned. As he walked, he dragged off his Stetson, shoved his fingers through his hair.

He hadn't seen Kathryn since the EMTs bundled her into an ambulance and sped away from the lake house, following close behind the one transporting the wounded deputy. Even though it grated to be away from Kat, Clay had stayed at the scene, walking Boudry and a crime scene tech through the events he knew about that led up to Brad Jordan's shooting death.

He'd spent the remainder of the afternoon at the sheriff's office. After answering more questions he gave his formal statement, then headed home to the Double Starr. And during all that time, a sense of urgency to see Kat had pulsed through him. Still, he wasn't expecting much of anything good to come out of this visit, so he'd waited to come until he knew she'd be alone.

That didn't mean he hadn't kept tabs on her. He'd talked to Willa several times throughout the afternoon and evening, so he knew that the E.R. doc had stitched up

Kathryn's thigh, then admitted her for overnight obser-vation. After Matthew received a clean bill of health, Willa and Johnny took him to his mother's room for a tearful reunion. Devin Mason arrived in time to join them. An hour ago, Mason took his son home to the Cross C.

As he neared Kathryn's room, Clay's stomach muscles began to tremble as he pictured her, kneeling beneath the rear of Jordan's car. The gun gripped in her hand shook while she desperately tried to squeeze the jammed trigger. Then Jordan crouched, and aimed his own weapon at her.

Clay knew he would never rid himself of those horrifying images. Or of the fear that pierced his chest like splinters when he thought about what might have happened if he'd raced up that driveway a few seconds later.

He stepped into the doorway of her room and paused. She wasn't lying in bed as he expected, but standing at the window, looking out on Layton's darkened Main Street. Instead of a hospital gown, she wore a silky blue robe that reached to her ankles. Her dark hair was brushed loosely back, and he could see one edge of a stark-white bandage on her left temple.

Framed in the dark square of the window, she looked small and fragile. Highly breakable. He knew she was anything but. She had not only survived her child getting kidnapped, but herself. She had gotten Matthew to safety by putting her own life at risk. And she'd had the inner strength to endure Brad Jordan.

Kathryn Conner Mason wasn't anybody's victim. Not Brad Jordan's and not *his*. Clay knew nothing could erase what he'd done to her ten years ago. But he'd had to come tonight. No matter the lumps he figured his heart was in for, he *had* to see for himself that she was all right.

Just then she turned. Her blue eyes widened when she saw him.

"Hello, Kat."

Emotion wedged in Kathryn's throat at the sight of Clay standing in the doorway. He wore jeans and a shirt as gray as the room's walls, its sleeves rolled on his forearms. His dark hair was mussed, his jaw freshly shaved. After what she had said to him before she galloped off on Dakota, she'd been afraid he'd never want to see her again.

"I was hoping you would come." With her nerves shimmering, she managed to take a step toward him. She stopped when she saw his shuttered expression. "I haven't heard an update on the deputy who got me out of that trunk. Do you know how he's doing?"

"He should make a full recovery."

"That's a relief."

"Yeah." Clay laid his Stetson beside the small built-in sink near the doorway, then moved to stand at the end of the bed. "How are you feeling?"

"I'm not sure which hurts worse, my head or my thigh."

"Shouldn't you be in bed?"

"I've been there for hours." Lying there, praying he would walk into the room. Now that he had, she wasn't sure how to tell him what she needed to say. Wasn't sure he'd want to hear it.

"According to Willa, Matthew seems to be doing pretty well," Clay said while digging into his shirt pocket.

"Yes." Kathryn swallowed against a swell of emotion. She still couldn't believe Matthew was back home. Safe. "I wish you had been here earlier so you could have seen him for yourself. He told me he got lost, and Mr. Turner helped him find the road."

"He's a brave little boy. I have a feeling if I hadn't run across him, he'd have managed to get home on his own." Clay held out his palm. "Do me a favor and give him this. I found it when I searched the outlaw tunnel."

Kathryn stared at the small plastic soldier lying in Clay's hand. "You could give it to Matthew yourself," she suggested softly.

He laid the soldier on the rolling table near the bed. "I'm not sure when I'll get a chance to get by the Cross C."

"I understand." And she did—yesterday she'd seen in his eyes exactly how much her words had hurt him.

She tried to force a smile, but it wouldn't gel. "I keep getting this sharp stab in my stomach when I let myself think about what might have happened. What could have happened if not for you."

"What could have happened *because* of me, don't you mean?" His voice roughened at the end, pulling at her heart.

"No." She closed her eyes on a swell of regret. "Clay, what I said to you was horrible. To blame you for Matthew's possible death because you went to the sheriff, when I'm the one who approved you doing that, is unforgivable. I'm so sorry."

He raised a shoulder. "You were upset."

"So were you. But you still faced me and told me the truth about what had happened to Nilo. And maybe to Matthew."

"I promised not to hold back news, good or bad."

"You've always been a man of your word," she

murmured. "So, despite the awful things I'd said to you, when I came to in that cellar, there was no doubt in my mind you were looking for Matthew and me. I knew you would find us, no matter how long it took. I trusted you to find us, and you did. You got Matthew to safety. You arrived at the lake house in time to save my life. You saved us both, and I was crying so hard today that I didn't even thank you for that."

"I didn't show up here so you could thank me."

"No, you're here because you gave me your word you won't walk away again, unless I tell you I want you to go. Is that what you're expecting, Clay? That I'll tell you to go?"

"There's baggage between us, Kat. A lot of hurt and pain. We lost a child."

"Yes." She shifted toward the window, staring out into the darkness, waiting until she was sure the right words were there.

"I loved you once, so much," she finally managed. "And when you left me, I made myself lock away that love. I couldn't have survived with it alive inside me. So, I moved on. From you, from Sam. I never wanted to see either of you again."

She stared at Clay's reflection in the window. He remained motionless, saying nothing.

When the silence stretched so long that her nerves rode on the surface of her skin, she turned slowly to face him. There was emotion in his eyes now, but she was at a loss to read it.

"But then I came back to the Cross C and ran into you at the café," she said. "Just looking at you hurt. I didn't want it to, but it did. And the lock I put on my feelings wouldn't hold. But this time, I had Matthew to think about. I wasn't going to open our lives to any man who might suddenly walk away."

When Clay's gaze shifted past her to the window behind her, she wondered if he was thinking about his parents, and all the guilt over their deaths that weighed so heavily on him.

"If I could," he said after a moment, "I would go back and change things. Erase all the pain. But I can't. Maybe what I did back then is too much for you to get past."

"I thought it was, even after we slept together again. I wasn't going to let you back in my life and give you a chance to hurt me a second time."

She lifted her hand, grazed her fingertips across the bandage on her temple. "When Brad locked me in the trunk of his car, it felt like I was lying in a coffin. I kept thinking this shouldn't be happening to me. But it was, and I knew if I died in there the world would go on, the seasons would change, the sun would rise on a new day. All without me. And that was so unfair. Because I wanted to watch my son grow up. And I desperately wanted to share a future with the man I love."

She moved to the end of the bed, pausing inches from him. "The man who still grieves for the child we created and lost," she added. "The man I've never, over all this time, stopped loving."

Although his dark eyes seemed to soften, he said nothing. Just stared down at her, as if he didn't quite believe what she'd said.

She raised a hand, cupped his cheek. "When you didn't show up here, I decided you'd changed your mind about wanting me. So, I was standing at the window, trying to figure out the best way to blow this joint, then hunt you down and see what I could do about changing your mind. Because I love you, Clay. I always have."

Careful of her injuries, he gathered her close, buried his face in her hair. "I thought you were going to die," he said, his voice thick and raw. "When I raced up that driveway and spotted you under the car, saw Jordan aim his automatic at you, I wasn't sure I could make the shot. I thought you would die right there."

"I'm all right now." She could do nothing but hold on, rocked by the emotions pulsing from him. "Because you made the shot. You saved my life. And I don't want to waste any more time."

He lifted his head. His smile was not much more than a faint curve of his mouth but there was an intimate quality to it that had everything inside her going warm. "Neither do I.

Rising on tiptoe, she touched her lips to his. "I was wrong when I said you belonged only in my past. You're my future. I want you to be a part of my life, of Matthew's. I want the three of us to be together."

He rested his brow against hers. "That's good, because I don't think I can live without you. I don't even want to try."

As their mouths joined, she felt the steady beat of his heart against hers. And for the first time since she'd set foot back in Texas, Kathryn felt like she'd truly come home.

* * * * *

Don't miss
THE PASSION OF SAM BROUSSARD,
the second book in Maggie's thrilling new Silhouette
Romantic Suspense miniseries
DATES WITH DESTINY.
Available early 2008,
whenever Silhouette Books are sold.

Melita had been expecting a chaste quick kiss of the generic variety. But this kiss with Sully was the kind that sparked a dying flame to life. The kind of kiss you can't plan for. The kind of kiss memories are built on.

The memory of her murdered lover, Nemo, came to her then and she made a starved little noise in the back of her throat. She raised her arms and threaded her fingers through Sully's hair, pulled him closer. Felt his body settle, then melt into her.

In that instant her hunger for him grew, and his for her. She pressed herself to him with more urgency, and he responded in kind.

Melita came out of her kiss-induced memory of Nemo with a start. "Wait a minute." She pushed Sully away from her. "You bastard!"

She spit two nasty words at him in Greek, then wiped his kiss from her lips.

"I thought you deserved some solid proof that I'm still in one piece." He started for the door. "The clock's ticking, honey. Come on, let's get out of here."

"That's it? You sucker me into kissing you, and that's all you have to say?"

"I'm sorry. How's that?"

He didn't sound sorry in the least. "You're—"

"Getting out of this godforsaken prison cell. Stop whining and let's go."

"Not if I was being shot at sunrise. Go. You deserve whatever you get if you walk out that door."

He turned back. "Freedom is what I'm going to get."

"A second of freedom before the guards in the hall shoot you." She jammed her hands on her hips. "And to think I was worried about you."

"If you're staying behind, it's no skin off my ass."

"Wait! What about our deal?"

"You just said you're not coming. Make up your mind."

"Have you forgotten we need a boat?"

"How could I? You keep harping on it."

"I'm not going without a boat. And those guards out there aren't going to just let you walk out of here. You need me and we need a plan."

"I already have a plan. I'm getting out of here. That's the plan."

"I should have realized that you never intended to take me with you from the very beginning. You're a liar and a coward."

Of everything she had read, there was nothing in Sully Paxton's file that hinted he was a coward, but it was the one word that seemed to register in that one-track mind of his. The look he nailed her with a second later was pure venom.

He came at her so quickly she didn't have time to get out of his way. "You know I'm not a coward."

"Prove it. Give me until dawn. I need one more night to put everything in place before we leave the island."

"You're asking me to stay in this cell one more night...and trust you?"

"Yes."

He snorted. "Yesterday you knew they were planning to harm me, but instead of doing something about it you went to bed and never gave me a second thought. Suppose tonight you do the same. By tomorrow I might damn well be in my grave."

"Okay, I screwed up. I won't do it again." Melita sucked in a ragged breath. "I can't leave this minute. Dawn, Sully. Wait until dawn." When he looked as if he was about to say no, she pleaded,"Please wait for me."

"You're asking a lot. The door's open now. I would be a fool to hang around here and trust that you'll be back."

"What you can trust is that I want off this island as badly as you do, and you're my only hope."

"I must be crazy."

"Is that a yes?"

"Dammit!" He turned his back on her. Swore twice more.

"You won't be sorry."

He turned around. "I already am. How about we seal this new deal?"

He was staring at her lips. Suddenly Melita knew what he expected. "We already sealed it."

"One more. You enjoyed it. Admit it."

"I enjoyed it because I was kissing someone else."

He laughed. "That's a good one."

"It's true. It might have been your lips, but it wasn't you I was kissing."

"If that's your excuse for wanting to kiss me, then—"

"I was kissing Nemo."

"What's a nemo?"

Melita gave Sully a look that clearly told him that he was trespassing on sacred ground. She was about to enforce it with a warning when a voice in the hall jerked them both to attention.

She bolted away from the wall. "Get back in bed. Hurry. I'll be here before dawn."

She didn't reach the door before he snagged her arm, pulled her up against him and planted a kiss on her lips that took her completely by surprise.

When he released her, he said, "If you're confused about who just kissed you, the name's Sully. I'll be here waiting at dawn. Don't be late."

Romantic
SUSPENSE

**Sparked by Danger,
Fueled by Passion.**

Onyxx agent Sully Paxton's only chance of
survival lies in the hands of his enemy's daughter
Melita Krizova. He doesn't know he's a pawn in the
beautiful island girl's own plan for escape. Can
they survive their ruses and their fiery attraction?

*Look for the next installment in the
Spy Games miniseries,*

*Sleeping with
Danger*

by Wendy Rosnau

Available November 2007 wherever you buy books.

HARLEQUIN®

Mediterranean NIGHTS™

Not everything is above board
on Alexandra's Dream!

Enjoy plenty of secrets, drama and sensuality
in the latest from Mediterranean Nights.

Coming in November 2007...

BELOW DECK

by

Dorien Kelly

Determined to protect her young son,
widow Mei Lin Wang keeps him hidden
aboard *Alexandra's Dream* under cover of
her job. But life gets extremely complicated
when the ship's security officer, Gideon Dayan,
is piqued by the mystery surrounding this
beautiful, haunted woman....

REQUEST YOUR
FREE BOOKS!

2 FREE NOVELS PLUS 2 FREE GIFTS!

Silhouette® Romantic

SUSPENSE

Sparked by Danger, Fueled by Passion!

YES! Please send me 2 FREE Silhouette® Romantic Suspense novels and my 2 FREE gifts. After receiving them, if I don't wish to receive any more books, I can return the shipping statement marked "cancel." If I don't cancel, I will receive 4 brand-new novels every month and be billed just $4.24 per book in the U.S., or $4.99 per book in Canada, plus 25¢ shipping and handling per book plus applicable taxes, if any*. That's a savings of at least 15% off the cover price! I understand that accepting the 2 free books and gifts places me under no obligation to buy anything. I can always return a shipment and cancel at any time. Even if I never buy another book from Silhouette, the two free books and gifts are mine to keep forever.

240 SDN EEX6 340 SDN EEYJ

Name	(PLEASE PRINT)

Address	Apt. #

City	State/Prov.	Zip/Postal Code

Signature (if under 18, a parent or guardian must sign)

Mail to the **Silhouette Reader Service™**:
IN U.S.A.: P.O. Box 1867, Buffalo, NY 14240-1867
IN CANADA: P.O. Box 609, Fort Erie, Ontario L2A 5X3

Not valid to current Silhouette Intimate Moments subscribers.

Want to try two free books from another line?
Call 1-800-873-8635 or visit www.morefreebooks.com.

* Terms and prices subject to change without notice. NY residents add applicable sales tax. Canadian residents will be charged applicable provincial taxes and GST. This offer is limited to one order per household. All orders subject to approval. Credit or debit balances in a customer's account(s) may be offset by any other outstanding balance owed by or to the customer. Please allow 4 to 6 weeks for delivery.

Your Privacy: Silhouette is committed to protecting your privacy. Our Privacy Policy is available online at www.eHarlequin.com or upon request from the Reader Service. From time to time we make our lists of customers available to reputable firms who may have a product or service of interest to you. If you would prefer we not share your name and address, please check here. ☐

SRS07

ATHENA FORCE
Heart-pounding romance and thrilling adventure.

History repeats itself...unless she can stop it.

Investigative reporter Winter Archer is thrown into writing a biography of Athena Academy's founder. But someone out there will stop at nothing—not even murder—to ensure that long-buried secrets remain hidden.

ATHENA FORCE

Will the women of Athena unravel Arachne's powerful web of blackmail and death...or succumb to their enemies' deadly secrets?

Look for

VENDETTA
by *Meredith Fletcher*

Available November wherever you buy books.

Silhouette®

SPECIAL EDITION™

**brings you a heartwarming
new McKettrick's story from**

NEW YORK TIMES BESTSELLING AUTHOR

LINDA LAEL MILLER

THE McKETTRICK
Way

Meg McKettrick is surprised to be reunited
with her high school flame, Brad O'Ballivan,
who has returned home to his family's
neighboring ranch. After seeing Meg again,
Brad realizes he still loves her. But the pride
of both manage to interfere with love...until
an unexpected matchmaker gets involved.

—— McKettrick Women ——

Available December wherever you buy books.